To
the
Moon

||||||||||||||||||||||||||||||||||||||||||||||||||||||||||||||||||||||||||||||||||||||||

L.L. Crane

Mark of Power Series

Book 2

www.llcrane.com

For Landon and Morgan…may you find your Power and forever love dragons.

To the Moon is a work of fiction. Names, places, characters, and incidents are either the product of the author's imagination or are used fictitiously. Any resemblance to actual persons, living or dead, events, or locales, are entirely coincidental.

©2015 L. L. Crane

Cover Design: Phatpuppy Art

Table of Contents

Inceptus...

I can remember bits and pieces of my mother, like flashes of lightning from the sky. The images come quickly, sharp and vivid, but disappear almost immediately. A hug. Her milky, coffee colored skin, upturned nose, high cheekbones. Sitting on her lap. Her long black hair sweeping around her face and tickling my nose. She and Entho embracing. Me in the middle.

I was four years old when she died. I have heard the story from Entho time and again, but deep down I just know there is something missing.

When I was a child I would beg Entho for information about her – anything I could hold onto. I wanted any scrap of knowledge about her – what she liked to eat, who her friends were, how she trained dragons. Yet, he always answered in a monotone, a factual display of events that left me craving more. He always ended the questions almost before they began. Case closed. But I wasn't needing facts. I wanted to know her – the real Pana Frain.

All I ever got from him was the same story. She was almost a Master Dragon Trainer. She was competing in her final test. It was back when dragons could fly, and her dragon was one she had hatched from an egg. He was a brilliant Emerald, loyal and true to my mother. But during the test, something went terribly wrong. Emory, her dragon, crashed to the ground with my mother on him. My mother's neck was broken, and Emory had to be destroyed. Entho was there and so was I.

That is it.

I remember that day, though. Snippets of it tickle my memory bank – smelling popcorn and cotton candy among the hordes of people jostling me around and the sounds of music playing – flutes and mandolins. I vividly recall a huge purple dragon and a gigantic spear. A man dressed in black. Someone grabbing me when I fell. In my mind, Entho dropped me, but he claims he didn't.

Entho says I am imagining things. That he was there and didn't see a purple dragon or any spears. After all, it was only a training test.

Real weapons couldn't have been used. He says I was just little and couldn't remember any of that.

But I do.

Medius...

My feet hit the muddy bottom of the tunnel floor, sloppily now, a sort of out of sync cadence with Thann's. At one time they were in perfect unison with his, almost like I was still in Weapons with my former team mates. Glendon in front. Me in the middle, and Pride behind me – training for Soldier Academy. That seems like it was in another life, although it was only a few short weeks ago.

I slip, falling to the ground on the slick mud beneath my feet, and Thann's thick arms pull me up. Again. I wonder if I would still be alive if he hadn't picked me up so many times…if I would have been trampled or left for dead in the dank tunnel beneath Mount Gareth – the one leading us to Harcourt and hopefully to safety.

I pant like a dog, desperately trying to suck air into my lungs, but the damp tunnel is not cooperating. My chest burns, a fire inside like I have never felt. We have been running for hours, and I wonder, yet again, if we will ever make it to Harcourt. Thump thump. Squish.

My feet pound like hammers on the slick floor, only to be met by gooey mud oozing up from the bottom of the tunnel.

It is dark – beyond dark, but I have given up on caring about that. Pure exhaustion threatens to overtake me, and images swirl in my mind like restless clouds as my feet strike the earthen tunnel floor. It isn't just physical exhaustion weighing me down.

As I run, the knowledge of the Purity Law crashes violently into my head. "All Light Skins are to be killed," the Destroyer told us. "Even if they have the Mark of Power." Instinctively, I draw my hand up to the crescent shaped mark on my left cheek. My Mark of Power. Or, as I think of it…my Mark of Powerless. Still, it has kept me alive all these years. But it won't now.

My mind flashes to my mother. She feels close to me for some arcane reason. It is as if I could reach out and touch her. As my feet pound up and down, slipping and sliding, I reach my hand along the muddy tunnel walls and pretend it is my mother's face…soft and smooth like rich, dark porcelain.

The thought shatters from my mind as rotten, fishy clay spatters down on my head. It trickles down my hair, and with it comes an odor so vile my stomach turns and I struggle not to retch. In direct contrast, memories of my mother's scent wage war with it… lilacs and dragons and sweetness. I have forgotten so much about her…but not that...not the way she smelled.

Another huge glob of mud splats from above and strikes my head, as if it were a lightning bolt shooting from the sky. I stumble, falling without grace, onto the ground. Yet again.

"Teak," Thann shouts. My name echoes in the tunnel, bouncing back and forth, ping ponging from one wall to the next. Then it lessens and fades to a real whisper. Teak…Teak…Teak. I am not sure if Thann has said my name several times or if it is a real echo.

I am face down in the mud. My knee aches fiercely from the fall I took earlier, and my bloody wrists mix with the mud beneath me, a gooey earth and blood soup.

"Get up, Teak," Thann orders, urgency in his voice. He is barely breathing hard.

I push against the mud with my hands, my left one throbbing in revolt. The rough clay dirt spills into my mouth, filling it like used coffee grounds or tea leaves. I cough and gag, then run my tongue along my teeth, spitting the dense grit out and trying not to swallow it. I turn my head, breathing in rancid air. I attempt to rise, but I fall back to the tunnel floor. I don't care anymore. I just don't care.

Thann's mammoth body is shadowing over me like a sentinel in the dark. He reaches down, grabs me by my pants and jerks me to my feet as if I were a rag doll.

"You okay?" he asks, concern in his deep voice. I struggle to stand, almost wishing I could fall back to the softness of the muddy tunnel floor.

"Yes, I guess so." My words are empty…shallow. To top it off, I am a liar. I am anything but okay.

Thann reaches a muddy hand toward mine, and I take it willingly, almost greedily. It is warm and rough and big. His fingers wrap around mine like a friend's. Or could it be something more?

I breathe out, the air from my lungs whipping around the stagnant air in front of me. I take my other arm and bring it to my face, wipe it over my mouth, and search for Thann's golden eyes. But in the tunnel they are only dark orbs, sinking into his face like dim, grey pebbles.

Echo calls him Golden Boy, but in the tunnels it is hard to find anything that resembles gold. Not in Thann, and certainly not in me. I wonder, not for the first time if Echo and the others made it to Harcourt safely. To Dragon Academy…where Thann and I should be. With them. Before the Destroyers came. Before Soot was killed.

I shiver, images of her pale face and reddish blonde hair darting before my eyes. Then, like someone snuck inside of my head and rewound a scene, I can see the Destroyer pull his sword and ruthlessly slash it across her neck. I watch helplessly, my bow and arrow ready but not quite fast enough as her body is sliced into two distinct pieces. That terrible feeling of failure drenches over me again, and I want to cry. For Soot. For Thann. And right now, even for myself.

Although I couldn't save Soot, I did save Thann's life, and my own, when I killed the Destroyers. It must mean something, to save a life - to swap one beating heart for another. Thann starts running again, and I have no choice but to fall into place beside him. Every step I take twinges with piercing pain as we sprint along, an agonizing rhythm of feet slamming into slick, mushy mud. I am used to running, have been trained to run for long periods of time. But not like this.

It isn't only my knee that hurts – my entire body is aching at this point, as if someone had flogged me with a club. Yaren told us to run and not to stop. But he didn't say for how long.

I somehow manage to put one step in front of the other, and my mind finds words to match the rhythm of my pounding feet. Winter. Winter. Entho. Entho. Mom. Mom. Canto. The names of the people I care about, even the dead ones, roll over and over in my mind with each step I take, like a nursery rhyme gone wrong.

Then it switches to the people I hate. Only, I can't quite get a rhythm to match my feet to the word Destroyer. So I break it into

little pieces, each part a step I take. De. Stroy. Er. Siv. Gar. Eth.
Reese. De. Stroy. Er. Siv. Gar. Eth. Reese.

I become lost in it, the only thing keeping me sane. Entho. Entho.
Winter. Winter. Mom. Mom. Canto. De. Stroy. Er. Siv Gar. Eth.
Reese. I am on the last set of the people I hate when Thann stops
abruptly. I hit the back of his body with mine, slamming into him
like an ancient bumper car. He rips his giant hand from mine,
untangling his thick fingers as if he had suddenly dropped something
hot, and for a minute I want to cry out, beg him to put his hand back.

Instead, I just stop, wheezing in and out as I try to catch my breath. I
bend over, touching my hands to my knees, fighting to squeeze air
into my burning lungs.

"The tunnel has ended," Thann tells me, in a matter of fact tone, as if
we run in tunnels every day of our lives.

"Are you sure?" I wheeze, disbelief shadowing my words. Thann is
thumping on the roof of the tunnel. He must have climbed up one of
the ladders.

Just then a sliver of light creeps into the tunnel, like waking at early dawn with the sun poking shyly through a window. We have been in the tunnel so long that the tiny shard of light burns my eyes. I squeeze them shut for just a moment, and once they have adjusted to the light, I slowly stand and slosh through the mud toward the ladder.

It took persuasion to get me down into the tunnel. Yaren actually had to push me down here, but now the thought of getting out is even more frightening. What if it isn't Harcourt? What if it is the wrong door and we end up where there are Destroyers? Yaren said there were hundreds, maybe thousands out…searching for Light Skins…their ruby handled swords ready to chop off our heads. Like Soot's. A tremble runs up my spine.

In what seems like another life, although it was only yesterday, I stained Thann and my skin with iodine and caked black mud in our hair, hoping to disguise our true skin color…the thought of having our heads chopped off trumping everything. But underneath it all, beneath the grime and filth and medicine, Thann and I both have deathly, pale white skin.

"Come on," Thann urges, his voice warbling in my ears like ocean waves crashing against the shore.

Suddenly I am dizzy, and I wonder if I will be able to make it up the small, rickety ladder. I grasp my hands onto it, the rough wood scraping against my skin. My left hand is useless, pounding with pain from when the Dorgan the Destroyer squeezed it so hard I thought he crushed every bone in it. I shake my head at the memory, drop my left hand to my side and let my right hand hold me up. I put a foot on the first rung, and slowly, step by step, rise up the shaky wooden ladder.

When I approach the top of the ladder, Thann grabs me by the armpits and yanks me upward. I land with a thud in the center of a strange room. I am face down, my nose pasted against hard wood floors that appear to have been polished repeatedly until they shine like mirrors.

I gulp, staring at my horrid reflection in them. Thann's mountainous body, distorted in the reflection of the mirrored floors, looms before me, and I can barely make out the perfect features of his face and his shaggy, mud encased blonde hair.

"We made it," Thann announces with a gigantic grin on his face.

"We made it to Harcourt."

Chapter 1

I open my dirt encrusted eyes slowly, a strange room spiraling wildly before me. I reach up with the sleeve of Koree's tunic and make a feeble attempt at wiping my eyes clean. It must be late, maybe the middle of the afternoon. Harsh rays of sunlight boldly blaze through a series of wide windows, simple blue curtains adorning them. Eventually, the room settles into focus. It is large and sparsely decorated with seven other beds lined up in a row beside the one I am in. There is a small dresser next to each bed.

Thoughts swirl in my foggy brain, confusion taking over like a tyrannical boss. I bolt upright, panicked, tossing a coarse blanket off of my filthy body in one swift movement. I catch my breath, though, as Thann's words echo in my mind. "We made it to Harcourt." Relief floods through my body as I gingerly place my bare feet on the dull, hard wood floor. My first thought is that I must get this filth and grime off of me, but then, like an uninvited guest, searing pain creeps through my entire body. My head spins with dizziness, and my stomach cramps into a tight ball.

I hurt everywhere. There isn't a bone or muscle on my body that isn't howling in pain. I glance at my wrists, cut deeply from the ropes that once bound them. Oddly, they don't hurt as much as my hand and knee, even though the cuts are fresh and angry, still oozing blood. I groan out loud, wishing I had my bags. If I did, I would find Entho's healing case and mix something for the pain.

I scan the bare room, and my heart leaps with joy. Nestled next to my bed are both of my bags. The last time I saw them they were strapped to Pebble's saddle, and she was running off alone, so far away from Harcourt I wasn't sure if I would ever see the gentle, red dragon again.

My eyes travel from my bags to the small oak dresser next to my bed. A basin of water, a tin cup, three cheese sandwiches, and a note are resting on it. Standing slowly, I grip the edge of the dresser as the room spins before me in gigantic spirals of blue and brown. I take a deep breath and shake my head. Once the room stops spinning, I grab the ladle from the basin and drink thirstily, sucking down the cool, sweet water. Suddenly, my stomach growls, a lion inside of me roaring for food. I reach for a sandwich, not even caring about the filth on my hands. Stuffing an enormous bite into my mouth, I grab the note and read it.

WELCOME! Drink the tea. It will help with any pain you might have. There are sandwiches for you to eat and a cleaning room at the back of the dormitory. When you are finished, find the door marked Office and ask for Kesper.

I gobble up the other two sandwiches, and drink the tea in about two gulps. It is cold and bitter, but I don't mind. Satisfied, I trudge toward the back of the room, searching for the cleaning room. I find a door, open it tentatively, and am greeted by a long counter with about ten pitchers of water and stacks of clean, white rags resting on it.

I wander in, grab one of the rags and scrub at the filth on my body. Once clean, I move to my long mess of hair. It takes several washings to rid it of the thick layers of mud, but eventually my blonde hair returns. I find a soft, grey towel hanging on a hook, dry off, and wrap it around myself as I venture back to my bed.

The pain in my body is already lessening as I kneel down to untie the cords on one of my bags. I fumble around for a few minutes, searching for a clean cloak. I spot some red fabric under three glistening daggers, my quiver of arrows, and my bow. I packed the bow and arrows myself, but Entho must have snuck the daggers into my bag before I left for Harcourt. I touch the daggers lovingly for just a moment and then pull my cloak out of the bag. I bring it up to my nose and breathe in the scent of home. A huge lump forms in my throat, and just for a moment it feels like tears might burst from my eyes…not for the city, but for Entho. I didn't know I could ever miss him this much.

I swallow deeply, tamping down tears while I slide the cloak over my head. Just then a pounding noise on the door diverts my attention. Barefoot, I traipse to the door and search for a viewing plate but can't find one. I end up just swinging the door open, not knowing what or whom to expect. A slight boy dressed in a matching red cloak greets me. His slanted eyes squeeze into tiny slits when he smiles, and his dark hair is glistening in the sunlight.

"Gunter!" I exclaim. "You made it."

"Well, snock, I wasn't the one who was captured by Destroyers."
For a second I think he is going to hug me.

"That is true," I agree, darkness clouding my mood at the mention of Destroyers.

"Thann told me how you got here."

"It was terrible, but I guess we are lucky to be alive." I furrow my brow. "Did Koree and Echo make it here with you?" Just mentioning Koree's name sends a strange tingle up my spine, and I shake it off, not understanding what it is all about. I am still confused about both Koree and Thann. I don't even bother asking about Reese, although I am curious if he made it to Harcourt or turned tail back to Bay City.

"Yeah, they're both in the Infirmary."

"Are they okay?" I ask him, concerned.

"They're fine. Koree will be released tomorrow. Echo has some stitches in her head."

"Oh, good." I sigh visibly.

Gunter changes the subject, his voice animated. "Geez, I thought you'd sleep all day."

"Me too." A yawn escapes from my mouth, as if on cue.

"The healers said you'll be fine. But they want to see you today to clean and wrap your wrists."

"Okay, sure." Gunter and I stare at each other for a moment. Too many thoughts are swirling around in my head, and I still haven't mastered the art of conversation with peers. As usual, Gunter comes to my rescue.

"Yesterday was rough, huh?" he asks, his voice now low and penetrating.

I pause, not wanting to relive the ghastly day. "You could say that again. At least you aren't a Light Skin. I thought Thann was going to die for sure. And me, too." I let out a huge, sad breath. "Like Soot…"

He hangs his dark head for a moment. "I know. Snock, that was awful." He sighs, stares at the ground then peers back up at me, his black eyes glistening. "We Red Cloakers aren't made for things like that," he adds.

I let out a small laugh. "I was trained for such things. But it didn't really help."

"Oh blazes, if you hadn't been there, I doubt if any of us would have made it here."

"Who knows?" I reply, pondering what he just said. "Did you have any problems getting here after Thann and I were abducted?"

"No." He purses his lips. "Just keeping Koree on the dragon was a bagger. He's freaking huge!"

"I know. I was worried you wouldn't make it." Koree isn't as big as Thann, but his muscular body and long legs quickly overtake my thoughts.

"Well, old Gunter here is stronger than he looks," he blares theatrically.

I can't help but laugh. "I am glad you made it."

"Hey, did you get a note about seeing someone named Kesper?" he queries, changing the subject.

"Yes. Did you?"

"Yep." He holds up his note. "You wanna go find this Kesper person together?"

"Sure," I reply, quickly slipping socks on my feet and stepping into my tall leather boots. I trail behind him out the door, and it shuts with a small bang. I follow him down a wooden staircase, our boots clomping in unison.

Curious, I ask, "How did you know how to find me?"

"I've been wandering around for a while, checking this place out." I found the sign that said Girl's Dormitory, so I guessed that's where you'd be. I'm in the boy's dormitory. So far I'm all alone."

"Me too," I answer. "Hey, do you know where Thann is?"

"Meetings," he answers in a matter of fact tone.

"Oh…" My voice trails off, and I hope that Gunter doesn't notice the disappointment in it.

"Missing the Golden Boy, are you?" Gunter's black eyes sparkle, and I realize he is teasing me. He raises his eyebrows up and down, and it brings a smile to my face. I haven't had a friend since I was six years old. I had given up on that long ago, soon after Entho enrolled me in Weapons Training School. Talking to Gunter like this…it is like drinking fresh, clean water.

"Well, we did go through a lot together – same as you and me," I answer a little too defensively.

Gunter flashes a wide grin at me. His teeth are gleaming white in the direct sun. But then a serious expression takes over and his slanted eyes widen, a frown forming. "They put Reese is in prison. Did you know they actually have a prison here?"

"No way!"

"Yep." He breathes deeply and lets out a long sigh. "I can't believe what he did to you and Thann."

"I know. If I would have had a weapon when he told the Destroyers we were Light Skins, I might have killed him," I say a little too seriously. Gunter sniggers.

He turns to me, then, peers up into my eyes. His eyes twinkle and his voice rises to a high pitch. "You have to check this place out! I can't believe we actually made it to snocking Dragon Academy!"

Chapter 2

Gunter takes off in a rapid blur, and I scurry to catch up with him. As I scan Harcourt, my breath is taken away at the stunning scene before me. Cobblestone roads lead to different buildings, most of them made of grey stone, resembling tiny castles with turrets and large windows. There are signs on the buildings. Each sign is rectangular, white with gold lettering, and announces the purpose of the building – Hatchery, Research, Nursery, Medical, Infirmary, Feeding, Training, and so on. Some of the signs have pictures of a dragon's head on them, all of varying colors.

White fences proudly enclose green pastures where dragons of different sizes and colors bask in the sun. Velvet green rolling hills nestle around the little settlement with huge oak trees scattered about like guards on duty.

"Wow," I breathe out. Then my mind shifts. "I wonder where Kesper is," I say, turning to Gunter. "Did you know that she is Thann's mom?"

"No freaking way!" he exclaims. "How do you know?"

"Well, Thann and I spent a lot of time together once we were captured." I don't tell him that I met Thann and Koree when they came to Entho's clinic for a package several weeks ago.

"Ooooo Lah Lah," Gunter teases. "You and Thann tied up now?"

I instantly blush, my face flushing with heat. "No, no, nothing like that." I think for a moment. Could something really happen between Thann and me? Everything about him is mesmerizing. His height and broad shoulders. The shaggy blonde hair that frames his face. The Mark of Power on his right cheek…similar to the one on my left. His golden eyes that sparkle with mischief. Could it ever be something else, something more than friendship?

Suddenly Koree's face enters my mind. Serious, Koree with his piercing green eyes, lopsided grin, copper curls and firm jaw. And that dimple. Just thinking about him sends a thrill through my entire body. "You look nice," he told me. Nobody has ever said anything like that to me – not to Teak the Freak. I shake my head, putting the two boys out of my mind and focus on Gunter again.

Gunter leads the way to one of the stone buildings. People, dressed mostly in tunics and pants of various colors, are milling about, some holding dragons, others talking in small groups, their voices wafting across the slight breeze that tickles my cheeks like a soft feather.

I wonder why they aren't wearing Alliance clothing. In Bay City I am required to wear red, because we are privileged. There are very few Red Cloakers, and even less Light Skins left in the world. I wait for the stares, name calling, or other abuse that Light Skinned people must endure, but I am mostly ignored. My red cloak and pale skin seem to mean nothing to these people.

We arrive at a door ornately marked "Office". Gunter reaches for the glistening golden knocker, twists his head toward mine and conspiratorially whispers to me, "I already asked around about where Kesper was. I was too chicken to come by myself."

"You weren't chicken yesterday. You were very brave."

"Yeah, well, you were there yesterday." Gunter raps the knocker several times. We wait for a minute and then he raps it again.

"Come in," a distinctly female voice calls out.

Gunter opens the door, and we step into a dark room, paneled richly in deep mahogany. I furrow my eyebrows, confused, biting on my lower lip. I scan the glossy hard wood floor, and suddenly I know without a doubt that this is the room that Thann and I entered from the tunnel. I search for the trap door that Thann and I came through, but I can't find it. I am puzzled. Why would the tunnel lead to Kesper's office?

Two overstuffed chairs with a rose floral pattern face a massive, neatly organized desk. A woman is seated behind the desk in a large, matching chair. She is obviously busy writing in a ledger of some sort, her face pinched down in concentration. She clears her throat and tips her head up, smiling at us.

Instantly, my mouth drops open in surprise as I study her face. Every inch of it. Over and over again as if it were a mistake or a cruel joke. I let out a gigantic, confused breath then squeeze my eyes shut for a second before opening them widely and continue gawking at Kesper's face.

It is as if I am looking at an older version of myself.

Chapter 3

Kesper is definitely a Light Skin, tall and lanky like me, with the same tangled blonde hair as mine, but hers is pulled up in a bun with tendrils spilling out around her face. Her eyes are the same gold-ish amber color as mine, and she has a crescent shaped mark on her left cheek, so similar to mine that my mouth hangs open in surprise. Her mouth is full, but her nose is longer, straighter than mine. She has tiny wrinkles in the corners of her eyes. She is dressed in a shiny golden cloak, those that only Master Dragon Trainers wear.

She smiles openly at us, revealing straight, white teeth. "You must be Gunter and Teak."

We stand numbly before her and just nod our heads, both of us struck mute.

"Come in, come, sit down." Her eyes are dancing with enjoyment. "She gestures at the two chairs, and we each find one, sitting obediently. Gunter appears to be as surprised as I am by Kesper's appearance. He keeps looking at her then back at me.

"I am Kesper," she begins. "Kesper Harcourt." She peers at us, a stern expression suddenly sprouting on her face. Gunter and I both remain speechless.

"I am in charge here…." Her voice trails off and she turns her head, looks directly at me. "I understand I have you to thank for saving my son, Thann." Her eyes cast down for a moment and then back up. "And Koree. He is like a son to me."

Silence lingers. I know I should say something, but I just keep staring at her, thinking how much I look like her, except not in such an elegant and self assured way. *Could I ever be beautiful like her?* I continue gawking at her shamelessly.

"She was totally smash," Gunter blurts out. "Pulls a knife out of Echo's head, throws it, and boom, it lands right in the chest of the Destroyer trying to kill Thann. Then two arrows right smack into the other one   just when he was going for Thann's head with his sword." Gunter's voice is animated, shrill, as if he were telling his friends about a fight at school.

I close my eyes, remembering the knife lodged in Echo's head – the one intended for me. And the Destroyer who was inches away from killing Thann. The other one who killed Soot. I cringe at the memories, still fresh in my mind.

"Well, thank you so much," Kesper replies in a matter of fact tone. Her eyes bore straight into mine. I feel like she is accusing me of something even though her words are polite. She pauses for a moment, strumming her long, delicate fingers on the desk.

"The death of the Destroyers does present a problem." She stops for a moment, tilting her head. "We do have tight security here…" Apparently deep in thought, she brings her hand up to her neck and fiddles with a necklace, a silver dragon with wings spread wide and a large white diamond for its eye. My hand immediately travels to my wrist – to the charm bracelet that Entho gave me before I left for Dragon Academy. It was my mother's bracelet, the one she used to "charm" the dragons she trained. I lovingly rub my fingers over each of the miniature golden dragons.

Kesper's voice rings in my ears as her eyes fix on mine. "You did the right thing, Teak." Her voice is so low I must strain to hear it. "You both have been through a lot," she adds. "I'm so sorry about the other girl...Soot. I'm sending a message and monetary compensation to her family, but I know it isn't enough."

She tilts her head to the side again, and a ray of sunlight catches in her hair, shimmering like gold. She speaks as if she were a holy person saying a prayer. "It could have been all three of you."

Gunter and I nod our heads in unison, words escaping us both again. She continues. "I am amazed that you and Thann survived. The Destroyers are....Powerful." Her face scrunches up, as if a painful image has overshadowed her thoughts. She gives her head a gentle shake and abruptly changes the subject.

"You can take today off. Go wander around. I'm sure Koree and the girl, Echo, will want to see you." She stands up, as if dismissing us. Then she opens one of the drawers in her desk.

She pulls out some coins and hands them to us – gold coins I have never seen before with pictures of dragons etched into them. "This is the currency we use here – the only one," she explains. "Go buy something fun for yourselves. Training will start tomorrow."

"Where do we go?" I blurt out.

"There are stores along the main path. But stay away from any sign that has a picture of a dragon on it – you don't have clearance for those rooms yet and could get yourselves into some trouble." At that her lips curve up, ever so slightly. "Be up and ready for training tomorrow at 6:00 in the morning. You'll hear the trumpets blaring."

Chapter 4

Gunter and I stumble out of Kesper's office, our boots hitting the cobblestone paths like small hammers. Without discussion, we wander into the first store we find – a dragon training equipment store. A stern man is perched at the counter. He is tall, lean and dressed in riding gear. The smell of leather, oil, and something metallic encompasses the room. I scrunch up my face.

"What's with you?" Gunter whispers, twisting his body toward mine.

"That smell."

Gunter laughs at me. "You'll get used to it."

Gunter and I fondle halters with gemstones, saddles, bridles, an assortment of books, dyed leather leg and shin guards, and an assortment of other items we have never seen before. We each buy a bag of dragon treats, hoping we will be allowed to give them to Pebble and the other dragons.

As we make our way out the door, I wonder how they can sell books here at Harcourt. Everyone knows that books have been banned unless they are for training purposes – authorized by Siv Gareth himself.

My thoughts are sidetracked by the next store we enter – a candy store. A chubby lady with grey hair and a white apron asks if she can help us. Shelves full of candy in jars tease us – chocolate shaped dinosaurs, fruit colored dragon eggs, spinning dinosaur heads, long licorice ropes that are shaped like riding reins. Little trading cards with candy dots glued to them, each boasting of a different breed of dragon. Paper thin dragon wings dipped in dark chocolate and glittery candy sprinkles. Fire red dragon flames, miniature marshmallow dragonlings. My mouth waters, wanting one of each. After much discussion, Gunter settles on the licorice reins, and I buy the colored dinosaur eggs. We leave with our purchases in little paper bags with dragons stamped on them, popping candy into our mouths as we go.

"This place really is fantastic," I say.

"I know. My dad forced me into Government. I hated it. All I wanted was to ride dragons. I was horrible. At Government. And a 'Big Disappointment' to Dad."

"I know the feeling. My mom was a dragon trainer. She died when I was four and my dad made me go to Weapons – he sent me away when I was six years old."

"I'd rather do Weapons than Government."

"Not me." I wrinkle my nose at the thought of it. "So, how did you get here if you are a Red Cloaker and trained in Government?" I ask him, curious about how he could have passed the Dragon Assessment.

"We have three dragons of our own. We live on the outskirts of the city. But snock, my dad hardly ever let me near them. I was only allowed to use the dragons with a driver and a cart. But I hung out with our stable hands a lot, picked up some stuff. Geez, was he mad when I failed Government and chose Dragons! Nobody in my family has ever failed Government."

"I am sorry about that." I try to think of something that might make Gunter feel better. "My dad spent a fortune on Weapons for me, and then I ended up taking the Assessment for Dragon Academy."

"Was he mad?"

"No. I thought for sure he would be. He actually apologized to me…for not letting me choose."

"Wow. Must be nice. My dad's a bagger most of the time."

"Entho hasn't always been that way. Most of the time he was just too busy for me."

"Entho?"

"My dad…his name is Entho."

"Oh. Weird." He raises his dark eyebrows and turns to me. "Why do you call him Entho?"

"I don't know. It happened after my mom died when I was a child. He was anything but a father at the time. I didn't think of him like a dad, so I just started calling him by his name."

"Still weird. My dad would have clobbered me for calling him by his name."

"Entho's not like that. He doesn't believe in striking people."

"Must be nice."

I nod my head at Gunter as we step into another store. Stacks of clothes are displayed neatly on racks, shelves, and an assortment of other interesting stands. They are mostly beige, like Thann and Koree's tunics. Some are shiny, glistening gold, like Kesper's. A short, kind faced man waddles over to us. It looks as if he has spent too much time next door in the candy store – his jowls hang low and his belly pushes against the apron he is wearing. A cloth tape measure is wrapped around his neck.

"NB's?" he asks us. Gunter and I look at each other, shrugging our shoulders.

"Short for newbies. Are you newbies? I don't recall seeing you before."

"Oh, yes, yes we are," Gunter replies, ever polite.

"I'm Jessup." He gets out a leather bound notebook, opens it.

"Names?" he asks as he reaches for a pencil.

"Gunter Longbird."

"Teak Frain."

"Hmmmm." The man closes the book with a quick snap, peers up at us with bleary blue eyes, the color of a cloudy day. "You both have already earned merits, I see. Well done." He smiles, waddles into a back room and comes out with two stacks of clothing – beige tunics and pants.

Next, he shuffles over to a drawer, pulls it open and brings out two dragon pins, similar to the ones on my bracelet. He hands them to me, reverently, as if they were holy objects. I clasp my hands around them, inspecting them closely. These dragons are silver instead of gold and are quite a bit larger than the dragons on my bracelet. They have fasteners on the back of them stamped with the numbers of our year – 2087. Both of them have a 168 stamped under the year, so tiny I can barely make it out. One of the dragons has blue eyes, and the other has red eyes, both made of gemstones just like those on my bracelet. He hands Gunter a dragon pin with blue eyes.

"We work on the merit system here," he explains. "You receive a dragon pin for each 100 merits you receive. Put them on the tunic you wear, by the neck opening." He winks at us then whispers, "The others will come in with no pins – real NB's, if you know what I mean." He chuckles to himself. Then, "Oh, and if you get 100 demerits, you have to give up a pin." He laughs again, as if it would be funny to actually have to part with one of the beautiful pins. He turns to me. "You have 20 extra merits waiting for you – must have done something spectacular."

I shrug my shoulders. "Not really," I respond.

"Well, I've never had an NB come in with 220 merits!" he exclaims. His eyes search mine for answers, but I really don't want to go into an explanation about what happened on the way to Harcourt.

We try to pay Jessup, but he explains that we have earned the clothing and pins with our merits. He hands us each a large cloth bag with our clothes and pins neatly stacked inside. We step out of the store, waving good-bye to him.

I breathe in the sweet country air of Harcourt as I grasp the bag tightly to my chest. It is weightless and glorious, and I can't help thinking about the heavy bag of weapons I carried over my shoulder since I was six years old. For me this bag holds more than just candy, clothes, and jewelry.

It holds a new life of dreams and hope, and I cling tightly to it…tighter than anything I have ever held in my life.

Chapter 5

"Let's check on Echo and Koree," Gunter says to me as I pop a candy egg in my mouth. He is gnawing on the licorice like a ravenous wolf.

"Sounds good," I answer. "Then we can go put this stuff up and find something to eat."

"Do you only think about food?"

"Not usually, but today I am famished." We chat back and forth, looking into store windows, calling off names of buildings. Eventually we find a sign displayed in front of a stone building marked Infirmary. We casually stroll in.

An elegant lady with dark hair pulled tightly around her face and wearing a white healer's robe is perched at the front counter. "May I help you?" She politely asks, as if she has practiced the words into perfection.

"We're here to see some friends – Koree and Echo," Gunter explains.

She inspects us with her deep black eyes, checks a leather book, and tells us their room numbers. "You will need to leave your bags with me. I'll place them behind the counter."

"Okay," I answer, reluctantly handing her my bag. Gunter does the same, and we take off around a bend that leads us through a long corridor. The walls are painted a sickly shade of green.

We reach Koree's room first, and my heart starts beating rapidly at the thought of seeing him again. Gunter enters first, and I follow, somewhat shyly behind him. Koree is lying in a white bed, looking as if he is dying of boredom. At the sound of our footsteps, he twists his coppery head around, and his lips breaks into an uneven smile. "Hey," he casually remarks, a dimple forming in his right cheek.

"How are you doing?" Gunter asks earnestly.

"Huge headache but ready to get out of here," he responds. His eyes appear normal – serious and piercing, yet still sparkling like green pools of water. I study his face. Yesterday it was pale, but today his olive colored complexion has returned. He turns to me, reddish brown curls draping over his forehead. "Thanks for what you did, especially for Thann."

"N...no...problem," I stutter, embarrassed by the attention. An awkward silence settles over us as Koree's eyes lock onto mine. I match his stare as my stomach flutters and my heartbeat races out of control. What is it about this boy, I wonder, as I struggle to find enough air to fill my lungs.

Koree gradually pulls his eyes away from mine, turning his attention to Gunter. "I get out in the morning. We start training then. Are you ready?"

"Yes," Gunter says so quickly that we all laugh. I try not to gawk at Koree, glancing out the window occasionally. Thoughts of yesterday creep into my mind – the good ones. Of how Koree used his Power to punish Reese for tormenting me, how he talked to me when we watered our dragons. How I tended to him after the Destroyer used his dark Power on him, sending him flying through the air. I reached for one of his coppery curls and tenderly moved it away from his eyes...

His husky voice interrupts my thoughts. "How did you and Thann escape the Destroyers?"

"Thann didn't tell you?" I ask.

"No, haven't seen him yet."

"It is a long story," I say nervously, making eye contact with him again. I bite my lower lip and furrow my brow before continuing. "We were tied to a tree and a little man named...Yaren cut us loose, flew us to Mount Gareth on a dragon and stuffed us in an underground tunnel. We ran here."

"Holy snock, you ran from Mount Gareth to here?"

"Umm, I guess we had no choice. Yaren said Destroyers were everywhere now that the Purity Law has passed." I fix my eyes onto Koree's, disturbed by a thought that has just flown into my head. "Do you think we are safe here...from them...from the Destroyers?"

Koree matches my gaze, his green eyes somber. "Nobody is ever safe from them." He lets out a giant sigh, and his curls swirl above his forehead. "Kesper has sealed the town off. There are guards everywhere. But…" His voice trails off.

"What?" Gunter questions, urgency in his voice.

"Nothing. Just none of us can leave here now."

"Well, who would want to?" Gunter exclaims, and Koree starts laughing, a rare chuckle that seems to come from his belly…more like one of Thann's laughs than his.

"We better go see Echo," Gunter interjects.

"Yeah, she's probably having fits with everyone," Koree agrees.

"You got that right," Gunter answers. Then, "See ya buds." Gunter reaches his hand out and smacks Koree's arm.

"See ya," Koree answers, whacking Gunter back.

"Bye, Koree," I tell him, turning to leave.

"See you later," he says, but it comes out more like a question than a statement. I twirl around and just for a moment our eyes meet again.

He cocks his head to the side, shoots me a lopsided grin, and like a gift just for me, his dimple appears.

I bite my lower lip, not knowing what to say, but I do manage to answer – a one word response. "Later," I barely breathe out, not even sure if he hears. I reluctantly pivot away from him, following Gunter out the door.

We find Echo's room easily. She is perched in a clean bed with a white bandage wrapped tightly around her head. When she sees us enter, she immediately launches into one of her tirades, and I can't help but laugh. "I'm going out of my snocking mind here", she complains. "I wish there was something to do. Dragonballs, I have to be here for a week. I'm going to miss out on training."

"A week isn't so bad," Gunter tells her, lifting his eyebrows up and down, almost in rhythm with his words. I wonder if he knows that he is doing this and how ridiculous he looks.

"Easy for you to say, hot shot," she quips. "You get to start training tomorrow." She makes a pouty face. "And I smell candy on the two of you. Pony up, Red Cloakers, I want some." Her misty blue eyes move back and forth between Gunter and me, accusing us of a crime.

"They took it from us…at the counter," I tell her. "Otherwise we would share, I promise," I tell her.

"Hmmmm." She crosses her arms over her chest. "I smell mutiny as well."

Gunter chuckles. "We'll bring you candy, okay?"

"Okay," she mutters. Then she looks at me. "Hey, how did you get here? Last time I saw you some ugly snocking Destroyers captured you and Thann." Her eyes open wide. "Is Golden Boy okay?"

"Yeah, he's here," Gunter answers.

"Oh, fireballs, that is good news," she breathes out.

Just then a healer walks in, so quietly I don't even hear footsteps. "You must leave the patient now," he tells us. He is short and chubby with a balding head.

"That's fine, Princess Teak needs some food," Gunter replies.

"Princess?" I ask. "Where did that come from?"

Gunter laughs. "You know, that's what Thann calls you. It kinda fits."

"Oh." I think about what Gunter just said. Do I really come off as a princess? I shake it off and turn to Echo. "We'll visit you as often as we can," I promise her.

"You'd better or I'll hunt you down like a Lav when I get out of here." I can't help but laugh at Echo as Gunter and I leave her room.

Chapter 6

As we round the corner toward the lobby, a woman in a white healing robe stops us. "Are you Teak Frain?" she asks. She is petite with dark skin and her grey streaked hair is tied up into a huge knot on her head, appearing almost comical. Her hazel eyes seem friendly, though, and she lifts her thin lips up in a slight smile.

"Um, yes," I answer.

"You need to come with me. We need to treat your wounds."

"Oh...okay." I look down at my mangled, bloody wrists, and suddenly, my hand and knee begin to throb.

"Can I come with her?" Gunter asks her.

"Sure," she answers, smiling fondly at him. She then turns to me. "We should have done this last night, but we decided that you were exhausted and needed sleep more than anything."

We follow her into a room that brings back vivid memories of Entho's clinic. "Have a seat here," she tells me, and I hop onto a white cot. She fiddles around with some bottles and a mortar and pestle for a while and then brings a bottle of medicine over. "Take three droppers full of this every hour until it is gone. It will take the inflammation away as well as the pain."

Next, she gently washes the gashes on my left wrist with an antiseptic solution. "This may sting a bit," she cautions. I nod my head, biting down on my cheek as the burning solution rinses blood and dried up mud into a basin she has placed under my arm. She repeats the process with my right wrist and then reaches for a stone bowl. She dips her fingers into the bowl and dabs salve on my festering wounds. Instantly, I feel coolness, letting out a sigh of relief. Finally, she wraps them with clean white bandages.

"There. All done." She smiles at me. "I understand you did a bit of healing work yourself on the way here."

"Just the basics. My dad is a healer."

"Yes. Entho Frain. I remember him." She lets out a gigantic sigh. "I wish he still worked here."

"Me too," I answer, thinking about Entho living here. I wonder what it would be like to grow up in Harcourt instead of Bay City.

"All better?" she asks.

I nod my head.

"Good. You may go now." She tips her head to the side, her eyes narrowing. "Be careful."

"All right," I answer. I thank her as Gunter and I wind our way through the halls and end up at the front counter. The lady hands us our packages without comment and we turn to leave.

We reach the dormitories in what seems like no time at all, and I throw my bags on my bed and rush back outside, the white sun almost blinding me on my way downstairs. I find Gunter waiting, and we decide to go to the game store and find something to keep Echo and Koree busy while they are in the Infirmary.

"I want to buy Echo that dragon training book," I tell Gunter, remembering how she barely passed the Assessment.

We stroll back to the dragon training store, and I quickly pay for the book. At the game store we decide on a deck of dragon cards for Echo and Koree. Each deck has different dragon breeds, the colors etched in metal. Directions for various versions of the game are printed in gold lettering on the back of the decks. I long for a deck for myself, but I am running low on dragon coins, and we promised Echo we would get her some candy. We venture back to the candy store, and decide that Echo would like the chocolate covered wings.

"No payment necessary," the kind lady tells us as Gunter and I both lay our last coins on the counter.

"Why not?" I question, puzzled.

"I heard you talking. They're for the girl in the Infirmary. I just can't take payment for someone who's hurt." Her voice quavers, almost like she is going to cry.

"Thank you so much," I tell her, hoping my voice reflects enough sincerity. I have never known anyone to do something like this, especially when a Light Skinned person was involved.

"You're welcome, and give the girl these." She reaches under the counter and brings out a huge bag and hands it to us. I open it, staring at the myriad of colorful candies and chocolates inside.

"Wow," I say as Gunter leans over, peeking into the bag.

"They're the ones I can't sell…just not pretty enough. But I promise they taste the same." A wide grin encompasses her chubby face and I can't help but smile back.

"Thanks," Gunter and I say together as we turn away. We return to the Infirmary with our gifts. Echo is excited, taking the deck of cards from us. "Thanks, guys, these are dragonific!" I hand her the book, but she doesn't seem too excited about it. "Uh…thanks," she tells me as she opens it. "It's got some pictures that are way smash."

"Oh Echo", Gunter says in a sing song voice, grabbing the bag of candy from me.

"What?"

"We have something for you." He is raising his eyebrows up and down again, and I look over at him as if he has lost his mind.

"Something else?"

"Yeah…you wanted candy…you got it." He hands her the bag and she lets out a squeal of delight.

"Holy dragon tits. You're the best!" She digs around in the bag and pulls out a chocolate wing, sticks it in her mouth and chews it slowly, obviously savoring the taste. Chocolate smears her lips, and she doesn't bother wiping it away.

"You Red Cloakers probably get candy all the time, but Blue Cloakers don't," she tells us with her mouth full, greedily reaching in the bag for more candy.

"Take it easy or you are going to get sick," I warn her, mimicking my father's healing voice. Then I think of Koree. "We had better get going."

"Yeah, we have dragon cards for Koree," Gunter offers.

"Thanks, guys," she tells us. I turn to leave, but notice Gunter dawdling.

"Come on, Gunter," I nag.

"Okay, okay." He waves good-bye to Echo and we tromp out the door toward Koree's room.

We reach his door, and I stop dead in my tracks when I hear a familiar voice. Thann. It is definitely Thann's voice I hear, and a wide grin spreads over my face. I peek into the doorway and Thann is standing next to Koree, apparently deep in conversation. Thann's mountainous frame seems to swallow the room, and I notice bandages on his wrists, just like mine. He is focused intently on Koree, and I suddenly don't want to disturb them. Apparently, Gunter doesn't seem to mind.

"Hey, are we interrupting something important?"

He and Koree immediately lift their heads in our direction, and Thann answers. "Naw. Just talking about some stuff for tomorrow. Come on in." A broad smile encompasses his face as Koree seems to disappear from my sight.

"Princess Teak!" Thann says to me, his golden eyes lit with fire and mischief.

"Hi Thann," I answer, suddenly shy.

"You look better than the last time I saw you," Gunter tells Thann.

"Yeah, that was some weird stuff yesterday," Thann answers. "I never want to see a Destroyer again in my life." Pensively, he rubs at his wrists, and for a moment there is an uncomfortable silence in the room.

"We brought you some dragon cards…so you won't get bored," Gunter announces. Koree's face falls, and I wonder if we have done something offensive.

"Thanks," Koree answers, taking the deck from Gunter. He tosses them up and down with one hand for a few minutes before he turns toward Thann. They both bust up laughing.

"Hey, what's so funny?" Gunter jabs at them.

Thann stops laughing long enough to answer. "We have about five decks each…grew up playing this game."

"Snock," Gunter tells him. "We didn't think about that."

Koree has stopped laughing, and a proverbial somber expression appears on his face. "It's okay. Each deck is different, and I haven't played in a long time." He slowly opens the metallic tin the cards are in and examines each dragon. After about ten cards, he holds out

one with a black dragon on it and shows it to Thann. "Look, an

Ebony…my favorite." He and Thann bust up laughing again, and

Gunter and I cast curious glances at each other, obviously not part of

their secret joke.

"Let's play a game," Thann offers, taking the deck from Koree.

"Um…I don't know how to play," I quietly tell them, embarrassed.

Heat flushes up my neck and onto my cheeks.

"Me neither," Gunter pipes in.

"We'll show you. Gather around Koree's bed," Thann orders. I

move to the other side of the bed. Thann shuffles the deck and

Koree explains the rules, but I only hear bits and pieces. I keep

glancing over at Thann. Then to Koree.

"We each get six cards, face down," Koree's voice drones in the

background. I reach for my cards.

"No," Koree's voice spits into my ears, as if I had just committed a crime. "Keep them face down until I say 'go'." His green eyes are intense, accusing, his eyebrows curving downward.

"Um, okay. Sorry." I feel as if I am about to cry, and I don't know why.

"It's all good," Thann interjects, his voice roaring. He whacks Koree on the arm.

"Sorry," Koree states flatly, turning to me. "I get a little carried away sometimes."

"It's okay," I answer. "I should have been paying attention."

Koree finishes explaining the rules, and I focus intently this time. Still, I can't seem to get the hang of matching the dragon breeds while adding and subtracting their wingspans and gestation periods while at the same time sorting the different colors into separate piles. Everybody is moving cards into piles, adding and subtracting out loud, and cards seem to be flying through the air. At one point I am sure that Koree and Thann are using their Power to make the cards fly into the correct piles. Still, Gunter is able to keep up better than me.

We play three games, and I lose every time. I make a pouty face on the final game, and Thann laughs heartily. "You'll catch on, I promise," he tells me.

"I hope so."

"We'd better get going," Gunter interrupts. "We need to get back to our dormitories."

"Koree yawns. "Yeah, new cadets are arriving as we speak, so I'd better get some sleep."

"Oh, we shouldn't have kept you," I interject.

"No. It was good." His green eyes fix onto mine. I am uncomfortable under his gaze, and I turn away, fidgeting with the hem of my cloak. I remember him walking by me on the journey here – before the Destroyers came – questioning me about weapons…how serious he can be.

"I gotta go, too," Thann says, breaking the awkward silence between Koree and me. He reaches his palm over toward Koree, and they execute an odd handshake, moving their palms together and then performing a crooked twisting motion. "See ya, buds," Thann tells Koree.

"Yeah, see ya."

Gunter and I both tell Koree good-bye. Awkwardly, I turn to leave, following the boys out the door.

"Teak," Koree calls out to me.

I spin back around.

"Yes?"

"See ya later," he tells me in a gravelly voice, nodding his head slightly, copper curls bouncing.

"Yes, later," I answer shyly. I stumble out the door and catch up with Gunter and Thann.

Thann and Gunter walk me to my dorm, and I smile inwardly, as if I need them to protect me. I say good-bye to them and as I tromp up the stairs, I realize the medicine has worn off, and my entire body is aching again, especially my knee. I am anxious to take another dose of the medicine the healer gave me and go to bed.

I open the door to the dormitory but stop short, shock and anger penetrating my body like a fast moving, poisonous snake.

Chapter 7

Three girls I have never seen before are sitting on my bed and their heads turn toward me in unison, gawking at me as if I were a circus sideshow freak. Teak the Freak…here we go again. They are all three wearing red cloaks and two of the cloaks are studded with dragon pins, one with red eyes, the other with blue…large silver dragon pins that I am sure are mine. My eyes quickly scan the rest of the room. It is a jumbled mess, and all of my belongings are scattered around the room.

My hands are shaking and my stomach clenches into a knot of rage. I tamp down my feelings, ignoring the girls in the room, as I approach my bed and begin to gather my belongings. To do this, I must crouch down by my bed, too close to the girls for my own comfort. I try to calm myself and control my temper as blood rushes violently through my head, pounding and swishing and throbbing through my veins like a turbulent river.

"Oh, look, a Ghost," one of the girls snidely announces, her voice almost a growl.

I keep my head down, doing my best to ignore her, a skill I have honed to perfection.

"An ugly Ghost," another girl howls. They all burst into horrid laughter. I drop to my hands and knees, gathering my new clothes, discarded on the floor like trash, when a solid kick to the side of my stomach launches me backward, pain streaking through the side of my body. Before I can think or stop myself, I grab the leg, twist it hard, and then yank it downward. A girl lands on her back with a thud right next to me.

"Enough," I breathe out like fire. The girl, tall with long black dirty hair, a flat face, high forehead, and a nose that resembles a pig lets out a squeal as shock washes over her face.

"Get up, Flame, you don't have to put up with that from a Ghost," one of the other girls shouts.

The girl who kicked me, Flame, glares at me but doesn't move. I stare down at her dark brown eyes, meeting them head on. We stay that way, squared off with our eyes battling each other for several moments. I refuse to be the first to look away as her name resounds repeatedly in my mind. Flame. Flame. Flame. Silently, I place her on my list right below Reese. Siv Gareth first. Destroyers second. Reese third, and then Flame.

Finally, she darts her eyes away from mine and hops up onto what was once my bed. "Stupid Ghost," she hisses, apparently needing the last word.

I wrinkle my forehead as I shoot all three girls my nastiest glare. I stand before them, an instant enemy for something I didn't do, breathing their foul air and hating them – so much that I want to kill them on the spot. Tears threaten to spill out, then, at the thought of killing them. I have killed…I truly am a killer, and now this is how I think. I gulp at stagnant air as I turn from them, surveying what is left of my belongings.

Entho's healing case is on another dresser, the bottles scattered about. The letter he wrote me is crumpled on the floor. My bow and quiver of arrows is on another bed, and I long to rush over and grab them, keep my bow next to me like the old friend it has always been. The three clean red cloaks I had folded neatly in my bag are gone, while two green cloaks and one blue, all dirty and soiled, are scattered on the floor. Apparently Flame and her friends like the idea of being Red Cloakers. What angers me the most, though, is seeing the dragon pins I earned on their bodies – peeking out from my cloaks – the dragon pins I earned.

Quickly, I gather up my new clothes, stuff them into my already opened bags, and limp over to the farthest bed in the dormitory. I tenderly set down what is left of my belongings on the floor and crawl under the covers of my new bed. I pull up the blanket around my neck and lie flat on my back, staring at the rough wooden ceiling. I might as well have gone to Soldier Academy. Nothing changes when you are a Light Skin.

I hold my body still, stiff…waiting for an attack. I know how the scene plays out all too well. Memories of the first assault I endured at Weapons when I was six years old creep into my memories. I wasn't prepared for the other children, older and stronger than me, who snuck silently into my room while I slept. I wailed in shock and fear and rage as fists and feet pummeled my tiny body. When the attack was finally over, I cried myself to sleep, bruises and cuts my only friends the next day. That never happened again. They tried – many times they tried – but after that I was always ready. To say I am ready now would be an understatement.

As each breath moves into my body and then out, with forced, controlled effort, I listen and wait. Whispering and giggling noises travel across the room to my hyper vigilant ears…but that is all.

My knee throbs in agonizing pain, and the past two days take hold of me like a tightly squeezing vice. Exhaustion creeps through my entire body. All I want to do is sleep, but right now I am not just a cadet at Dragon Academy with instant enemies in the same room. I am a soldier with ten years of Weapons training. Sleep is not allowed if I am to survive.

More memories crash through my skull…of being at Weapons and sleeping in the wilderness, daggers, a bow and arrows, and spears my only bedfellows as I sat up all night waiting…watching…waiting. And more recent memories of when Thann and I were captured by Destroyers and brutally tied to a tree. We waited until the Destroyers fell asleep, rubbing our wrists against the tree bark until they were bloody and raw. There was no sleep that night, and I silently resign myself to the same fate once again.

The hours tick by slowly, and I fight to keep my senses alert and my eyes open. At some point, though, the room becomes still and quiet. I listen intently and crane my neck around the room. The only sounds are the steady breathing of the other three girls, deep in slumber, their bodies cocooned by the rough navy blue blankets.

It is then, and only then, that I allow my eyes to close, and when I finally relax, I fall into a rare, deep slumber.

Chapter 8

I am flying on a Crimson; it must be Pebble. I swoop down from the sky, and find the orphanage. There she is…Winter…playing in the desolate yard with the other children. Dressed in brown – dirty, filthy, ugly brown. I swoop down on Pebble and grab her, easily settling her safely on the dragon as ruby red wings stretch out so far they block the sky. Once Winter is settled in front of me, away from her Guardian and the terrible orphanage, I stop for Entho, landing the dragon by his clinic.

I rush in, grab his hand, and he runs with me and leaps onto the back of the scarlet dragon, her soulful black eyes staring placidly at us. Pebble then turns back to me, opens and closes her eyes a couple of times as if waiting for a command. I nod my head at her – that is all it takes because we are bonded – and then she flaps her enormous wings a few times and in an instant we are in the air. Together, Entho, Winter and I leave Bay City behind, the crumbling sky scrapers and blackened buildings disappearing from our sight the higher up we go. I am filled with happiness as we soar through the air, hanging on as Pebble performs acrobatics in the night sky.

The dream ends abruptly with a smack – a large hand covering my mouth. At first I don't know if it is part of my dream or real, but soon enough I understand. It is definitely real. My heart thunders in my chest and I pop my eyes open, struggling to fill my lungs with air.

Instinctively I know it is a male hand clamping over my mouth. Reese, of course. I knew he wouldn't back down so easily. I struggle to breathe… and to understand. I thought Reese was in prison. My mind whirrs like a machine, and it takes me several seconds to orient myself to the situation.

I reach out my hand from under the covers, make a fist, and bring a strong blow upward, quick as lightning, not sure what I might strike in the darkness, but knowing it has to hit something. A groan fills the still night air, along with a solid thump. I feel a surge of satisfaction rise up inside of me. Maybe Reese will finally leave me alone now.

I jump out of bed and perch next to the figure that has dropped to the ground. I narrow my eyes in the dim grey light, trying to focus. I am not sure who it is, but after scrutinizing the prone figure for a few minutes, I realize it can't be Reese. The person on the floor is way too tall. I kneel down closer, inspecting the long body on my bedroom floor. Shock grabs me by the throat when I recognize who it is.

Koree is lying flat on his back. Yes, it is definitely Koree. I struggle to understand why he is here.

"What are you doing?" I hiss at him.

"Geez, you didn't need to clock me," he moans, sitting up.

"What did you expect, sneaking in here at night?" I ask. My voice has risen and I can start to see him a little better in the darkness, the outline of his face as he rubs his firm jaw. At last he stands, a tall solid figure in the darkness.

I rise with him, somehow registering that I am matching his movements with my own. I cross my arms over my chest.

He leans close to me, and a very masculine scent overtakes my sense. He pauses. Shifts on his feet for a few seconds. As I stare at the fidgeting outline of his body, anger and shock flood through me. How dare he sneak into my room and scare the daylights out of me, clamp his hand over my mouth. Who does he think he is?

He gets right to the point. "I…I…need your help," he whispers, desperation creeping out of his voice like the last breath of a dying man.

"With what?" I ask, tapping my foot on the floor.

"Shhh. Don't wake them up." He inhales deeply, exhales slowly, all the while glancing around the room. Then he confesses what he wants. "I need help with some healing. I'll have to take you somewhere else."

"I am no healer. And besides, you have healers here." I am baffled. "Why don't you go to them…the healers at Harcourt? Maybe in the daylight hours?" Sarcasm drips from my whispering voice. "And speaking of healers, aren't you supposed to be in the Infirmary?"

"It's a long story…but I really need help. Will you bring your healing case and come with me?" I blink my eyes in the dim light. I can't see his penetrating emerald eyes, but I somehow hear them, and they are begging. He speaks again, urgency in his voice. "Please?"

I don't know why I agree – it must be something in his voice. Or the eyes I can't see but know are there. I have only known Koree for a short time, but he has always been strong and self- assured. This is more like actual begging and is definitely a side of him I have never seen before. I give in. "Okay, but those stupid girls took my healing case…and a bunch of my other things."

"I'll help you find them," he whispers, relief obviously flowing through the cords of his voice.

Koree and I wander around as quietly as we can, searching for Entho's case like two criminals trying not to be discovered. After bumbling around for a while, we locate the healing case in one of the dressers. Koree gathers the bottles together, and closes the case. He then tucks it into the front of his tunic and tiptoes toward the door. I follow in a sort of trance. Koree shuts the door behind us like a secret that is kept between friends. Only the softest swishing noise can be heard along with a quiet thump.

The night is ghostly silent except for the creaking of our feet on the steps. I follow his tall figure until he stops at the end of the dormitory. Koree fiddles with something in front of him for a minute, then turns around, facing me, a granite silhouette in the darkness. He thrusts something into my hands.

"Put this on over your clothes." It is a quiet order.

Without complaint I slip a sleek black cloak with a hood over my body – it is loose and baggy on my lean frame. "Do you want me to put the hood over my head?" I ask.

"Yeah, we don't want to be seen." Koree slips into a similar cloak and turns to me while I stuff my long, unruly hair up into the hood. "We're getting on a dragon, he's right here, but you probably can't see him. He's an Ebony."

"Okay. What's his name?

"Onxy." He lets out a sigh. "What's your deal with dragon names?" he asks. I wonder if he is angry, but all I can detect is curiosity.

"Um…I don't know. I just like to know what their names are."

"Okay." He pauses for the briefest of moments. "Are you afraid of heights?" He is serious, intent. The Koree I have come to know.

I don't answer right away, not because I am afraid, but because I am not sure. Have I ever been up high? Certainly not in Weapons. Everything we did was on the ground. I have flown on dragons two times, but it wasn't the height that scared me, it was the Destroyers. "No," I answer confidently.

"Good." Koree's voice is serene, floating on the night air like a feather in a breeze. "Onyx is right here. And we're both going to get on him and take off. It's hard to see him in the night, but that's what I want. I'll help you on."

Koree enfolds my hand in his, wrapping his long fingers around mine. A tingle travels up my arm, and my first instinct is to pull my hand away. But I don't. This is so different than when Thann held my hand in the tunnel. My hand fit Thann's like they were molded for each other. But Koree's hand is different. Smaller for sure, but his fingers enfold mine perfectly, not like they were molded together...more like they fit together like two puzzle pieces.

Blanketed in darkness, I blindly follow Koree until we reach the black dragon. Koree lets go of my hand, and a feeling of desolation wipes through me. But before I can think about it too much, he lifts me up, as if I were a real princess, and actually places me on the dragon. I feel small next to him, feminine, perhaps for the first time in my life. There is no saddle on this dragon, and I am confused. "Where is the saddle?" I ask him.

"Don't need one the way we're going," he replies, hopping easily up onto the dragon in front of me. He turns around. "Put your arms around my waist and hold on tight. We'll be catching air in a few minutes."

"Catching air?" I know this is against the law. When Yaren flew with us on dragons in the middle of the night it was to save our lives. At the time I didn't think too much about the flying dragons, but now I am confused. "You mean...this dragon flies...we're going to fly?"

"Yep, hold on tight."

I tentatively reach my arms around Koree's waist, holding on tightly just as he told me to. Firm muscles explode under my fingertips and I struggle to catch my breath as the black dragon flaps his enormous wings and launches us off the ground. In an instant we are in the air.

The wind washes over me, cleansing me like a cool summer rain. I close my eyes as the earth leaves us behind and the dragon soars higher and higher into the black, starless sky. The warm night air brushes against my entire body, a fresh dark breeze that turns me into a person I don't even know. I am strong, confident, invincible.

"So, what do you think?" Koree asks, turning around. He holds his hands firmly on the dragon's neck.

"It is fantastic…the best feeling I have ever had," I answer quickly, honestly. But, as I grip Koree's waist, I am not sure if that is the only wonderful feeling I have. Touching Koree…it is like a fire has been lit inside of me.

"Well, watch this!" Koree shouts. I marvel at the difference in him…watching as the sullen boy I know disappears when he squeezes his legs then touches the dragon's neck. "Hold on," he orders, and suddenly we are flying upside down. The dragon launches into a loop and then a spin. I feel like I might be sick for a minute as my stomach seems to rise up into my throat, but at the same time I let out a squeal of delight.

"Do it again," I scream. He laughs deeply and it so contagious that I can't help but giggle along with him. He spins the dragon again, this time in a wider loop with three fast spins. I let out a whoop of delight, feeling like a bird that has been let out of its cage for the first time.

Koree rights the dragon, turns around. "We'll be landing soon," he tells me, the wind whipping his chestnut curls around his face.

Instantly I wilt like a dying flower. I want to stay out all night and fly, to keep spinning forever. I want to soar into the clouds on my own dragon and never get off of it. Koree's words break my thoughts into little bursts of nothing that disappear as quickly as they came.

As I clutch Koree's waist, curiosity takes over. I bend my head around the back of his body. "Where did you get a flying dragon? And why aren't his wings clipped?"

As the black earth materializes before us, Koree answers, his voice tight and thin against the wind. "That's part of the long story. I'll tell you when we land.

Chapter 9

Onxy lands smoothly a few moments later, only a slight bump an indication that we are actually on the ground. I am disoriented. Between the flying and darkness, time has taken on a new dimension for me. Koree dismounts the dragon then reaches for my hand again, helping me down off of Onyx.

"It's dark, so I'll guide you there."

His words sting as disappointment washes over me. Of course. He just needs my healing abilities. How stupid of me. "Okay," I answer. *What a fool I have been! As if a boy like Koree would be interested in me.*

Koree leads me through a maze of trees, grasping my hand and pulling me along. The trees appear to be planted in rows on purpose. He turns back to me, "Kesper's grandfather planted this orchard years ago. The trees are…well, you'll see in a minute."

He navigates somehow to a specific tree, knocks on the tree trunk five times in a certain rhythm: knock knock, rapppppp, rappppp, tap. Almost immediately a rope ladder is dropped down from the tree.

"Follow me," Koree orders, dropping my hand as he grabs the edges of the ladder between both hands and scales it as if he does this every day. Maybe he does, how would I know?

For a split second doubt encompasses me, and I wonder what I am doing out here in the middle of the night…arriving on an illegal flying dragon no less. Tentatively, I take hold of the rope ladder with both hands, step onto the first rung, and am immediately unnerved when it begins to sway. I clutch the rope tightly, my fingers turning white as I swing back and forth.

Koree is leaning from some sort of platform up in the tree. "Just climb," he tells me in his patient voice, the same one he used to teach me how to ride a dragon on the ground. "And don't worry about the movement of the ladder." His voice fades away against the light wind like trying to talk to someone during a windy storm.

I put one foot in the rope step, sway a little, and then climb to the next. I reach a sort of rhythm, swaying and climbing. My stomach seems to have traveled up to my throat with each step I take. How is it that I am not afraid of flying on a dragon, but a rope ladder sends bolts of fear through me? With shaking hands I reach the platform, and Koree takes me by the waist and easily lifts me into a small house. He shuts a door behind us.

I blink my eyes in the dim light, not sure of where I am. A candle flickers on a rough wooden counter, and I blink my eyes again, this time in surprise. There are two Light Skinned adults and a Light Skinned boy staring at me. I notice the woman is holding an extremely small toddler. I immediately deduce that the child is lethargic and unresponsive, limp in her mother's arms with her eyes closed.

"She's terribly sick," the mother flatly states, but her grey eyes seem to be asking me for something. For help I assume. I let out a huge sigh. So this is what Koree wanted me for. I am still puzzled why he wouldn't take this terribly sick child to the healers at Harcourt.

"Lay her on the bed," I tell her mother, my voice firm. There are four small cots in the little tree house, a table and chairs, and a small sofa. The woman gently places the toddler on one of the cots. She looks to be about two or three, and I am dismayed that she doesn't stir when placed on the cot. Her eyes stare vacantly into space, similar to Thann's when the Destroyers came…when they used their dark Power on him. I didn't know what to do for Thann. What If I can't help this child? I feel my chest tighten into a ball, fear of making a mistake clenching it tighter and tighter.

Anger at Koree blazes through me and I struggle to tamp it down. How could he put me into this situation? How can he endanger this child's life when there are real healers so close? I don't have the answers to these questions, but I intend to find out. I wipe my brow and set to work. The little girl needs attention…and fast.

I reach down and feel her forehead. "She is on fire," I declare to Koree, glaring into his green eyes. "She needs liquids. I turn to the girl's mother. "I need a wet cloth. And take her clothes off. You can leave her diaper." My words are singing to another person's song – Entho's. If only I could be sure the tune I am singing is the right one.

I begin my analysis of the toddler, and I realize that the blank stare is from a high fever and not some kind of Power that was placed on her, a spell I don't know how to undo. This time I breathe a sigh of relief. At least I know what to do with fevers.

Koree pulls Entho's healing case out of his tunic, as if reading my mind. I dig out an assortment of herbs – lemon balm, catnip, yarrow, peppermint. Then I add Echinacea, which will also help fight infection as well as a small dose of antibiotic. Entho mixes his own antibiotics, but I never learned how to do it. I frown, my eyebrows furrowing at the sight of so little of the precious medicine.

"I need water, to mix these herbs – warm or hot is best." The child's father, a man of medium height and light brown hair, turns to leave, rushing across the room. "Oh, and garlic if you have some," I call after him.

"I'll be right back with whatever you need," he answers, his voice solemn, as he lowers the ladder, scales it like a monkey, and disappears from view. The little girl's mother returns with a cool cloth. I place it on the toddler's forehead, noticing that her mother has already stripped the clothes from her body, leaving a small diaper. The toddler seems so tiny, lying on the cot…like a miniature porcelain white doll. The blue veins in her forehead are enlarged and seem to be pulsing with every one of her heartbeats, a true living map. Her small chest rises and falls with each slow, labored breath. "Keep her cool with the water," I order.

"Yes, of course, whatever you say," her mother replies, a small tear forming in her eye. I want to reassure her, like Entho does with his patients, but I am not that confident with my healing abilities. Just then the child's father arrives, rushing up the ladder with a bag of water that is warm and a garlic clove. I quickly mix the herbs and garlic in the water. I know the toddler isn't going to take the medicine willingly, that the terrible taste will bother her. "Do you have honey, or syrup, something sweet?" I ask, thinking of Entho's tea. I suddenly miss him more than ever. I shake off the feeling, knowing that it won't help right now. The man strides over to a small cupboard and hands me a crock of syrup. I pour some of it into the bag and mix it thoroughly, shaking the bag back and forth until I am satisfied that the medicine and herbs are combined.

I discover a small dropper in Entho's case. Perfect. I fill the dropper with the syrupy medicine, prop the little girl up with a pillow and start painstakingly dripping the liquid into her mouth, knowing that I need to place the dropper almost in the back of her throat to make her swallow. At first she just gags, and the medicine drips down her chin. I am so dismayed I want to cry, but I keep trying.

Eventually she swallows, just a tiny bit. Then she coughs and sputters. I wait a second and place some more medicine in her throat. She swallows again, coughs and gags. This goes on for quite some time. Her mother is beside me working silently, following my directions without comment, working like the lowliest of servants while constantly keeping cool rags on the toddler's forehead.

"What's her name?" I ask her mother.

"Autumn," she replies. I stop in my tracks thinking of Winter…alone in the Bay City orphanage. *Am I cursed by the seasons?* I shake my head. "Autumn is the most beautiful child I have ever seen," I tell her mother. Then I add, "I think she is going to be fine." I show her how to put the medicine down Autumn's throat.

"Can you get more water for me?" I ask Autumn's father.

"Certainly," he answers, returning quickly with another water bag. I mix up a second batch of medicine and herbs for Autumn then prepare a bag of Echinacea tea for the rest of the family.

"You all need to drink this tea…twice a day. Two spoons full," I tell the family, moving my eyes from one person to the next, even the little boy who is now hiding shyly behind a cupboard.

"Yes, yes…anything you say," the mother answers. The father nods his head solemnly.

Koree has been silent in the corner of the room, watching intently. I had actually forgotten about him until he walks over to me, standing nervously with his hands in his pants pockets. "There are others…" he says quietly. "Will it spread to them?"

I look up at him in horror. "Others?" I ask in a muted tone. "How many?"

"Hundreds."

"Hundreds?" I ask, shocked, wondering where they are. "Do they all have fevers?" I blurt out, thinking I will never be able to leave this place.

"No, none yet. But the fever will spread, right?" He fiddles his thumbs together nervously.

"Like wildfire." I whisper. "This family has to stay here. Alone. They can't spread this to the others."

"They all meet together as a community – you know cook, share chores." Koree lowers his eyebrows as if he is pondering the situation. "I'll be back in a minute." He almost jumps out of the tree house and is gone. While I wait, I talk quietly to Autumn's mother, find out her name is Asha, the little boy's name is Caylib, and the father is Destin.

"You must watch Caylib for signs of fever and get medicine in him quickly if he gets hot or becomes lethargic," I explain. "And you need to stay away from anyone else. This fever could spread."

"It's not a problem," Destin tells me, authority in his voice. "We'll do what you say." Just then Autumn begins to stir, moaning a little.

A smile creeps over my face, and I let out a sigh of relief. "That's a good sign," I tell Asha and Destin. "Keep up with this regime…place cool rags on her and give her medicine every thirty minutes," I yawn. "All through the night."

They both nod their heads, blonde and light brown with pure white skin. A familiar yet strange combination. I think of my lone pale face among all of the Dark Skinned people in Bay City, and a part of me wants to stay in this tree house with them. For the first time in my life, I don't feel like a Ghost.

Just then Koree bounds into the tree house. "Food and water will be delivered to your door three times a day," he announces. "Send a note to Anker if you need something else. We'll be back tomorrow to check on you." He scoops up Entho's healing case, stuffs it in his tunic again and strides with long legs toward the door. "Ready to go?" he asks me, his emerald eyes sparkling in the candle light. I nod my head, following him to the door, stopping to check on Autumn one more time before I leave.

I follow Koree down the ladder, and this time it is easier. My feet hit the soft dirt below the tree house, and we both stop, facing each other as the rope ladder rises, disappearing into the leaves of the enormous tree. Darkness surrounds us like a thick black breath of air, and we stand face to face, peering into the dimness of each other's eyes.

Finally I speak, my voice an audible whisper. "You have a bit of explaining to do.

Chapter 10

Koree's hand finds mine in the darkness, and he laces his fingers through them, as if it is the most natural thing to do. *Could this mean something? Or is he just being a polite guide, like before?* All my life I have studied hands, and if I were an artist I know I would draw them, over and over again. I love to look at people's hands, to wonder what they are feeling when they touch something. When they are idle or at work. When they are stroking the face of someone they love...

I have stared at my porcelain white hands numerous times, hating them – the purplish veins that creep up, long fingers that seem too large for a girl's, thick knuckles from so much hand-to-hand combat. I can picture Entho's hands in my mind...long slender fingers, sensitive healing hands.

Koree's voice breaks into my thoughts. "Okay, come with me. You deserve some answers." He charges ahead through the odd orchard, and I barely keep up with him, leaves crunching beneath my feet and a slight breeze blowing through my hair. We arrive at another tree house, almost by itself on the edge of the orchard. A ladder is already dangling from it, and Koree untangles his hand from mine. He climbs up the ladder first as before. I follow, and this time it is easier climbing the swaying ladder. Once again he helps me into a little house, firmly grabbing my waist and launching me up.

He finds a candle and lights it. I am expecting others, more people, perhaps Light Skins, but the little tree house is empty. "Have a seat," he says, pointing to a small brown couch.

I sink into it, and Koree plunks down right beside me, nonchalantly putting his arm around the back of the couch and rotating toward me. My heart begins to thump in my chest as I turn toward him. His face is outlined in the yellow glow of candle light as if it were chiseled out of stone. His jaw is square with a trace of stubble, and coppery curls fall loosely onto his forehead. His green eyes are deep emeralds, serious yet challenging, as if you'd like to dig them up and keep them for yourself. He smiles at me, then, his dimple appears, and instantly dizziness takes over me. His words are muffling in the background but I seem to be in a trance. A Koree trance.

"You were great…with Autumn," I hear him say to me, and I shake my head a little, forcing myself to pay attention. "Thank you," he continues. "I really appreciate it." His mood is serious, and his eyes are bolted tightly onto mine. As I meet his gaze, my heart continues to pound in my chest and I struggle to catch my breath.

"No problem. I think she will be okay," I answer stiffly.

"Yeah. She looked a lot better when we left."

I clear my throat, curiosity overriding every other emotion that seems to be crashing through my body and mind, like a rainstorm pelting down on me from all angles. "So…you were going to explain…" My voice trails off.

Koree pauses then takes a deep breath. "Yes, I owe you that…and I did promise." He grins at me then, that lopsided smile that sets my heart beating like thunder. He reaches for my hand again and stares earnestly into my eyes. "We chose you…because of your Light Skin…and because you already know about the tunnels." He pauses. "And you know a lot about healing and weapons."

I interrupt. "Who is 'we'?"

He sighs. "Kesper, Thann, and me. And Yaren. That's it."

"I don't see how it all fits…you chose me? For what?"

"Well, when Autumn got sick, we needed help. We've been lucky so far with so many people here in the tree houses. You were awesome when you saved Thann, although I don't remember that." He shoots me another crooked grin, then continues. "But I do remember you healing me, and Echo too. After we all got to Harcourt, we had a meeting and decided we needed you and were willing to take the risk of bringing you into the fold…to save Autumn and maybe others. We can't use our healers. They would know….word would get out, and…it…it would all be over."

I fold my eyebrows down, confused. "What would be over?" I interrupt.

He hesitates, bouncing his leg nervously and clenching his jaw. Eventually he cocks his head to the side and speaks in a hushed tone. "We have almost three hundred Light Skinned people we've saved…living in the tree houses."

"Fortheloveofangels!" It comes out as one word. "How?"

"You're sworn to secrecy from this moment on." Koree is stern, his green eyes more serious than I have ever seen them.

"Who would I tell? The loads of friends I have?" I don't mean to sound so sarcastic – it just creeps out of me sometimes.

"Echo. Gunter. Your new roommates."

"Right, like I would tell those idiots anything. Echo and Gunter have been great, but I just met them." *Why do I sound defensive?*

Koree sighs again, deeply, his chest heaving up and down, and I stare at the muscles that seem to explode through his beige tunic. I catch my breath as his eyes dart back and forth between me and something I can't see. "Kesper started it years ago. Before the Purification Law passed. Her husband was killed by Destroyers because he didn't have the Mark of Power. After that she started funneling Light Skinned people to Harcourt. As many unmarked people as she could. It's the perfect place. We're remote, and we're practically self-sufficient." I nod my head, listening intently. He continues.

"It is her passion…to take care of these people. There was a healer –
here at the tree houses – but he died a few months ago. Like I said,
so far we've been lucky. Yaren has been filling in, doing what he
can, but he's a dragon healer and his methods are primitive at best.
When Kesper found out about your healing abilities, she thought it
would be a good idea to take you into the fold. Your Light Skin was
a bonus." He furtively trains his eyes onto mine. "And now you
know about the tunnels, so you might as well be a part of it all." A
deep breath follows as he runs his long fingers through the curls on
his forehead. "If you want to."

"I have *never* thought being Light Skinned could be a bonus."

"It makes no difference." He turns his face toward mine, slowly
moves in closer to me. I find it difficult to breathe as he nears me. I
am not sure what he is going to do as his face shadows before
mine…only inches away now. I can feel the softness of his breath on
my face, and it is sweet and minty and masculine. Rapidly then, he
jerks his head back, settling back into the fold of the couch. I let out
a huge breath.

He starts talking again. "Thann and I grew up like this. Training dragons, helping the Light Skinned people. Building tree houses. You name it." He stops for a moment, closing his eyes as if he is trying to remember something. "I don't know when we started clipping the dragon's wings incorrectly. It was Kesper's idea. She figured out how to clip their wings well enough to pass inspection, but all of our dragons can fly. We've just trained them not to fly unless they have the proper cue."

"All the dragons here can fly?" My eyes pop wide open. "But that is illegal!"

He flashes a brilliant but slightly crooked smile at me. "I know, but isn't it great?"

"Well, yes. But it is scary, too." I answer, recalling the death penalty that goes along with keeping more than five flying dragons. I think about Koree for a minute, puzzled at his position at Harcourt. He definitely seems to be instrumental in the decision making here. "Have you lived here all your life?" I ask him. I remember Kesper telling Gunter and me that Koree was like a son to her.

His stiffens, and his eyes move downward, toward the floor. "No."
An uncomfortable blanket of silence settles over the tree house. I
wonder if I have said something wrong. His mood has obviously
shifted, and it is as if the room has suddenly become cold. A small
shiver runs up my spine.

Eventually he speaks, his voice thick and deep as he continues to
stare at the floor. "I came here when I was seven. My mother was a
Light Skin, my father dark." He turns his green eyes toward mine,
anger shooting out of them like a glistening green weapon. I
shudder, thinking it is directed at me, but then I realize he is waiting
for my reaction.

Before I can comment, more words tumble out of his mouth. "The
Destroyers killed them…both."

I gasp. "Who?"

"My parents."

It is quiet again but he doesn't take his eyes away from mine. "I hate
them…the Destroyers. And Siv Gareth for what he's done."

I think back to Soot, of what Koree said when he saw her body. How he fell to his knees in despair. It all makes sense now.

"I am so sorry," I softly whisper.

He doesn't acknowledge what I say. "Kesper took me in." His eyes glimmer in the candlelight and his leg bounces up and down nervously. With a furrowed brow he continues, his voice low. "Kesper and my mother were friends." He tilts his head and pauses, as if he is playing a scene over and over in his mind. "I was alone after my parents were killed. It took days to get here, but she took me in." He twiddles his thumbs with each other, his elbows resting on his knees as he leans forward.

"Oh how sad." I can't think of any other words. He meets my eyes and they shine with accusation. I wonder what I did to make him so angry. "She didn't have to, you know...take me in."

"You were lucky."

Anger flares from his eyes again, and his lip curls up in a sneer. "Lucky? You've got to be kidding."

"I…I am sorry," I stammer foolishly. "I didn't mean it that way. It is just…there is a little girl I know…Winter. She is in an orphanage in Bay City. It haunts me. Nobody cares about her. Nobody can take her in, adopt her. It is the law." I breathe out deeply, my tangled hair brushing against my mouth. I can't seem to stop talking, the ghost of Winter haunting me. "And they're training her to be a soldier – she and about a hundred other children without parents." I pause again. "Orphans…from the Final War."

Koree's voice softens. "Oh, snock. I must sound so selfish."

"No, no. It is just that I want to help her…help all of them." I cast my eyes downward. "But I don't know how to."

Koree sighs deeply, rubbing his hand over his forehead. "I guess I *am* lucky when you put it that way." He pauses, fiddles with the bottom of his tunic, bounces his leg again.

"You might as well know it all." He leans close to me again, and I can feel his breath on my face, a light fresh wind. His eyes widen, and he whispers lowly, as if someone could hear us talking. "There's a Rebellion…against Siv Gareth and the Alliance. It's based here…at the tree houses. Kesper is leading it."

My eyes match his in size now, shocked. "A Rebellion?"

He nods his head slowly. "Are you in?" he asks soberly. He lifts his chin up and his lips curl down. His green eyes shimmer at me, waiting for an answer.

Embedded in my memories are images of Siv Gareth…Lord Gareth…taking over what is left of our country, enacting laws that killed my friends as a child just for being Light Skinned…and Soot. Poor Soot's head being sliced away from her body like she was nothing more than meat…the latest law he passed…the Purity Law…where all Light Skins are to be destroyed…killed. Entho's pale face flashes in my mind. Is he even alive?

I don't need any more time to think as I stare back at them. As if saying a prayer, I answer reverently, quietly, sincerely.

"I am in."

Chapter 11

Koree and I scramble out of the tree house and hop onto Onyx – this time I am able to mount the dragon without help. Another squeal of excitement escapes my lips as we take air, the black dragon's wings flapping against the invisible night sky. Koree chuckles. "It's great, isn't it?"

"Oh, yessss," I let out. "Do some more spins!" Koree obliges my request, and we spin and loop again, over and over. I watch the world turn into different angles as I hang upside down, and sideways, grabbing Koree's waist tightly, wind rushing over me, blowing my hair in all directions.

In what seems like no time at all, we land discreetly behind the dorms. Koree and I dismount Onyx wordlessly. We stand next to the black dragon, invisible in the dark night. Wordlessly, we face each other by the wooden steps for a while. *Should I say something? Or just leave?*

Koree's voice breaks my trance. "Meet me out here tomorrow night, after your roommates fall asleep….maybe around 11:00. We need to check on Autumn." His voice is a combination whisper and deep throaty growl. My skin prickles at his words. Then he grins at me, a toothless, lopsided smile, and I am transfixed once again by the dimple in his cheek. His words wave in and out of my ears, as if I am under water. "I'm glad you're on board."

I hesitate, unsure of myself. "Me, too," I answer, waiting for him to leave. But he doesn't. Instead, he cocks his head to one side and stares at me, his emerald eyes piercing through me as if they were a sharp needle. *Should I say something? And why is he just staring at me like that?*

"You look…" It is barely a whisper.

"What?" I interrupt, my voice way too loud. Every nerve in my body is tingling and on edge. I am finding it difficult to breathe and my heart beats like thunder in my chest. I have never felt like this about anyone – it thrills and confuses me at the same time.

Koree launches me another grin. "Nothing." He lingers, then changes the subject. "You were great tonight…with Autumn." I am locked in place, not sure what to say or do. He leans his head toward mine, and I freeze, immobilized. *What can he possibly be doing?* His face lingers, close to mine, and I shiver with excitement. I feel his breath on mine again – that mixture of mint and sweetness – and a leathery, very masculine smell to go with it.

"See you later," he says, his eyes flashing in the dim light. He steps back with long legs and I stand shivering in the warm night air, unable to move, the remnants of his breath still on mine.

"Later," I breathe out, not knowing if he even hears me.

I watch the outline of Koree and Onyx disappear quietly into the night as I stand there, speechless, rooted in place with a wonderful feeling crashing through my entire body, as if I were waiting for Christmas or my birthday.

I finally stumble up the stairs, wash up, and land in bed with a thump. Scraps of the night keep flashing through my mind, and I can't seem to settle down. I see the tree houses with Asha and Destin. Then it is Koree sitting on the couch with me. The Rebellion. *Did I really just agree to join a Rebellion?* I feel Koree's breath on my face, and I my stomach clenches, not with fear but excitement.

I toss and turn most of the night but finally fall into a light sleep. I am awakened all too soon by a cacophony of trumpets. I open my eyes slowly, and through the open window I can tell that the sun is barely up. I groan, turning over in my bed, pulling my covers over my head for just a moment, reveling in the warmth and darkness. In time I kick them off with a flourish and sit up in my bed, rubbing my eyes.

I get out of bed, favoring my knee as I stand and find my way to the back of the room so I can wash up. I make a point of ignoring the other girls. I find a mirror and am dismayed at the sight of my puffy eyes and messy hair. I make a futile attempt at brushing it and try to arrange it neatly but give up as I pull my beige tunic over my head and slip into the matching pants. I wander downstairs, following the sound of trumpets.

People are gathering in a nearby arena. I walk briskly toward them in an effort to be on time. When I reach the arena I find a spot to stand, nervous among all of the strangers. A moving hand a few feet away catches my attention. It is Gunter, waving me over. I squeeze through the horde of people and stand next to him. "You look rough," he smiles, his eyes disappearing into little slits.

"Yes. Roommate problems." It seems like a good enough excuse. I notice Gunter is wearing his pin, and for a moment I am angry and hurt, wishing I had my dragon pins.

"Reese and three other guys live with me – all of them about as big as mountains. So far they haven't been bad, though."

"Reese is out of prison?" I ask, immediately on edge.

"Yeah, I guess they just wanted to scare him or something."

"Is he behaving? Did it work?"

"So far, so good. I just keep away from him."

"Good call." I bite my lip, then, thinking of my dragon pins. "You're lucky. My roommates seem to think what's mine is theirs."

"I've seen you in action. Why don't you just nail them to the wall?"

"Tempting."

My attention is turned to the crowd of people that has gathered – there must be over fifty people standing by the huge stage in the middle of the arena. When the trumpets stop, it immediately becomes quiet, a pulse of excitement resonating in the air.

Just then four figures in shiny golden cloaks emerge onto the stage, holding hands. Golden cloaks that only Master Dragon Trainers can wear. I am stunned to see who they are: Kesper, Thann, Koree, and an older girl, maybe in her late teens. She is dark skinned and beautiful with long black hair, huge black eyes with long lashes, and high cheek bones. She is holding Koree's hand, and suddenly a wave of jealousy shoots through my entire body. I want to jump up on the stage and tackle her. I breathe deeply then, chiding myself silently. I have no claim on Koree. What am I thinking?

Kesper is on the other side of Koree, holding his hand along with Thann's. Kesper and Thann look spectacular in their golden cloaks, pale skin and blonde hair contrasted by the shimmering golden cloaks.

But it is Koree I can't seem to take my eyes off of. I had no idea he was a Master Trainer. His cloak is filled with dragon pins – more than Thann's or the other girl's. I assumed that Thann would be more advanced than Koree, just by his birthright, but I was obviously wrong.

"Welcome new cadets," Kesper begins, her voice shattering the noise of the crowd. Peace settles over us all, as if a switch had been flipped. "And welcome to all Harcourt citizens. Our fifty- second induction ceremony will now take place. Thank you all for coming…new cadets as well as experienced trainers, workers, and members of our wonderful community."

Kesper gives a short speech about the history of Harcourt and then announces each new cadet by name and calls us up onto the stage. When I hear my name, my heart beats in my chest as I walk up the stairs and find a place to stand. Kesper calls a few more names and then Gunter's. He hustles up the steps and lands right next to me. She finishes calling the cadets and the crowd breaks out in applause.

Kesper continues with her speech, telling of Echo's injury and Koree's concussion – how difficult our journey was. "We're lucky to have someone trained in Weapons who helped us out… saved Echo and our boys." She smiles, looking toward me and then Thann and Koree. Thankfully, she doesn't say my name. I don't want everybody staring at me. I have had enough of that in my life. "But sadly, we lost a cadet on the journey here. Soot Janker was destroyed for being Light Skinned." She asks us to take a moment to think of Soot, even if we didn't know her, to understand and appreciate how precious the gift of life is and how easily it can be taken away.

Everyone bows their heads, and I do the same, trying to block the image of Soot's severed body, lying in two bloody pieces on the ground, from my mind. An enormous wave of sadness washes over me, and tears threaten to spill out for Soot. For failing her. She should be standing on the stage with the rest of us. But I wasn't fast enough. I couldn't kill the Destroyer in time.

After a few minutes Kesper speaks again, and heads slowly move up, eyes on her, mine included. "Okay, back to business." She smiles out at the crowd. "There are basic rules here at Harcourt. To start with, we are all equal. Skin color, wealth, status…there is no room for that here. You see us all holding hands because we are one – one unit of Master Trainers. And the rest of you are all one unit as well…cadets, trainers…workers…all of you."

She goes on to tell us about the merit system, which Gunter and I already know about. She explains that there are different ways to earn merits, and we will learn more about that in our classes. Then she warns us, "You will also be receiving demerits for poor behavior or breaking the rules. For every 100 demerits you receive, you will spend a week in isolation. And lose a dragon pin."

Isolation, I think. Is that the same as the prison Reese was in? I can't help myself. I search the stage for Reese. Sure enough, he is here – standing alone, short and stocky and sultry with his arms crossed over his chest. Hate for him burns deeply in my chest, but I quickly dart my eyes away, not sure if he notices me.

"You receive your pay for the week every Sunday," Kesper continues. "And, every evening after feeding time you have free time." She stops, licks her lips. "But you are not allowed in any of the dragon related rooms until you achieve clearance. Please stick to the stores or other buildings and areas that are not designated for dragons. A picture of a dragon will appear on the doors you aren't allowed in."

Kesper takes a breath. "We are a self-contained community. We produce everything we need, except for a few things. Because of this, your performance will determine your job posting at the end of training. You might be chosen for training dragons or cleaning pens. All jobs are of equal importance. In the past, cadets were allowed to leave if they didn't like their positions or wanted to go somewhere else, but this year..." Her voice trembles for the slightest of moments.

She scans the crowd, rallying. "This year we have a serious problem that needs to be addressed before I turn you over to your trainers. As you might have heard, there's a new law...The Purity Law. It is a ludicrous law stating that all Light Skins are to be destroyed. As you can see, we have some Light Skinned members at Harcourt, including me. Because of this, we have sealed the gates. No one leaves. No one comes in. Until the law is changed." She hesitates. "Which I'm sure will be soon. Now, I'll leave you to your trainers. Good luck."

Kesper turns with a flurry of quick golden movement and disappears from the stage.

Chapter 12

Koree speaks first, his voice blaring confidently. "I'm Lead Trainer. My name is Koree Timbrel. I'm responsible for the cadets who have little practical experience. I'll call your name and come stand by me." He calls my name first, and I step next to him. He doesn't acknowledge me in any fashion. Then he calls Reese and Gunter and to my dismay, the girl named Flame. Both appear out of the back of the crowd and stand next to us. I immediately stiffen.

Next, the female trainer announces her name – Persia Shank. I immediately bristle. Even her name is beautiful. Persia. It sounds so exotic. Much better than Teak the Freak. She calls the people with limited dragon experience, including Echo. She explains that she will be conducting a mixture of field work as well as book work.

Finally, Thann announces his name and calls forth his charges, those with the most practical experience. The three large boys Gunter was talking about as well as one of my roommates gather around him. They will be spending most of their time in classes instead of on dragons.

We stand idly in our assigned groups, waiting for instruction. Thann and Persia begin to leave with their cadets when Koree's voice booms over to them. "Wait," he calls out. He marches over to Flame, who still has my dragon pin on her tunic. "Where did you get this?" he asks, pointing to it.

"Um, my grandmother gave it to me," Flame answers. "She gave me two, and I let Loris wear one."

"Where is Loris?" he asks, scanning the cadets, his eyes squinting into the sunlight. One of my roommates raises her hand, the one in Persia's group. "Come over here, Koree orders." She timidly walks over. I try to keep a smile from appearing on my lips but find it difficult. I think back to the kick I took from Flame...my clothes and belongings scattered everywhere.

"So," Koree continues, "Your grandmother gave you these two pins?"

"That's what I said," Flame responds icily.

Koree reaches toward her tunic, slowly, unclasping the pin. His face leans into hers as he speaks, his voice a steely weapon. "I'm not sure if you know this, but each pin is stamped and coded with the year and the student it belongs to. He tips the pin upside down and inspects it. I'm guessing your grandmother's pin wouldn't have the year 2087 on it, now, would it?" He shoves the pin toward her face. "What year do you see?" he asks her, his eyes now a deep jade, arrows of anger shooting out of them.

"2087," she replies weakly, casting her eyes downward.

He reaches in his tunic, pulls out a leather book, opens it. "Teak Frain, number 168."

"What number do you see under the year?" he asks Flame.

"168," she answers, this time defiantly glaring at him.

Koree marches over to the other girl, Loris, and repeats the same process, removing the pin from her tunic. Then he brings both pins back to me, slowly opens my palm and places them in it, keeping his hand on mine for just a second. It is a familiar feeling from last night…warm and safe and raspy. I examine his hand curled around mine and barely hear what he is saying to Loris.

When I hear him speak my name, my attention is immediately diverted. "Do you have any idea how these girls ended up with your pins?" he asks me, as if he didn't know. Even though the weather is warm, a coldness like I have never known shoots through me.

I swallow. Hard. I am not sure what to say. I think of the consequences, of how I will be tormented by Flame and Loris if I play a part in their punishment. I also think of how I have to live in the same room with them, how miserable they can make my life...have already made it. Then I think of lying to Koree... how he held my hand...flying on a dragon with him...being asked to join the Rebellion. I am pulled in two distinct directions. My heart beats wildly as I hesitate, thinking of which direction to turn. In an instant I make the only choice I know how to make.

"I... I loaned them to them. They really liked them so I let them use them," I stammer, refusing to look into Koree's eyes – eyes that I know have become deadly green arrows aimed directly at me.

Koree closes my hand, firmly, just a little too hard. "20 demerits for you, then, Teak." I know he is looking straight at me, searching for my eyes, but I continue to keep them diverted from his, staring downward. If I look at him, I know that I will break down, confess the truth. As I study my dusty brown boots, as if they could possibly hold any interest for me, I hear him stomp closer to the other girls. His feet are hammers pounding into the ground, anger emanating off of him in waves that can only be felt. "And 100 demerits for you, Flame – for stealing and lying to a trainer." He calls a guard over to take her away.

"And you get 50 demerits, Loris, for not speaking up when you knew these were Teak's pins." It is deadly quiet everywhere. I can barely hear the soft wind brushing through my hair and the occasional far away yowl of a dragon. So many people are staring at me and at the other girl, Loris. I gain the courage to look up, to face Koree's eyes. He glares at me – if his eyes were arrows before, they have become lethal spears shooting directly into my eyes now.

"My cadets need to come with me," he orders. I place the pins on my tunic as I follow his directions, trudging behind Gunter and dragging my feet like a naughty toddler.

Chapter 13

Koree leads us to a building labeled "Tack". We follow him inside, and he gives us instructions on bridles, halters, lead ropes, shin guards, and other items used for training dragons. His voice holds no expression, and he rattles off the instructions in a monotone. I wait for a smile, a sign that everything is fine between us. I get nothing.

"Once you pick out a halter, come outside," he tells us, twisting his tall frame around and tromping out the door. I grab a green halter from the wall and step outside, blinking my eyes at the bright sun. Koree is leaning against the building, and I catch my breath at the sight of him. He is still wearing the golden cloak, and it brings out the golden edges of his dark green eyes. I wonder how he can be so mad over a little lie…a lie to protect myself. Of all the people here, I thought Koree would understand. I guess I was wrong. I walk past him and stand next to Gunter, my heart aching as if someone were pressing against it.

"Today will be spent on ground work, which is the most important part of dragon training," he explains. He shows us how to halter a dragon, groom it, saddle it, and lead it around. "The dragon must respect you at all times. If it doesn't respect you on the ground, it won't respect you when you're on its back," he tells us.

I think back to my early attempts at riding a dragon...how I was launched in the air for mounting on the wrong side...how it was Koree who helped me. Thann and the others laughed, especially Reese, but Koree patiently walked me through the steps of ground riding a dragon. A lump forms in my throat at the thought, and I swallow, trying to put it out of my mind.

We practice catching various dragons, putting halters on them, and then setting them free. Gunter and I start out slowly, but after a while we become adept at it and are able to halter the dragons with ease. Reese, on the other hand, struggles immensely. He seems to want to dominate each dragon, and not one of them will cooperate with him. Not even Pebble. Koree leans against the fence, the slight wind brushing his curls against his face as he offers suggestions to Reese.

"Don't look her in the eye. You are threatening her."

"Walk slower." His voice is calm, patient, and I glance over at him when I think he isn't watching. But Koree…Koree is always watching. His green eyes smolder every time I meet them with mine, and instantly I look away.

Finally, we are given a break and lunch, which we eat at an outside table. Koree hands us each a brown paper sack. When I take mine from him, our fingers touch, and he instantly pulls his back, as if he might get burned if he touched me. I try not to show disappointment and turn away from him.

A warm breeze blows around us and the sun is shining, but my stomach is so tense I am only able to nibble at my sandwich. I wish I could take back the past few hours of my life, change it around, like chess pieces on a chess board. As I slowly put the sandwich to my mouth, Koree's voice carries across the slight breeze.

"I have a meeting to attend. I'll be back in thirty minutes."

"Righto," Gunter tells him as he takes a huge bite of his sandwich. Koree stomps away, his boots hitting the cobblestone path, every step an accusation – surely directed at me.

"Someone woke up on the wrong side of the bed," Gunter tells me after Koree has disappeared.

"I am sorry," I tell him, my head hanging low. "I am just tired today." I hope the excuse works.

"Not you. Koree." Gunter tells me. I pop my head up. "He is snocking crabby today. I don't know what crawled up his butt."

"Yes, I guess so." I let it go at that.

Gunter and I finish eating and stroll wordlessly to a patch of grass. Reese stays put on a bench by the table. We lounge on the grass, lying flat on our backs, and I breathe out deeply, my sad breath mixing with the slight wind.

"Let's make shapes out of the clouds, "Gunter offers. It is something I couldn't do in the city. The clouds were hidden behind dust and dirt, ash and cinders.

"Okay," I answer, wanting to take my mind off of Koree. I narrow my eyes, peering up at the fluffy white clouds blocking the pale blue background.

"I see a kangaroo, I swear," Gunter tells me. I squint my eyes, peering up at the fluffy clouds.

"No, I think it is a dragon. A dragon breathing fire."

"Get real." Gunter cranes his neck. "At very best it's a hippopotamus."

Before I can answer, Koree's voice interrupts us, and I leap up as if I were a puppet connected to strings. Strings that only Koree's voice holds.

"Okay, break's over. Now we'll go into the pasture and practice tacking up dragons some more," he tells us. "Remember to use correct body language." Koree speaks to all of us but refuses to look directly into my eyes. We continue as before lunch, catching dragon after dragon until it eventually becomes boring. Even Reese is getting better at it.

"We'll meet in the cafeteria for dinner," Koree finally announces as the sun begins to set. "But before you're done for the day, I need to show you how to feed the dragons and clean the pens, which you will be expected do from here on out every morning and evening."

Koree leads us to a dragon pen and hands us shovels and rakes. Gunter and I begin scooping dragon poop into a wheel barrow. I don't mind the work, and when we finish up, we stroll to the cafeteria. My stomach rumbles as the smell of homemade bread, meats, cheeses, and vegetables wafts through the air.

Gunter opens the door for me, and I immediately spot Koree, standing with his arms crossed over his chest, leaning against the food counter, and my heart begins to race. *What is he doing, just standing there? Why isn't he eating?*

"I have some things I have to do," Koree tells us as we approach the counter. "You can have free time now." He turns around and clomps away.

We line up and fill our plates with the steaming assortment of foods displayed before us then find a place to sit down. I keep seeing

Koree's face. The disappointment. The accusation. The burning anger. I take my fork and pick at my beef and broccoli, making an effort to make small talk with Gunter.

"Hey, what's wrong with you?" he asks as I move the food around my plate.

"What?"

"You're acting weird," he tells me. "And you aren't eating."

I cast my eyes downward. "Just tired. It's been a busy day."

"You thinking about Soot...you know...all of that?"

"Well, yes, of course." I don't dare tell him what is really bothering me.

"Yeah, me, too, but you gotta move on. It's over."

"I know." I stuff some food in my mouth just to make him happy. He finishes eating, and we dump our trays and walk outside.

"I'll walk you to your dormitory," Gunter tells me, ever the gentleman.

"Sure," I answer. It is silent as we traverse through the paved paths at Harcourt, talking back and forth about our day. In no time at all we arrive at the girls' dormitory.

"See you tomorrow," Gunter tells me.

"Yes, see you tomorrow. It has been a long day."

"A good one, though. I learned a lot." He smiles at me, glistening white teeth reflecting off the last strands of sunlight.

"Yes," I tell him, thinking just the opposite. "Good-bye Gunter." I hear his farewell as I trudge up the steps to the girl's dormitory, open the door, and head for my bed.

"Hey, Teak." It is Loris, and I slowly move my head to face her.

"What," I reply, my voice cold. Instinctively, I bristle.

"Thanks…for what you did. Flame gets a little carried away sometimes."

I plop on my bed and look at her to see if it is a trick. Her dark eyes, as round as coins, seem sincere. She is actually pretty, in an elfish sort of way. Her hair is short and tucked behind her ears, which seem to turn up at the ends a bit. Her nose is a tiny button and her lips are thin, a dark pink.

"It is okay," I say, turning back toward the wall. I just want to get to bed and forget this terrible day.

"Do you want to play Dragon Cards?" she asks. I think about it for a second, and then something occurs to me. Dragon Cards.

"No," I answer abruptly. "Maybe another time. I forgot I have to do something." I jump out of bed and race out of the dormitory, taking the steps two at a time, then run as fast as I can through the paved paths of Harcourt.

Chapter 14

I reach the Infirmary just before it closes and ask to see Echo. I am escorted to her room by the same balding healer. He still doesn't speak to me but simply leads me there, dissolving back into the hallway as I enter her room. Echo is paging through the book I gave her, which makes me happy.

"Teak," she almost squeals as I walk in.

"How are you?"

"Bored as dragon balls. I wish I could get out of here." She scrunches up her face. "Hey, how 'bout you break me out?"

I let out a giant sigh. "I have already gotten in enough trouble today."

"Do tell." She leans forward, placing her chin on her hand. The bandage on her head makes her look silly. Or tough. I can't tell which. But I am relieved that there is no blood on it, that the wound must be healing.

I tell her about Flame, Loris and the other girl, whose name I still don't know. I go on and explain about the pins and how it angered Koree when I lied to him, how I got 20 demerits. I don't tell her about the night with Koree. Or holding hands. Or the Rebellion. Or all the Light Skinned people in the tree houses.

"How did he know they stole them?" she asks

I am caught. I swallow hard, thinking of what to say. I remember Koree's warning in the tree house – not to tell anyone about the Rebellion. "Umm…I don't know. He is a Master Trainer, did you know that? So is Thann, and another girl named Persia. You'll be in Persia's group."

"No way, Thann and Koree are Master Trainers?"

"Yes way. They were even wearing golden cloaks."

"Wow, that's smash!" I am flooded with relief when Echo changes the subject. "What do you think about Gunter?"

"He is very nice."

"Do you like him?"

"Of course, who wouldn't?"

"No, like him…you know…*like* him."

"Like a boyfriend?"

"Yeah." She grins shyly, something I have never seen her do.

I furrow my brows, thinking about Gunter. "No, I just like him as a friend."

"Well good, 'cause I think I might like him."

"Like a boyfriend?"

She nods her head and a goofy grin erupts on her face. "He is kind of cute."

"Yes," I agree. "And he is a lot of fun."

We talk and play Dragon Cards for a while, which I discover once again that I am very bad at. "Have you been practicing?" I ask her, bending over to pick the cards up off of her bed.

"Fire balls, yeah, there's nothing else to do here." Then her eyes become serious, a grayish blue. She looks down at her lap. "Teak...I have a confession," she chokes out.

This is so unlike Echo that I immediately snap my head up. "What?" I ask.

"I...ah...I don't know how to read...that's why I couldn't pass the Assessment." We stare at each other in silence for a moment, her blue eyes misting with emotion, perhaps even embarrassment.

I think for a minute. "I can teach you how. It really isn't that hard."

"Really?"

"Sure. If you can play Dragon Cards, you can read."

"Sweet dragon balls! When?"

"We can start tomorrow, after I am done with feeding and cleaning."

"Cock and balls, yes! I'm ready." Echo makes me laugh, something I desperately need. We talk for a while and then I tell her I have got to go.

"Come back soon. I'm losing my freaking mind."

"I will," I let out, feeling a little better. I may have lost Koree, but at least I have two friends…Echo and Gunter. I wave to Echo, turn into the hall and exit the Infirmary.

As I stroll back to the dormitory, I think about how I am going to keep up with everything – teaching Echo to read, learning about dragons, healing at night.

Then it occurs to me. I wonder if Koree will even show up tonight.

Chapter 15

I make it back to the dorm, crawl into bed and doze off for a few hours. I jump up at some point, grab the black cloak from under my pillow, and sneak out of the dorm and down the stairs. I have no idea what time it is, and I glance around for Koree and Onyx but see nothing except darkness. I sit on the bottom stair, thinking I will wait for a while and then go back to bed.

As I hold my head in my hands, resting my elbows on my knees, I think of little Autumn and wonder how she is doing. Then my mind jumps to Winter and how I am ever going to get her out of that terrible orphanage in Bay City. Next, I think of Koree and the wonderful night I spent with him...and then the lie I told – the one that destroyed everything. It rolls over and over in my mind. I keep hearing my voice tell him I loaned the pins to Flame and Loris. I keep seeing his eyes shoot green daggers at me...feeling the icy coldness that erupted from him almost like a wildfire out of control.

"Took you long enough." It is a hoarse whisper, but I bolt up, spotting Koree's silhouette framing the darkness like a picture on a wall.

My heart leaps into my chest. Koree. He came. "Have you been waiting long?" I try to smile.

"A bit. No biggie."

Silence settles between us like a sharp knife cutting through the thick black air. I try again. "I didn't know you were a Master Trainer."

His response is a little too quick, his voice harsh and grating against my ears. "I didn't know you were a liar."

I open my mouth, try to explain, but any words I have are stuck in my throat. A wave of disappointment crashes over me. And anger. Anger at myself. Anger at Koree. *Why is he making such a big deal over this?*

"Let's go," he orders before I can say anything in my defense. Still all business.

I hop on Onyx by myself watching as he easily stretches his long legs over the black dragon, settling in front of me without a word. Or a touch. He doesn't remind me to hold on as we catch air. Tentatively, I grab his waist anyway, feeling the firmness of his stomach against my hands and hating the silence between us. There are no loops or spins tonight, just eerie silence in the black sky, the only sound the wind whistling around us. Eventually we land by the tree houses.

Koree dismounts and walks briskly ahead of me to Autumn's tree house, his feet crunching on the leaves like stepping on burned toast. I try to keep up in the darkness but I find it difficult. He knocks on the tree trunk and I follow the patterned sound. The ladder drops just as I arrive. Koree climbs first and I follow, landing on the platform with a plop. I struggle to stand as I enter the little house.

I catch sight of Autumn, sitting up on the bed. She is lucid, awake, and her cheeks are turning pink. Destin and Asha are smiling. Caylib is playing with some wooden toys on the floor. I tend to Autumn, mix up some more medicine, and give it to them.

"The fever has broken," I tell Asha. "You can put clothes back on her. Just keep up with the medicine every thirty minutes. Even through the night."

"I will," she tells me. "And thank you so much…for saving our daughter."

"I am just glad she is okay." I ruffle Autumn's blonde head, marveling at her big blue eyes.

Koree's voice takes over. "I'll check on you tomorrow night…see if you need anything."

I snap my head up. *He'll check on them. Alone.* My chest tightens into a ball and I fight back the tears that want to spill out. I purse my lips together, holding my emotions in, something else I have honed to perfection.

We say good-bye to Autumn's family, and I exit the tree house behind Koree, climb down the ladder and follow him wordlessly back to Onyx. It only takes us an instant to hop on him, and then we immediately catch air, the only sound the black dragon's wings flapping against the breeze. We fly for a while and land without a word spoken between us. Koree dismounts, stands with his arms crossed over his chest. I dismount and turn toward the girl's dormitory.

"Thank you for helping Autumn," he says from behind me, his voice cool and formal.

I twist around, facing him again. "Sure, no problem," I respond, wishing I could say something to make it right between us. It feels like someone has taken a dagger and is twisting it in my chest as I turn back around and tiptoe toward the wooden steps, knowing that Koree is gone, vanishing silently into the night.

I crawl into my bed and try to sleep but thoughts keep flashing through my mind. Different thoughts than the night before. The feeling of excitement has been replaced with dread, sadness, and emptiness. I can still feel Koree's hand in mind. I see us talking on the tree house couch. I hear him ask me to be involved in the Rebellion...his lopsided smile and dimple. Then images of his eyes appear – full of scorn for me. All because I lied.

My stomach sours as I toss and turn fitfully, feeling nothing but the

coldness of Koree.

Chapter 16

All too soon, trumpets blast like enemy fire. After cleaning up, I stumble downstairs in a daze and start my chores. I feed the dragons assigned to me, clean their pens, and then tromp silently to the cafeteria. I mechanically put food on my plate and sit down next to Gunter. I stare at my scrambled eggs, stirring them absent mindedly with my fork.

"Still not eating, I see," Gunter comments, turning his head toward me.

"Just not hungry today. You want my eggs and toast?"

"I'll take your toast. Snock, they'll work you to death here." I hand him my toast.

"I know." I try to keep my voice chipper, but I know I am failing.

A large boy with shiny black hair and broad shoulders sits down across from us. He smiles at me, and I make an effort to smile back.

"Teak, this is River. His family owns and operates a large dragon ranch. He's in Thann's group."

"Hi." My voice is shallow, easily mistaken for aloofness, but it is all I can muster at the moment.

Gunter is right, River looks like a mountain. "Guess what today is?" River asks, leaning toward me, his grey eyes twinkling.

"I have no idea. I think we're going to actually ride dragons today," I respond.

"Oh, it's better than that," Gunter chimes in.

"What?" I am curious. It sounds exciting, and I could use something to keep my thoughts off of Koree.

"You'll have to wait and see," River teases.

"Tell me!" I am leaning toward him, almost reaching across the table.

"You're cute."

I fall back. Did he just call me cute?

"Um, thanks. So what is it we're doing today? It is a flimsy question. No boy has ever called me cute before. Koree said I looked nice once…but he had a concussion at the time, and I am not sure if that counts.

"We're going to pick out dragon eggs…or rather they'll pick you." It isn't River who answers, and the voice is one I recognize all too well. When I hear it my chest tightens and my heart thumps rapidly in my chest. It is Koree. I immediately turn around, facing him as he stands directly behind me. He doesn't acknowledge my presence. "I need my group to finish up and meet me in front of the Incubation Room. We drew first pick."

Then Koree shoots River a death glare. "What's your name?"

River eyes him steadily. "River Coan"

"Well, *River Coan*, ten demerits for revealing privileged information without permission." Koree stresses River's name as if it were a bug he might want to squash. He makes a rapid turn and stomps away. I stuff a few bites of egg into my mouth and take a drink of apple juice. Gunter and I clear our plates and wave to River, who whistles at me when I walk by.

"Is he like that with all the girls?" I ask Gunter on our way to the Incubation Room.

"No, I think he...you know…likes you." Gunter is grinning widely, which means I can barely see his eyes. To top it off, he is lifting his eyebrows up and down like he does when he is around Echo.

"No way," I tell him. "No boy has ever liked me before." I think of Koree. Did he like me…before? Maybe I was just imagining things. Maybe he has a girlfriend…like Persia. A pretty Dark Skinned girl who isn't tall and gangly and Light Skinned.

"You've got to be kidding," Gunter exclaims, looking up at me.

"No. You know how things are in the city. Everyone calls me a Ghost and a bunch of other stuff. It just gets old."

"I never thought about it like that," Gunter confesses. "I just thought you were ultra smash when you saved Thann and did all that healing. I guessed that all the boys had crushes on you."

"I wish." I ponder what Gunter has said. Me? Ultra smash? If only he knew.

We arrive at the front door of the Incubation Room. Koree and Reese are already there. "Took you long enough," Reese complains. Gunter and I ignore him.

Koree looks up from his leather bound book. "Okay, here are the rules for choosing an egg," he begins. "You will go in one at a time. There are numerous eggs in different stages of incubation. A sign will let you know what stage the egg is at. The older the egg, the sooner you'll have a dragon to train, but you won't have as much bonding time with the egg."

He is animated now, his voice rising. "Here's the great part. You don't really choose the egg – it chooses you. You need to be very still, very quiet. Look for changes in the color of the egg, the pulse of the heartbeat, a feeling you'll get when you walk by one. Don't try too hard. Let the egg choose you."

"Your lineup to choose is based on the merits you've earned so far, so Teak, you get to go first." My heart leaps in my chest. I get my own dragon egg to take care of? I bite my lip, wondering how to take care of a dragon egg. Do I dare ask Koree? I decide to keep quiet.

"I'll walk you in, then wait out here with the others while you choose."

He opens the door for me and I tentatively step into a room that is warm and dimly lit. Shelves line each wall and on the shelves are huge eggs, all of different colors and sizes neatly tucked into wooden boxes filled with straw. A small card by each egg announces the breed and its stage of incubation.

The door shuts quietly, and I realize that Koree has left. I wander around the room, which seems to have a thousand heartbeats humming at me. I feel like I am in a trance. How will I choose just one? Just then a stooped man with pure white hair hobbles up to me. "Are you Teak?" he asks, his voice warm but raspy.

"Yes," I whisper, afraid to disturb the eggs. He smiles at me, almost laughing and I see his crooked yellow teeth reflecting in the pale golden light.

"You don't have to whisper – the noise is good for them. It gets them accustomed to humans before they even hatch." He chuckles.

"Oh, I am sorry."

"No need to be sorry. My name is Kebb. I'll be at my desk. When you find your egg, let me know, and I'll mark it. After you choose your egg, you're to sign up for a time each day to come and bond with it."

"Okay. Thank you." I am a little overwhelmed with yet another chore on my list but also excited about the egg. I wander slowly beside the shelves, examining each egg. There are mottled red eggs, speckled black eggs, metallic eggs, shiny eggs, plain eggs of an assortment of colors. Nothing happens.

I am beginning to think I need to just select one, that this egg choosing you is a joke or a myth, when I am drawn to a pearly white egg. It seems to be on the smaller scale of size as far as the other eggs go, but I am no expert. I stop in front of the white egg and breathe in its smell…a mixture of rain and leaves. No, more like raindrops falling on leaves. And the smallest hint of roses. How can an egg smell like that? I am mesmerized by the egg. The incubation card reads 9 months. That is pretty old. I was hoping for a younger egg so that I would have more bonding time, but I can't seem to take my eyes off of the pearly egg. I reach out to touch it, stroke it, when I hear a voice behind me.

"That one's not a good choice." It is Kebb.

"Why not?" I question.

"Well, it's an albino egg, and they don't have a very good survival rate. I'm afraid you're setting yourself up for heart break there, little miss."

"An albino egg?" I ask. "How do you know?"

He chortles. "I've been doing this a long time. They're very rare, but like I said, only a few have ever lived." His smoky eyes squint into a frown on his wrinkled face. He coughs into a rag then speaks again. "Look at how small it is for nine months. I'm surprised it's made it this long." He reaches into his tunic pocket and pulls out an instrument, puts an end in each ear and places a round disk that is hooked to a tube up to the egg and listens intently for a while.

"Hmmm......still has a solid heartbeat in there...125."

"125? What's that?"

"Beats per minute."

"Oh." He pulls back from the egg. "Why don't you look at some other eggs?"

"Okay." I walk through the room again, hoping that another egg will catch my attention. Nothing happens.

"Try again," Kebb urges.

I do. I try three more times and again, nothing happens. I end up stopping by the pearly egg, staring at it, stroking it, feeling its heart beat and watching, mesmerized by the glow that is emanating from it. Kebb hobbles over to me.

"Look, it's lighting up....it's choosing you."

I smile widely, hardly able to contain my excitement. "Really?"

"Yes," I'd better mark it. He slowly limps over to a desk and returns with a card. "Full name and spelling," he says to me.

"Teak Frain. T. e. a. k. F. r. a. i. n." He shakily prints my name on the card, places it next to the beautiful pearl egg. I stroke the egg lovingly, as if I were actually its mother.

"Now, missy, I have to warn you again about this egg. Odds are against it making it two more months. I want you to sign up for three visits per day instead of one."

"Not a problem," I firmly answer.

He shakes his head. "I've never seen an egg light up so brightly. That's a good sign. That egg likes you, that's for sure. The more time you spend with it, the better odds it has."

"Can I stay with it now?" I ask, almost breathing out the words.

Kebb chuckles again. "No, you have to leave. Everybody picks an egg today. They need their turns too."

"Oh, you are right. I am sorry," I sputter, feeling selfish. I give the egg one last stroke, breathing in its scent like cool, wet rain. I think of names in my head for it. Pearl? Raindrop? Moonlight? No, those names don't sound right.

Kebb chuckles again and takes me to his desk where I sign up for three time slots. I am to tell my Master Trainer the times and I will be released from my duties to come bond with my egg.

I open the door, smiling widely. For the moment I have forgotten about Koree's anger, his coldness toward me. I look him directly in the eye and say, "That was smash!"

Chapter 17

Gunter and Reese gawk at me as if I have lost my mind.

"Ghosts must like eggs," Reese grumbles under his breath. He outwardly sneers, then in a loud, obnoxious voice asks, "Did you choose a white one?"

"That's enough, *Reese.*" Koree spits out, glaring at him with green fire in his eyes. "Twenty demerits. I think we already talked about using the term "Ghost" here." He opens his leather book and writes in it.

"Gunter, you're next," Koree announces, taking his eyes away from Reese. I can't remember the last time I saw him smile. Koree leads Gunter into the Incubation Room, which leaves me alone with Reese.

I stiffen, not wanting to deal with him.

"Your babysitter isn't here, Teak the Freak," he sneers. "And you are still an ugly Ghost no matter what anybody says."

"Shut up, Reese." The last thing I want is to tangle with him. I know all about his dark Power…his hate for Light Skins. It is hard to believe we were once friends.

"You better watch your back, Teak the Freak. I am going to get even with you…for all you did on the way here. I haven't forgotten." His words are precise and succinct, like mine. We have spent ten years together in Weapons and the training is as much a part of us as the blood running though our veins. "And I am going to kill that bagger, Koree, too. You can tell him that." He raises his eyebrows, and his face contorts into something beyond ugly.

It feels as if a spear has penetrated my heart when he threatens Koree. Reese and I are not evenly matched. I am better at Weapons than he is…I chose dragons, but he didn't even make the top three in Weapons. He is here because he failed. I glare at him. But he has Power…a lot of it. And I have none. "I am not afraid of you, *Reese*." I mimic Koree's use of the word Reese. It feels good rolling off of my lips.

Just then Koree opens the door and strides up to us. Since Koree is here I turn my back to Reese and bite my lower lip, thinking. I am supposed to tell Koree about needing three time slots instead of one. But approaching Koree now…I think I would have better luck talking to an iceberg. I clear my throat anyway, and muster up the courage to talk to him.

"Kebb says I need to sign up for three time slots." My voice is quivering as I stare blankly at him.

Koree launches one of his serious green eyed looks at me, raising both eyebrows. There is the slightest hint of accusation seeping out of his voice when he speaks. *"Three* time slots?"

I explain about the albino egg that chose me and the odds of its survival. Koree nods his head, writes the times down. 11:00, 3:00, and 6:00. "I'll be double checking with Kebb," he snips at me – as if I might be lying again.

Gunter slides out of the door just then. "I've got a Metallic," he almost shouts. "It just lit up when I walked by. Only seven months along, so I have a long time to bond with it." He shakes his fist in the air. "Holy snock, that *was* smash!"

I can't help but let a giggle erupt at Gunter's animation. Reese enters next and returns within a few minutes. We all stare at him, Koree included, as if we need an explanation for why he came out so quickly.

"What? I chose a green egg. I hope it is an Ebony," he mumbles under his breath, as if talking to us is too much of an effort.

Koree changes the subject. "Fine. Let's move along now." He leads us to the tack room and tells us to get our tack and a saddle. We follow his directions and then traipse behind him to a dragon pen not too far away. I notice Pebble right away. Koree tells us to go catch a dragon, tack it up and bring it back out. We are going to ride in the arena today.

I follow Reese and Gunter and am relieved when they choose other dragons. I slowly approach Pebble and put a halter on her, brush her glistening red scales, then put on her saddle and bridle. I notice a huge horizontal scar across her neck and wonder why I haven't seen it before. My first reaction is to ask Koree about it, but then I think about how cold he has been to me, and I decide I had better wait and ask Thann the next time I see him. I lead Pebble out of the pen. I am the first one out. "Five merits," is all Koree says to me, writing in his book again. Well, at least he is being fair. Reese and Gunter each follow with a dragon plodding behind them.

We reach the arena together, Gunter and me side by side with Reese following. Koree is already in the center of the arena. "Mount your dragons," Koree orders, his voice like steel. He is mounted on Onyx, and memories of flying on the black dragon with Koree flash into my head. I feel a lump form in my throat, not just for Koree, but because I want to fly on a dragon again. I can almost feel the wind blow over my face when I think of it. I shake my head, look over at Pebble, and with a sinking heart I lift my leg over her back and settle in the saddle.

"We're going to play follow the leader, and I'm the leader," Koree announces.

Koree leads us with a slow walk and we fall into place. Gunter first, me second, and Reese behind me. I am a little nervous having him behind me, but I try to just follow Gunter, having Pebble do what Koree and Gunter are doing. Gunter is agile, and his dragon responds easily. Pebble is larger, but she seems willing to do what I ask.

"Squeeze your legs and give the dragons a small kick with your heels," Koree tells us, turning back from Onyx. "We are moving into a trot, so keep your heels down and stay balanced. Look where you want to go and the dragon will take you there." I follow his instructions, and soon I find myself bouncing up and down on Pebble, and a feeling of exhilaration rushes through my body. It is not quite like real flying, but a definite second best.

We travel in circles, and my legs are starting to tire, actually trembling as I continue balancing and trotting. "Okay, stop," Koree tells us. "You're doing great, Teak." I smile inwardly at the praise. At least it is something. "Reese, you need to work on balancing a little better."

"Whatever," Reese answers rudely. Koree's eyes flash green ice at him.

"Twenty demerits, Reese," he almost snarls. "Watch your tone with me." He turns back around on Onyx and I catch Reese shooting a nasty look to his back. Part of me is relieved that Reese is targeting someone else, and another part of me is actually frightened for Koree. I have been on the losing end of Reese's fury way too many times.

Gunter guides his dragon next to mine, leans over and whispers, "Someone's crabby again today." I just nod my head.

As we wait, Koree dismounts Onyx and takes long Koree strides around the edge of the arena and sets up an obstacle course. There are huge logs, round hoops that are perched high in the air, a bridge, and an assortment of other objects scattered around. We watch as Koree fluidly jumps back on Onyx. "We'll continue as before," he tells us in a matter of fact tone.

We follow him through the course. I am scared and excited all at once, concentrating on each obstacle. When we get to the first round hoop, all I can think to do is hold on as Pebble soars through it, and it reminds me of flying on Onyx. We land easily, and I feel a thrill of delight. Just then I hear a thud and a curse behind me. I turn back to see Reese sprawled on the ground.

I glance down at him and squeeze my legs, moving the dragon forward. Pebble trots away, stirring up a tornado of dust…directly in Reese's face.

The slightest of smiles creeps up on my lips.

Chapter 18

Koree's voice pulls my attention to the center of the arena, where he has stopped. The sun is shining on his chestnut curls, and he is perched on the sleek black dragon, leaning slightly forward.

"Teak, you need to bond with your egg," he tells me. There is no emotion in his voice.

"Okay," I answer as I throw my leg off of Pebble and land on the ground with a soft thud. I take Pebble to her pen, quickly groom her with a soft brush and rush to the Incubation Room. I sign in at Kebb's desk and immediately find the pearly white egg. It lights up for me as I caress it tenderly.

"Hi little buddy," I tell it. "What should I name you?"

"That's good." It is Kebb standing behind me. "It needs to hear your voice as often as possible. You're a natural."

"Um…thanks," I answer as I continue to pet the egg. Kebb checks the little egg out again. "Seems fine," he says, as if he is talking to himself and not me. He wobbles away, muttering something under his breath as I continue to stroke my egg. Then, all too soon I hear Kebb's voice from across the room. "Time's up little missy." I get up to leave, giving my egg one last pat. When I step outside, I am blinded by the bright light as I search for my group.

I fetch Pebble from her pen and head back to the arena. I ride up to find Koree holding Onyx as he stands in the middle of the group. "Tomorrow we will be playing dragon games with Persia's group," he flatly tells us. Persia's group. I think of Persia, how petite and pretty she is. Of course Koree would be interested in her and not me. I was so stupid to think otherwise. I swallow back a lump in my throat as I listen to him speak. "You are doing better than any group I've ever had, but that might change once Flame gets out of isolation. It might set us back as a group."

Koree releases us and storms off. I shrug it off as I rush off to the supplies store. I only have 15 minutes before it closes. I search around and find some parchment paper and a charcoal pencil. I quickly part with my last coins and race to the Infirmary.

I ask to see Echo and this time I am led into her room by a tall, elegant woman with black hair, a white streak cutting through the middle, just like a skunk's tail. I am breathless when I reach Echo's room. She smiles widely when she sees me.

"It's about time. Snock, I am bored out of my skull here."

"It has been a busy day. We got to choose eggs...dragon eggs of our own," I exhale.

"No way."

"Yes way." I answer. "You get to go into a room and if one lights up...it chooses you. Mine is an albino egg." I stop there for a minute. "Kebb, the man in charge, says it doesn't have a very good chance of making it, though."

"Oh dragon tits, what does he know!"

"Well, more than me."

"Just give it a lot of attention. It'll be fine."

"How do you know?"

"I grew up on a dragon farm. I had to take care of a lot of eggs."

"Oh, that is right." I breathe out a sigh of relief at her words of encouragement. "Oh, and tomorrow your group and my group are going to have a competition."

"Snock, it's not fair."

"You will be out soon," I tell her. Then, "Are you ready to learn to read?" A smile crops up on my face.

"Yep, let me finish eating and we'll start. She gobbles her food while I rip the paper into little squares and write the alphabet on them with big letters.

I give Echo her first reading lesson, showing and telling her each letter and the sound it makes. I have her trace them with the charcoal pencil as she says each sound out loud, thinking back to how I learned to read from Entho. It doesn't take long for her to memorize the letters and sounds. "Tomorrow I will teach you how to blend the sounds together," I tell her. I say good-bye and stroll back to the dormitory.

I open the door and find Loris and the other girl playing Dragon Cards. I agree to play with them and find out the other girl's name is Celerie. She is oddly quiet, her dark eyes darting at me and then back to Loris. She is dark skinned, short, and chunky with wavy brown hair. I remind myself to keep my guard up around her.

"Where do you go every night?" Loris asks.

"I am visiting a friend in the Infirmary. She will be here in a few days."

"Oh, smash," Loris answers.

"I am sure you will like her," I answer, yawning.

Celerie and Loris continue to play cards as I stand up and get ready for bed. I wash up and put on some pajamas. As I crawl into bed, I feel under my pillow and stroke the black cloak with my fingers, remembering my night with Koree. I wonder if he will come in the night so that I can check on Autumn. But his words replay over and over in my mind…*I'll come back tomorrow night to check on Autumn…I'll…I'll…I'll…*

I hear the words, as if chanting lunatic resides in my head, as I toss and turn, wishing I could just close my eyes and fall asleep.

Chapter 19

I must have fallen asleep, because at some point I awake to trumpets blaring, wondering if I will ever get used to them. As I step out of bed, I feel like an empty container. I silently scold myself. Koree has made his feelings for me clear, and he didn't come for me in the night to help with Autumn, so it is time for me to move on. I only wish I could get my heart to follow my head. *He is out of your league anyway, I silently tell myself.*

The day follows as the previous one did, rushing to my egg, riding Pebble through the course, and ending with the competition. Persia's group is definitely better at dragon riding than we are, but I think that is what the competition is about. We watch and learn from them as they glide effortlessly through the obstacle course. Gunter is by far the best rider in our group and he handles the Metallic with ease, as if he has been riding dragons his entire life. I am second best, feeling a little smug to be better than Reese, who misses his loop again and falls to the ground. His scowl is deep and his face turns massively red while both groups watch.

We lose the competition, of course, but we don't mind. Gunter and I lead our dragons back to their pens, groom them and go about our chores.

"That was smash," Gunter exclaims.

"Yes, it was," I agree. "Will you put Pebble up for me? I have to go to my egg, and I am running late."

"Sure," Gunter agrees. He takes Pebble as I turn to leave, racing to the Incubation Room.

The next few days pass like this, and finally Echo is released from the Infirmary and Flame returns to our group. Flame seems a little more humble, but I do not trust her at all. Echo and I stay close in the dormitory, and Loris and Celerie return to ignoring me. I figured that it would work out this way. I fuss over Echo's bandage and check her wound often.

"Quit flipping checking on me all the time. It's creeping me out." She throws a dirty sock at my face, and then we both start laughing.

"Okay…"

"Let's go outside." Echo nods to the door. We both get up and leave the dormitory, three sets of eyes watching us silently as we leave. Echo settles on the bottom step and I plunk down beside her.

"Snock, those girls are a bunch of creepers. They weird me out….staring at us like we're a couple of baggers." I grin, nodding my head in agreement. "Hey," she turns to me, "Where are we going to do the…reading stuff? I don't want those lollies knowing about it. I might have to kill them and bury their bodies."

"Well, let's go check around," I laugh. Together, Echo and I stand up and start wandering around Harcourt. We read each building name, wondering if it will be suitable. Finally, we see an ornate sign that says "Dragon Library". There isn't a dragon head on the sign, so we know we can enter without any problems.

"This will be perfect," I tell Echo. I had no idea that Harcourt had a library. Books…I think, could they really have books in there? I think of the times I had to sneak books from under Entho's bed so that I could read…how he would have been punished for keeping my mom's dragon training books had anyone found out.

"You think? Echo inquires.

"Yes, I do. Let's go inside and ask." We traipse up some brick steps and enter the library. A librarian is sitting at the main desk busily sorting some cards and placing them in books. Her face looks like it is permanently pinched and I wonder if she has ever smiled.

I scan the enormous room and am shocked to see shelves of books on every wall. I try to read the titles from where I stand but can't tell what they are. *Could they all be dragon related books? And why are they out in the open...so many of them?*

"Excuse me," Echo politely interrupts. The librarian's head shoots up and she glares at us with grayish green eyes.

"Yes," she answers in a voice to match her expression.

"Um...uh...could we study here...in the evenings? I manage to ask her, hoping my voice isn't shaking.

She takes a minute, as if to assess us. "Yes, but only if you are quiet." She returns to her cards and books.

"That is not a problem," I promise her. Echo only nods her head, quiet for a change, and we turn around, walk out of the building like perfect ladies until we hit the cobblestone pavement. Echo lets out a loud whoop and takes off running back toward the dorm. I follow at her heels, a smile forming on my lips.

The following evenings, after riding, chores, and checking on my egg three times, I meet Echo in the library. I have already taught her to read basic words. She is delighted. "You are a great student," I whisper to her from across the table.

"Thanks. I always thought I was just dumb."

"You're not dumb!" I tell her. Then, "How is it that you never learned to read?"

"Well…we didn't go to school, that's only for the Red Cloakers. And I'm the last of six kids, so nobody ever got around to teaching me. My brother tried for a while, but he lost patience quickly. I just couldn't seem to pick it up."

"Well, you are learning it now."

"Thanks to you," she grins. I smile back at her…at my friend.

Echo and I walk briskly back to the dormitory, clean up, put on our pajamas, and crawl into bed. She has chosen the bed next to mine, and I feel more at ease with her between Flame and me. I am exhausted from the day and I fall into a deep, dreamless sleep.

Chapter 20

It isn't trumpets that awaken me. At some point I feel a hand on my shoulder, gently shaking it. I turn away, trying to go back to sleep. I feel the shaking movement again, leap out of bed, and immediately launch myself into a fighting stance. I pull my arms up in fists in front of my face, ready to strike.

"Teak...don't...it's me." The voice is a whisper...and a familiar one at that. It is Koree, and my heart skips a beat as I stare at him in the grey light of the girls' dormitory. Slowly, I drop my arms. But not my guard.

"I need your help. Three more children have fevers." He is still whispering as if nothing has happened between us...as if we don't have a thick wall separating us, dividing us like warring countries.

I spread my legs and cross my arms over my chest, facing him in the dimly lit room. "No," I whisper back to him.

"NO?" His whisper turns into a deep growl.

I nod my head, glaring at him.

He grabs my arm firmly and starts pulling me toward the door. My first reaction is to slam his elbow, forcing a release. But I rein it in…there is something in me that just can't hurt him. Not on purpose, anyway. Just then Echo stirs, sitting up in bed. Koree immediately drops to the floor. I am standing by the foot of her bed. "Is everything okay?" she groggily asks.

"Yes, I am just going to the bathroom," I tell her in a whisper that I hope doesn't sound frantic.

"Oh, okay. I thought I heard a boy's voice." She yawns, rubbing her eyes.

"No, just me. I was probably talking in my sleep."

She cuddles up in bed, turning her back to us, and Koree waits a few minutes before gingerly standing up. He nods his head toward the door, and I follow him, tiptoeing across the wooden floor. *Why am I doing this? I don't owe him anything.* But I continue slinking across the room like a rat in the night…silently scolding myself with every step.

I step outside and the warm evening air wraps around me like a light jacket. Koree takes my arm again, his long fingers wrapping around it like a long lost friend. Or enemy. I can't be sure. "Come with me," he seethes. "We're going to have a little chat."

"We can chat here," I tell him in my most snarky voice, the one I have usually kept reserved for my former Weapons Instructor, Bello. I start to pull free from his grasp, but he tightens his grip on my arm.

"No, it should be private. I don't want anyone to see us."

"Afraid to be seen with a Ghost?" I taunt.

"That does it." He takes off walking at a fast pace, his long strides forcing me to scurry beside him. We walk briskly and silently through Harcourt, Koree's hand gripping my arm. The only sounds between us are our footsteps on the cobblestone paths. Feelings of relief and anger wage war inside of me. His touch…it feels so good, even if it is just his hand on my arm. But he is so confusing…and infuriating.

We end up at the Incubation Room. Koree lets go of my arm, digs around in his pants pocket for a second and pulls out a ring of keys.

He unlocks the door, leads the way inside. I follow him and he closes the door behind me.

"Why here?" I ask, crossing my arms and glaring at him, the yellowish light casting shadows of eggs and nests and light flames behind him.

"Because no one is here at night." He lets out a long sigh. "And because it's good for the eggs to hear human voices."

"Alright…" Silence settles between us as he matches my nasty look with one of his own.

"Okay…I've had about enough of you," he finally spits out.

"Then why did you drag me here?"

"Because I thought you'd help those kids." "But you tell me no?" It is a question and an accusation rolled into one.

"You can figure it out another way. You have healers. You saw the medicine I made. Figure it out yourself."

"Yeah, right. Like I know what to do." He rubs his hand on the back of his neck, twisting his head sideways, his loose brownish red curls dangling like leaves on a willow tree. "And I already told you about the Rebellion and that we can't involve the healers from Harcourt."

Something inside me breaks apart at this…memories of the night we spent together blazing through me. "That's right, you ask me to help a sick girl, tell me about the Rebellion, hold my hand, confide in me about other things, then just forget me because you think I'm a liar," I shout at him. My chest is heaving, and I am holding my fists into tight balls. "You've been horrible to me, treating me like…like snock, and then you expect me just to jump when you need me."

"YOU *ARE* A LIAR." He yells, accentuating the word "are".

I glare at him in the dim light. "I AM NOT A LIAR. I AM A SURVIVOR." I scream back.

"A SURVIVOR?"

I feel like I am going to cry. Tears threaten to spill out of my eyes, and I find it hard to breathe. Once again words are trapped in my throat like a caged animal. I swallow over and over again, but it doesn't help. Silence surrounds us except for the soft beating of hearts…the enormous eggs that soon will hatch into dragons. I cast my eyes downward, biting my lower lip. Thinking. And hurting. For some reason my heart feels like claws are shredding it to pieces.

Then I glance up, find Koree's eyes and gaze into the greenness of them that is reflecting against the soft lights that keep the eggs warm. Soft…soft…soft… The word plays over and over in my mind. When I finally speak, my voice is soft, just like the lights. I tilt my head up, my eyes still fastened on his.

"You don't know what it is like…being the only Light Skin." I stop for a second, not sure if I should go on, but his eyes have not left mine. I don't know if I am imagining it or not, but his harsh, piercing stare has become more tender, if only just slightly. I breathe out, my voice a misty fog. "I have been bitten, pinched, shoved, called ruthless names… I could go on. A few weeks ago Reese shoved me into a dragon statue at Assessment and I had a concussion and 17 stitches in my head. All for being a Ghost."

"Don't say that word." Green eyes flash at me, but the anger seems to have faded out of them.

"Well, that is what they all call me. Even my new roommates. The first thing they said when I walked in the room was, "Ghost. Ugly Ghost". I hesitate, looking down. But you were not there…you don't understand." I purse my lips and then take a deep breath. "You don't know what it is like." I pause for a moment, breathing heavily. Words slip out of my mouth, my voice a whisper. "Growing up…they called me Teak the Freak." Shame floods through my body. I have never told this to anyone, not even Entho.

Koree hangs his head for a minute then rubs his forehead. His russet curls are messy, tangled, and I feel an unexpected urge to reach out and straighten them. Instead, I keep my hands and arms crossed against my chest.

"You never explained it…like that," he whispers, sheepishly.

I wait a minute or two before answering in a voice so low, I am not even sure if he can hear it. "You never gave me a chance."

He sighs, rubs his hand through his hair again. "I know…I was just so…so disappointed."

"I know the feeling."

We face each other in the dim golden light, so close that our breath blends together, and a piece of me wants to drink it up like sweet lemonade on a hot day. I don't know what else to say and my eyes start to mist over with tears of frustration. Then words stream out of Koree's mouth, like they have been locked up in prison and have just been released.

"When I first saw you…in your dad's clinic… you were covered in blood. You were…so smart and pretty…I couldn't take my eyes off you."

My jaw drops. *Pretty? Me? He thought I was pretty?* I can't help but interrupt. "You didn't say a word to me. Thann did all the talking."

His lips curl up ever so slightly. "Thann is smooth with the ladies. I just let him do his thing."

"Well, you seemed…so…so…hostile."

He smiles a little then, a lopsided grin shadowing his face. His dimple jumps out at me, and I find it difficult to breathe.

"You weren't exactly friendly either. If I remember correctly, you had a dagger in your hand most of the time," he quips.

"You were strangers…"

"I know." He cocks his head to the side and stares at me. In the yellow light his copper curls glisten like precious metal. When he speaks, his voice is deep, husky. "The next time I saw you…when you came out of that mansion… I didn't realize it was you…that the clinic was behind where you lived. I saw right away that you were a Red Cloaker. I thought that you were just another spoiled girl whose daddy bought her way to Dragon Academy." He stops for a few seconds, clenches his jaw, glances down to the floor for a slow moment and then moves his head back up, as if it were heavy.

"When I woke up on the ground, after the Destroyers came…your face was the first thing I saw…and…and I thought I had gone to the moon and back."

"To the moon?"

He reaches both hands out then and gently places them against my neck, pulling me close to him.

"To the moon," he answers in the huskiest voice I have ever heard. We stay that way for a few minutes, our hearts beating in a rhythm I didn't know possible. I can't seem to take my eyes off of his, as if his green rays of light are streaking into my golden eyes, mixing with them and creating a Power of their own. He slowly leans back, then, and lets his arms fall to his side. I let out a long breath I didn't even know I was holding

He takes in a deep breath and then lets it out, the air spinning before me with hints of mint and something so masculine it could only be Koree. My stomach is turning over and over, as if something were inside of me doing somersaults.

"When I figured out that you weren't just a spoiled rich kid…that you cared about people – you healed me, Echo, and Autumn…" He stops again, his eyes almost pleading in the dim light. "You saved Thann's life…and that night with you…I thought something was happening between us…and then I caught you in that lie…and it ruined everything."

I gulp air into my lungs. "I only lied to protect myself."

"I get it now. It's just…"

"You thought I was pretty?" I interrupt. I can't seem to move past the pretty part.

"Still do." He grins at me, a hint of mischief in his emerald eyes. "I was so jealous when River was flirting with you I almost gave him 100 demerits."

"Really?" *Someone…Koree…was jealous. Of me?* I feel something move out of me, then, something that has been locked up tight, as if the lid of a huge box was just opened. "I…I…am sorry I lied.…I just didn't want anything else stolen or any more problems with those awful girls. I am so sick of it…you have no idea."

"I'm sorry I didn't listen." He grasps both of my hands and pulls me toward him. My heart is racing and my breath is caught, as if I am paralyzed, rooted in this place without a chance of ever moving again. We are facing each other, only a few inches apart. "Will you please come with me and help those sick kids?"

"Ofcourse," I breathe out as if it is one word.

Koree wrenches away from me, still holding my hand and begins to lead me out the door.

"Hurry, Onyx is waiting. Maybe we can do some spins."

"Wait," I say, feeling pulled in two distinct directions. "I need to check on my egg first."

"Good idea…that little guy…"

His words trail off behind me as I scuttle over to my pearl egg. I bend down and place my hand on it, but immediately draw it back. The egg's light is shining, but only a tiny glimmer that weakly turns off and then on like a flickering flame. I stare at the small white egg, not knowing what to do, and then a sick feeling seeps through my body, settling in my stomach as the light dims completely. I put my hand back on it, running my fingers over it. There is no mistaking what I feel. It is a crack. My precious egg is cracked.

"Koree, come quickly." My voice can't hide the panic I feel.

He is at my side so quickly I didn't even hear him move. "What?"

"Something is wrong with my egg."

Koree kneels down and places his hands expertly over the diminutive egg, his long fingers feeling all around it. Then, he stands quickly, grabs Kebb's instrument from the desk and returns in a flurry of motion. He bends down next to me, placing the instrument on the egg.

He turns to me, his expression grave. "This egg is hatching...prematurely." I detect fear in his voice. "Stay here. I'm getting Kebb.

Chapter 21

I stroke the egg lovingly. "Hang on little buddy…please hang on." I tell it this over and over again, the widening crack scraping harshly against my fingertips. At last the door swings open and Koree runs up to me, bends down beside me and checks the temperature of the egg with a thermometer. He listens for the egg's heartbeat and takes his long fingers and feels all over the egg.

"Heartbeat is still strong, but there are more cracks. Kebb will be here in a few minutes."

"Will it be okay?" I ask, fear drenching over me.

Koree lets out a deep breath, a story of darkness and shadows. "Don't know…" he answers, rubbing his fingers through his hair and wrinkling his brow. Then, after pausing for a brief moment, his lips curl up, ever so slightly. "One way or another it looks like you're about to become a mother."

"What do you mean?"

"Premature dragons require constant care if they're going to survive. You'll have to bottle feed it, carry it with you everywhere you go, check its vitals…there's a whole list of things to do. Just like a real mother."

"Oh," I sigh, far from disappointed,

"Do you think you can handle it?"

"I can handle it," I say with determination.

Just then Kebb limps in. He doesn't say a word but hobbles directly to the egg. He runs a series of tests on it as Koree and I watch. He listens to the heartbeat several times, fiddles with the flames in the room to warm it up, and takes the egg's temperature several more times.

"You kids can run along. I've got it from here."

"Will it be okay…will it live?" I ask Kebb.

"Don't know little missy, only time will tell. These albinos….I warned you about them."

"I know." I hang my head, sadness washing over me. "Can I stay here with it?"

"No, it's better with me. I know what to do."

"But, we're bonded…right?"

Kebb narrows his eyes as if deep in thought, but doesn't take them off of the egg. "Yes. But you would only be in the way." His words sting like someone slapped me in the face, and a giant lump forms in my throat. "It's not your fault," he continues. "You don't have the proper training." He continues to monitor the egg, expertly tending to it. "Go get some sleep and come check with me first thing in the morning," Kebb orders, his voice gruff for a change.

Koree tenderly reaches for my hand, walking me toward the door, and I grudgingly leave, looking back at my pearly egg, knowing it might be the last time I see it.

Chapter 22

The door shuts quietly behind us, as if it knows to only whisper at a time like this. Koree takes his thumb and slowly rubs circles on my hand as we stand side by side outside the Incubation Room. "It will be okay...one way or another," he comforts, twisting his body so that we are now facing each other. A tear reluctantly leaks out of my eye, and I feel foolish for crying, but before I can swipe it away, Koree drops my hand, reaches toward my face and wipes the tear away with the same thumb. Just for a moment, he rests it on my face.

"I know what you're feeling," he comforts. I just sniff in return, wondering how he really could know what I am feeling. He tips his head sideways. "Kebb is the best. If anyone can save that egg, he can." His eyes flash at me, only not with anger like before but with an intensity that is unsettling. "We still have some sick kids, though. Let's get your case and get going."

It takes me a few seconds to shift gears, to go from my egg hatching prematurely to helping sick children. "Koree, we have a problem."

"What now?"

"I am almost out of the herbs and medicine I need to treat fevers and infection. Entho only packed me a small amount of everything."

"Oh, snock." He narrows his eyes, deep in thought. "Do you know what you need?"

"Of course."

"We can get whatever you need from the Apothecary. Let's go."

Together, Koree and I, hand in hand, bolt to the Apothecary. Koree unlocks the door, opens it for me. "We've been filtering what we need from the stores here at Harcourt for the Rebellion. They haven't missed a thing yet."

We step foot in the Apothecary, and Koree lights a flame. Numerous jars of herbs and medicines line shelves that travel up to the ceiling. I point out to Koree which ones I need and he pours the herbs and medicines into smaller jars. He finds a sturdy bag and places all of the jars in it. "Okay, let's get going," he urges.

We race to Onyx as quietly as we can and jump on him at once, as if we were both singing the same melody of a song. Onyx flaps his wings and we take off, soaring into the still night sky. I grab Koree's waist, feeling his stomach muscles flexing under my fingers again, and I breathe a sigh of relief – I didn't know if I would ever touch Koree again – or fly on a dragon. Koree spins the dragon several times, loops him, and lands him with a sliding stop. I catch my breath as I jump off the black dragon, my hood flying off of my head, spilling my hair out like a butterfly emerging from a cocoon.

We dash through the orchard until we reach a tree trunk. Koree repeats the knocking rhythm, the ladder falls down, and we climb up. I treat a little boy who is feverish but not as bad as Autumn was. His name is Drake and he has the whitest hair and skin I have ever seen. We make it to two other tree houses and repeat the process with two other children, another boy about Drake's age and a little girl, about nine or ten years old.

When we climb out of the last tree house, our feet hit the soft dirt almost in unison, and this time we leisurely traipse back through the orchard toward Onyx. I let out a yawn, thinking of all that has happened in such a short time.

"This way," Koree whispers, his voice a deep song on the soft breeze. He clasps my hand in his and turns me in a different direction, leading me to the empty tree house. He climbs up the ladder, and I follow him, reaching the platform right behind him. He wraps his hands around my waist and lifts me into the same tree house we were in before. With a swift kick of his leg, he slams the door shut.

"Have a seat," he tells me. Curious, I sit down on the couch, and he plops down right next to me, turning to face me. "We're having a Rebellion meeting at lunch tomorrow. Do you want to come?"

"Sure," I answer. Suddenly it becomes quiet. Koree fiddles his thumbs, bounces his left leg. Then he turns his head toward me. "I want to tell you something."

My heart sinks into my stomach. His eyes are so serious that it can't be good news. "What?" I ask.

He clenches his jaw, never taking his eyes off of me. When he finally speaks, his voice is husky, full of emotion. "You're the first person I've told this to, but I want you to understand where I'm coming from…about my issues."

"What issues?"

"You know…my hang up…about being lied to…" He closes his eyes, scrunching them together as if it hurts to keep them open. "…why I was such an ass to you." The last words bleed with finality.

"Oh, that."

Then, like oysters revealing pearls, his eyes open wide. Two green pearls blazing into me. I swallow, confusion settling over me again. He speaks, his words reverent, almost holy whispers. "They lied to me."

"Who?" I crane my neck forward, straining to hear what he says.

"My parents…the Destroyers…Siv Gareth. All of them."

"What are you talking about?

He lets out a raspy breath and swipes at his forehead. "I was seven years old," he starts, his voice now a monotone, like when Entho tells me the story of my mother's death. "Siv Gareth was friends with my parents. He was at our house a lot back then. He and my parents were part of the first Alliance. They were restructuring the government... for the good of the country, you know because of the wars and all. They wanted to restore electricity, technology, all of the things we lost." Koree clears his throat then purses his lips, as if he had just eaten something distasteful.

"I was listening...to a meeting they were having...eavesdropping behind the door. Siv Gareth started talking about making the Alliance pure by getting rid of the Light Skinned people." Koree stops then, as if expecting a reaction from me. But I remain still and silent. This is not news to me. I have endured it for the past ten years of my life.

After a while, he swallows and continues. "My dad had a fit, started yelling about it being wrong. They got into this huge argument. But they finally agreed to take the matter up with the New Alliance Commission."

"They all made promises. Siv told me he was taking my parents to a meeting and that I was to stay home and wait for them. If I was good, he was going to give me my own dragon – one of his personal Lavs, and when I grew up I could join his elite army. I was excited at first, but something just didn't seem right. Then, my parents left me. They said they'd be back in a while…to wait for them. They promised they'd return."

Koree hangs his head and sighs deeply, as if a deadly snake was slithering out of his mouth instead of air. "I followed them…twisting and turning through the trees and paths. They ended up outside of an empty building I had never seen before. I peeked my head around the building, watching. Two Destroyers grabbed my mother, and she was screaming and fighting against them. I wanted to run to her and help her, but I just stood there watching."

Koree stops for a sad moment, and the expression on his face feels as if it might compress my heart into a small box of nothing. I find his eyes, and he continues. "My dad went crazy and was attacking them, but he had no weapons. He was trying to protect my mother…screaming about her Light Skin not mattering. Then another Destroyer came up from behind and stabbed my dad in the back with a red handled sword. He fell to the ground and I watched as he quit moving, my mother screaming over and over for him."

Koree stops, again, his chest heaving. "I didn't move…didn't do a thing to help. I just stood there. Then the same Destroyer who killed my dad crept up behind my mother and…and sliced her head off."

"Oh no…"

"I did nothing."

"You couldn't have. They would have killed you, too."

"I know," he answers, his eyes flashing dark green cinders at me. "But it doesn't make it any easier."

"I am so sorry," I tell him. I reach for his hand, a move that is awkward for me. He wraps his fingers tightly around mine.

"The thing that's always burned me is that they lied to me…all of them. My parents promised me they'd return, and they didn't. And Siv Gareth promised me that if I waited like a good boy he'd let me have my own dragon. You can guess I never got that dragon," Koree exhales, stirring the stagnant air in front of us.

"I am so sorry," I say again. "Soot…" I say. "Seeing Soot must have been horrible…"

He nods his head. "It brought back so much. I never thought I'd have to see something like that again. No one should."

He squeezes his hand tightly around mine now, almost squishing it. "I'm going to stop them…stop them all…somehow." He stubbornly sticks his chin out, staring into space at a place that he isn't sharing with anyone. The flicker of the candle burns down in the corner of the small tree house casting eerie shadows on the rough wooden walls.

After a while I break the silence. "I watched my mom die, too, only not like…not like Soot or your mom. No person…nobody should die that way." I swallow, afraid to go on, afraid to reveal the part of me that I have kept locked up for years. I squeeze his hand, a gesture I hope he understands. "And then I watched my dad die daily to the point where he wasn't even a dad any more – just a man who provided for me. I was sent away to Weapons when I was six years old, and I hated every minute of it. That is when I started calling him Entho instead of Dad."

"You watched your mom die?" He faces me, eyes wide and shoulders stiff.

I am in no hurry to speak but finally the words tumble out. "Yes, I was a small child…four or so. She fell off a dragon and broke her neck."

"Holy snock, that's as bad as what I saw."

"No…no, it was an accident." I pause for a minute, thinking…remembering. "Or so they say."

Koree's eyebrows shoot up. "What do you mean?"

"I just saw some stuff. But nobody believes me."

"What did you see?" he presses, his green eyes cutting through me.

I struggle to answer. I have kept this imbedded inside of me for so long. Still, I am tired of secrets. "I…I swear it was Siv Gareth who struck a spear into her dragon. And then she went down. I recognized him when he came to the school yard and they took us away to be killed…when I was six years old." I gulp, memories of that day speeding like a dragon out of control through my mind. "Entho saved me, though. I was the only one who was Marked with Power."

His eyes are earnest as he slowly speaks. He wraps his hands behind my head and turns it toward his so that we are eye to eye. "Siv Gareth? You're sure?"

I nod my head. "I am positive now. I saw him recently…and I knew it was him.

Right before I tried to kill him."

Chapter 23

"You what?" Koree sputters, the room falling silent as his jaw drops.

I smile at his reaction, but it isn't one of satisfaction. Steel forms inside of me at the thought of Siv Gareth. "I shot an arrow at his heart. And I never miss my mark."

"Fireballs…what happened? I know he's still alive."

"He grabbed the arrow from the sky…just reached out with his hand and caught it."

"He's very Powerful." Koree's voice trails off. "You must have a lot of Power…to still be alive after that."

I laugh then, almost a snort. "I don't know what happened. But I placed first in the competition and he didn't even bother me about it…said it must have been a mistake. And I have absolutely no Power."

"But when those Destroyers captured you and Thann…I remember them saying Siv Gareth wanted you." He fiddles his fingers on his leg for a few minutes. "You have no Power?"

I hang my head. "None."

"But, you're Marked." With that he reaches up and gently strokes the crescent shaped mark on my cheek. It seems to sizzle where his fingers touch, and I gradually turn my face toward his, moving closer to him, reveling in his leather and woods and musky warm scent.

"I believe you," he says, slowly pulling his finger down.

"You do?"

"Yeah." He flashes me a lopsided grin. "I guess we're alike – only different – like bookends that don't match but still…" He tips his head to the side. "…work well together." Maybe that's why I liked you so much from the start." He pauses for quite a while, as if he is pondering a difficult decision. "From the start," he repeats, nodding his head slightly.

We are already so close we are almost touching, but he leans into me, wraps his arm around my back, and pulls me to him, my chest rubbing up against his. Then both of his hands connect with the back of my neck and I am held in place by them, his green eyes glistening. My heart races out of control and I swear I stop breathing all together. A shock wave runs through my entire body when his lips softly brush against mine. I close my eyes, not knowing what to do, and I feel his lips again and again, each time pressing a little harder, moving over mine with a rhythm that I learn to match. A fire moves through the inside of my body like none I ever could have imagined.

Suddenly he pulls away from me, quickly, as if he were burned. I have never been kissed before, never thought it possible, but I can't imagine why he would do this. I stare at his lips, slightly swollen, and I can still taste them, feel them on mine. My eyes blaze at him, confused.

"Snock, we need to go," he stammers. "It's starting to get light out." He jumps up from the couch in one swift movement, reaching for my hand. "Hurry," he calls back to me.

I follow him to the door of the tree house, scaling the ladder quickly, hating that I had to let go of his hand to do so. Too much has happened and it all jumbles around in my head as we run toward Onyx, jump on him and catch air almost immediately.

Koree turns back to me, "We have to go really high so nobody sees us." I nod my head and hold onto his waist tightly as we soar through the now yellowish red sky. I lose track of time, recalling the feel of his lips on mine time and again. Just then my cracked egg flashes into my mind, and I go back and forth between the pleasure of Koree's kisses and the pain of knowing my little egg has cracked and I may never see it again.

Soon we start to descend, and Onyx lands in a remote field behind a huge stone barn. Koree slows Onyx to a walk, as if we might have been out on a leisurely morning dragon stroll. We both jump down to the ground as we near Onyx's pen, standing face to face again.

"There's no need for sleep now," Koree tells me. He grabs my waist and pulls me close to him. That same, wonderful feeling rushes through my body as I stare up into his eyes. He reaches in toward me and kisses me again, long and slow. This time my lips seem to know what to do.

At last Koree pulls away from me and flashes me a gigantic smile, teasing me with his dimple. I slowly reach my hand up and touch it, resting my fingers against his cheek.

"See you later," he whispers in my ear.

"Later," I breathe out. Then he twirls around so quickly I barely notice, and his tall figure strides away into the early dawn, his footsteps fading like hushed whispers.

For a moment I stand in the morning of a new day, reflecting back on all that has happened in a short amount of time. I have been kissed. Me, Teak Frain…Teak the Freak…I have been kissed by a boy. And not just any boy… by Koree. I play the scene of Koree kissing me over and over in my mind.

Suddenly, a different image shoots into my head – one of a cracked egg. I can almost feel a heartbeat calling to me, a different heartbeat that Koree's. I turn around as fast as I can and run full speed toward the Incubation Room.

Chapter 24

"Please be alive…please be alive…" The words tumble over and over in my mind in perfect sync with my feet hitting the cobblestone path as I thunder toward the Incubation Room.

When I reach the building, a wave of fear drenches over me, and I stand transfixed, my hand stuck to the doorknob. What if my egg hatched and the hatchling died? I am frozen in place, too afraid to turn the knob. After staring at the plain wooden door for several minutes, I take a deep breath, square my shoulders, and tentatively step inside. Warm yellow light wraps around me like a discolored ocean breeze, and I struggle to focus. I search the room for Kebb or my egg. Or a hatchling. Mostly a hatchling. But it is eerily still. And quiet. As I move toward my egg's box, I spot a stooped figure in a rocking chair and tiptoe toward it.

My body tenses the closer I get, and I bite my lower lip, preparing for the worst. I peek at the figure, and let out a small breath. It is Kebb, and he is sound asleep…with the tiniest pure white dragon lying motionless in his lap. It is curled up in a little ball, and instinctively I know it is my dragon – that my egg must have hatched. But is it alive?

I shake Kebb's shoulder, hating to wake him, but I just have to know if my baby dragon is alive. Kebb snaps his head up, turns to me with foggy, sleep filled eyes.

"Is it alive?" I croak.

He cackles and coughs and clears his throat. "Well, so far…he's a strong little thing for as tiny as he is." He strokes the miniature dragon's back, and it slowly opens its eyes… the most beautiful brilliant blue eyes I have ever seen.

"Oh….his eyes look like clouds." And then, "Is it a boy?"

"It's a boy, alright," Kebb chuckles.

The little dragon's blue eyes locate mine, and he lets out a tiny, almost pathetic squeal, like a cat's meow. "I think he wants you," Kebb smiles. "Do you want to take a turn?"

"Oh yesssss…" Kebb hands me the little dragon, wrapped in a soft blanket. He gets up, tells me to sit in the rocking chair and hobbles off. I sit down and hold the hatchling, stroking his smooth, damp skin – it feels like the softest of leather. His indigo eyes open and close slowly, contentedly. It is like holding a soft hairless cat with wings. We stay that way for a while, and I inspect every inch of him. But suddenly he starts squealing and squirming, thrashing his tail back and forth. His wings spread out, and I try to calm him, but it isn't working.

At that precise moment, Kebb arrives with a bottle. "Even though they aren't nursed by their mothers after they hatch, we've found the best way to keep premature dragons alive is by giving them proper nutrition, the kind they would get in an egg – only from a bottle. Also, you're going to be carrying him everywhere you go, since he's chosen you."

"I don't mind."

"You say that now." He chuckles again. Kebb shows me how to feed him out of the bottle, and it is awkward at first. The small squirming dragon seems hesitant to eat and wants to nibble on the nipple of the bottle with his tiny, pointed teeth instead of actually swallowing the mixture. "Keep at it," Kebb urges. I'll be back in a while to check on you. I'm going to get some breakfast. Do you want some?

"Sure," I say, just now registering that I am hungry.

I hold the baby dragon and caress him as he learns to drink out of the bottle. We make some progress – he finally swallows some of the formula and then becomes greedy. When he is finished, he stretches out, curls up in my lap, and goes to sleep. I wrap him in the blanket and rock him in the chair, trying to think of a name that is suitable for an albino dragon.

At some point I fall asleep and wake up groggy and confused. There is some cold food on a table by the chair. I don't know what time it is, and I am hoping I don't get demerits for missing my chores and training with the group. Then I think of my dragon, and I shake my head, panicked that I might not have taken proper care of him while I slept.

I let out a sigh when I discover that he is still sound asleep in my lap, breathing short little breaths. He smells like raindrops in a forest. I think of names for him with half closed eyes. Raindrop? Forest? Indigo? No, those names won't work. Then I panic again. What if I name him and he dies? My eyes open wide instantly, fear racing through me when a voice interrupts my thoughts.

"I was watching…thought you needed a little cat nap. I've already talked to Koree and you're released from duties today to tend to this little guy." It is sweet Kebb, watching over us both. I realize he must be exhausted, and I am sure he doesn't know that Koree and I were up all night as well.

"Thanks, so much," I tell him.

The morning passes with me feeding the tiny white dragon, checking his temperature, rocking him to sleep. At lunch time, Koree enters with some sandwiches for me, grinning like a fool when he spots us. He reaches down and strokes the dragon's soft baby skin – no scales have appeared yet.

"He's a good looking dragon."

"Oh…I know," I tell him, looking up into his eyes.

"Here, I'll hold him while you eat." I hand the baby to Koree, and the white dragon snuggles into his lap while Koree briskly strokes his back.

"You need to do this every few hours, to stimulate his nervous system."

"Oh, okay," I respond, reaching for a sandwich. The baby dragon wakes up, starts swishing his tail and spitting in the air. Koree and I both laugh at his antics, then Koree reaches for a bottle and expertly places it in the little dragon's mouth. The dragon guzzles the mixture greedily.

"You've done this before, haven't you?" I ask while taking a bite of sandwich, chewing thoughtfully as I watch Koree with the baby dragon. My baby dragon.

"Yeah, a few times," he laughs.

Kebb wobbles over to us, handing me a funny looking contraption made of fabric and buttons. "Here's a pack for the little albino. You'll put him in it and carry him next to your heart. The heartbeat is what seems to help these little guys pull through. Koree said you had an important meeting, so take him with you." He hands me two bottles and shows me where to put them in the carrier. He straps the carrier to the front of me, tenderly takes the dragon from Koree, and places the tiny, wrinkled creature in the carrier. The dragon doesn't fuss at all but closes his eyes and falls asleep, nestled next to my heart. A wave of love I have never known travels through me as I peer down at him.

"Be sure to keep him out of the sun as much as possible – his skin can't take it yet." Kebb warns. He hands me a blanket to put over the sleeping hatchling. "Good luck. If you need anything, let me know."

I thank Kebb yet again, and Koree and I leave the Incubation Room together. He closes the door and takes my hand, lacing his fingers through mine.

Koree leads me to Kesper's office and opens the door, dropping my hand. The room is empty. He locks Kesper's door from the inside and hurries over to a spot behind her desk. He slides her chair out of the way, pulls back a rug, and opens a trap door in the floor. I bite my lower lip, remembering the trap door…knowing what is underneath.

"Down we go," Koree says. "We don't have to worry about sun for the hatchling where we're going." He steps down into the dark, rectangular hole, his head stationed at floor level. "I'll help you down." He holds his hand out for mine, but I can't seem to move.

"Koree…I can't," I call down to him.

"What?"

"Go down there…again…it was terrible."

"Oh," he answers. His voice is soft. "I'll be right here with you. I won't let anything happen, I promise."

I think for a moment – of how Thann kept me alive in the tunnel when we ran here from Mount Gareth. The very same tunnel I am going back into. "Okay," I say tentatively, biting my lip and snuggling the tiny dragon closer to me. I turn around and take a step down into the tunnel.

Step by step we make our way down the rustic wooden ladder. There are rails for me to hold on to and I am relieved that this time both I can use both of my hands. But still, I am frightened at the thought of being in the tunnel. Koree must sense it, because I feel his hands on my waist, holding me steady as we descend into the black abyss.

The cold earth meets my feet with a soft thump, only this time there isn't water and sloshing mud like before. I wonder how the mud could have dried up. The hatchling stirs in the carrier, and I worry that I have awakened him. "I'm going to light a torch. Stay here," Koree explains, squeezing my shoulder lightly. He leaves me for a minute, and I stroke the little dragon. Then a flame lights the black earthen walls, and I let out a breath of relief. Koree returns to me and takes my hand.

"Koree?" I whisper, as if I am going to disturb the dead.

"What?" He answers, turning to me. "Is the hatchling okay?"

"Yes, I was just wondering…when Thann and I came here I remember mud and water. Now it is dry."

"Oh, that." He swallows and then clears his throat. "If there have been a lot of people in the tunnels, they get muddy. You and Thann came right behind a large group. But there haven't been many since you and Thann got here. Kesper is trying, but it's getting harder and harder."

"Oh, how terrible." I have been so caught up in my new life that I have all but forgotten that there are still Light Skinned people out there...and that the Purity Law calls for their deaths...as well as mine.

"I know," Koree answers. He reaches for my hand and squeezes his long fingers around mine. "That's why we're doing this. Let's go, okay?"

"Okay," I answer with more confidence than I feel as Koree leads me through the damp, chilly tunnel.

Finally, after we turn through numerous dirt encased corridors, we reach a room. Koree doesn't knock but just opens the door. He tugs me through the entrance and I blink my eyes, adjusting to the light. Thann and Kesper sit at a wooden table with papers scattered about.

Yaren sits in the corner of the room on a rustic wooden chair, his eyes closed as if he is sleeping.

"Well, if it isn't the Princess," Thann smiles. I realize I haven't talked to him in days. "Bring me that hatchling and let me inspect him." I walk over and kneel down so Thann can see the baby dragon. The hatchling opens his bright blue eyes, slowly turning them toward Thann.

Thann studies the dragon intently then tilts his head up, his pale golden eyes searing into mine.

Then he speaks in a quiet, solemn voice – words I never thought I would hear.

Chapter 25

"I don't think this hatchling is an albino. He has blue eyes. Albinos have red eyes. Or pink."

Kesper and Koree come running over and inspect the little dragon, who turns his head to each of them as if he is part of this important meeting. "I think you're right," Kesper answers. She jumps up, almost runs to a bookshelf, and returns with a thick volume. She rifles through it, finds a page, and reads out loud to us. "Albino dragons are always born with red or pink eyes."

"So what kind of a dragon is he?" I ask.

She flips through the book again and stops on a page. "A very rare one. An Opal."

"I've never heard of that breed," Thann tells his mother.

"Me neither," Koree pipes up. "But the good news is that he isn't an albino." He furrows his brow. "I should have picked up on it."

Yaren is at the dragon's side by now, but I have no idea how he got there. "Dis be de rare one," he comments. "Dis not be de al-bino."

"His survival rate just increased by about seventy percent," Kesper tells us, peering up from the book. She is smiling radiantly, and I can't help but grin foolishly back at her.

"Ok, let's get down to business," Kesper closes the book and Koree and I take a seat. Yaren pulls up a chair beside us.

"Teak, you've been invited into a very private organization…one that can be dangerous," Kesper begins. "I have to warn you right now of how important it is that everything about this meeting and what we are doing is kept secret."

"I can keep a secret," I tell her, looking directly in her eyes.

"I hope so. For your sake. So far you have kept everything secret as far as we know, but I must warn you…we have a prison here, and we will put you in it if you leak any information. Understood?"

I nod my head. "Understood."

Attention is diverted from me, and I caress the miniature dragon as I listen. Kesper, Koree, Yaren, and Thann are talking, pointing at maps and papers on the table. Kesper turns to Koree. "How many trained Lavs do we have by the tree houses?" My jaw drops. *Lavs?*

By the tree houses?

"One hundred and seventy two," Koree answers. I stare at him.
Somewhere they have one hundred and seventy two Lavs...dragons
that can fly and breathe fire. Dragons that are especially trained for
battle. Illegal dragons...

"Not enough," Kesper answers. "How many battle trained soldiers
do we have?

"About seventy five," Thann responds, in an unusually dismal voice.

Kesper taps her fingers on the table, apparently in frustration.
Yellow light spills over her face and the only sound is from a clock
ticking relentlessly on the wall. She lifts her head and stares directly
at me.

"You've achieved Level Four in Weapons, correct?"

I nod my head.

"You can shoot a bow and arrow decently, I assume."

For some reason I bristle at this, but then I realize she wouldn't

know that I placed first in the Weapons Competition and that I was

best at bow and arrows. "Yes," I answer.

"Good. Spears?"

"Yes."

"Blades?"

"Yes."

"Can you teach others to use these weapons?"

I think for a moment, images of Bello flashing in my mind. "I don't

see why not," I tell her.

"Good." She taps her fingers on the table again, her nails rattling

against the wood. "Siv's soldiers are trained primarily in

swords…some blades. He's getting cocky and lazy. If we can attack

from the sky, with arrows, spears, and blades….we'll have a fighting

chance."

She continues, her face stern. "We need to form a new plan. This

hatchling has put a kink in the works." As if on cue, the little white dragon opens his eyes and lets out a long squeal. He shakes his tiny head and starts chewing on the carrier strap. I reach for a bottle, shake it, and pull him out of the carrier as he wriggles in my arms.

"Do you mind?" Kesper asks, reaching for the dragon. "We haven't had a bottle baby in a couple years." Before I can answer, she takes the little dragon, plops him on his back, nestles him to her, and feeds him. A look of total contentment fills her face.

"Anyway, is there anybody, a friend of yours with dragon experience, you could trust to babysit for small periods of time while you learn to ride...so you can then train soldiers? Our soldiers must be able to use bows and arrows as well as spears and blades while flying Lavs."

I pause for a minute. Flying Lavs? While shooting bows and arrows? Even Siv Gareth hasn't attempted this...to my knowledge. "Um...Echo was raised on a dragon farm...and she is loyal...honest."

"Find out if she's willing to help with the hatchling."

I nod my head. "Okay."

"What is our weapons count right now?" Kesper asks, turning to Koree.

"Blades…about a thousand…and some spears, although not as many," Koree answers. "The blacksmiths at the tree houses have been working on them."

"What about bows and arrows?"

Koree speaks again. "We need a model…haven't been able to find one. We can't seem to get it right The arrows don't fly straight." Koree, Thann, and Kesper all turn to me, three sets of eyes asking me a silent question.

"Well, I did bring my bow and some arrows, but…"

"But what?" Kesper asks curtly.

"My roommates…Flame…they took them and I don't know where they are."

Thann and Koree turn their heads, eyes meeting. They break into infectious grins simultaneously. "We can handle that, huh Kor?" Thann asks, laughing like only he can.

"Oh, yeah," Koree answers. "Nothing like a surprise weapons inspection to make some girls sweat in their boots."

"Okay, fair enough, you boys handle that and get a prototype to the woodworkers as soon as possible. We'll need hundreds of bows and thousands of arrows." She clears her throat, changes the subject. "Koree, you need to start training the Lavs. How many untrained do we have down there?"

"About a hundred…they've had some ground work and are pretty tame, but not ready to go…" Koree sighs, letting the air flow up from his mouth, blowing his curls across his forehead. "The tree house people are working on them, but…"

"That's a lot." She scratches the baby dragon under his chin, a pensive look taking over her face. "I have an idea. I'm going to say you're studying for your next level of training….let's see, I'll make it up now. Master Trainer Level 10. How does that sound?"

Koree nods his head, seriously. "Sounds official."

"Pretty awesome," Thann pipes in. What am I, Level 8?"

"Sure, that sounds good," Kesper smiles, beaming at her son, two golden statues in the dimly lit room.

Yaren finally speaks. "Persia, dat girl might be' de prob-lem."

"I'll tell her that new Master Trainer qualifications have just come through and give her…let's say…Level 3. With the gates sealed she won't be able to know otherwise. What do you think?

Yaren nods his head. "Dat be good."

"Perfect," Thann agrees along with Koree. I watch intently, not knowing entirely what is going on.

"Koree you'll need to go back and forth, make appearances in the library and research room. I'll work out something that looks official tomorrow. With Koree gone, we'll need to split the group of cadets differently." My heart sinks with the words, "Koree gone."

"Thann, you'll take the least experienced dragon cadets. We'll split them in half. Persia can take the more experienced ones. That will hopefully distract her…make her think she is getting a promotion."

All business, Kesper turns to Koree. "How good is Teak at riding? Can she gallop a dragon?"

"No...but we haven't covered that skill yet," Koree answers, almost defensively. "She's second best in my group, so I think she'll be able to pick it up quickly. Thann's a better teacher than I am, so that's a good plan for him to teach her."

"Solo flight yet?"

"No, but she's flown with me a few times at night on the way to the tree houses. She seems to get a thrill out of loops and spins...so that's a good sign." He grins widely, like a proud father.

"Can she solo tonight?"

"Yeah, but what about the hatchling?"

"De hatchlin' be fine in dis' weather," Yaren interjects.

"Yaren is right," Kesper agrees. The temperature is ideal for a premature dragon if he's in a carrier. Bundle him up and he'll be fine. Just strap him down so he won't fall off." She clears her throat and looks directly at me. "And strap Teak down, too. We don't want to lose her."

My eyes widen. *Solo? Tonight? I am going to fly on a dragon by myself?*

"How long before she can gallop, be experienced enough to train from a dragon's back?

Thann and Koree let out a breath together, as if their thoughts are the same. Koree speaks first. "Couple weeks, I'd bet."

"Okay, two weeks, then we'll assign Teak to research." She smiles, her lips curving up slowly. Then she turns her head to me. "We'll make a big deal about how well you scored on your Assessment, which you did, by the way. "You have the highest Assessment score of any cadet ever. But, instead of doing research, you'll be training soldiers."

"Wow," I breathe out – the thought of actually training soldiers piercing me with discomfort. Talking about it was one thing, but actually doing it is another.

She turns to Koree. "Get the woodworkers onto those bows and arrows and start tomorrow on the Lavs." Then her face pinches into a tight ball. "How are the children with fevers doing? Is it spreading?

"Seems to be contained right now," Koree answers. "But if it spreads we're going to need some help. Teak's going to be worn out if she doesn't get some sleep." He reaches for my hand under the table, squeezes it. "She can't train all day and be up all night with sick people and take care of a premature dragon."

"We'll work something out. Start with this girl Echo. Relieve Teak and Echo of feeding, other chores. Use the hatchling as an excuse. Just concentrate on getting Teak to ride well." She turns to me, concluding the meeting. "Have you thought of a name for him yet?"

I have been so afraid to name him, scared that he might die if I do. I start to say no when a name flashes into my head, a name so pure and white that I instantly know it is perfect.

"Diamond…I want to name him Diamond."

It is totally quiet for a few minutes. Then I hear her say, "Perfect. I love it." She hands Diamond back to me as Thann and Koree both nod their heads.

Yaren grins toothlessly. "I be likin' de name. I be likin' it good."

Chapter 26

I meet Echo in the library, Diamond tucked happily in his carrier.

She squeals with delight when she sees him. I take him out of his

pouch, hand him to her, and she lovingly pets his wrinkly skin.

"You're so lucky," she comments, her blue eyes wide. "I loved

taking care of the preemies."

"Well, he's not out of the woods yet, and he might not even be a

preemie. He's an Opal, a rare dragon. Not an albino."

She examines him. "Wow, I've never heard of that breed before."

She scrunches her eyes up, examining him. "He looks pretty strong

to me."

"That's what everyone says." I proudly reply. "Oh, Echo, I love him

so much."

"Yeah, he's a looker, that's for sure." She contorts her face. "My

egg won't hatch for two months."

I laugh at her as I carefully place Diamond back in his carrier and we

sit down at a table in the back of the library that we have claimed. I show her how to blend words together for about an hour. She is just finishing her last word.

"Hey, Echo…"

"What?" She looks up from her papers.

"Kesper wants me to pick someone to help me take care of Diamond…you know so that I don't miss out on training. I was wondering…"

She interrupts me before I can finish. "Sweet dragon balls, yes!" She smiles widely. "You picked the best nanny available!"

"I know. But how did you know I was going to ask you?"

"I don't see anyone else around. And I'm obviously the best choice." She grins radiantly at me.

"That you are," I agree. "I will tell Kesper. I glance at the clock on the wall. "I have to go. I will see you tomorrow."

"Ta ta," she answers, waving at me.

I venture back to the Incubation Room where Kebb has set up a bed for me. The temperature and environment is better for Diamond, and if he wakes up at night, which I am told he will do several times, he won't bother the other girls. Someone has already brought my belongings in and left them by the bed. I feed Diamond, wash up, put on the black cloak, and fall into a deep sleep with him nestled to my chest, taking one or two breaths to his ten.

I am awakened at some point in the night by a gentle shoulder shaking. I don't want to wake up, but I know who it is and force myself to sit up, smiling at Koree in the dim yellow light. His eyes are soft, and he sits on the corner of the bed, stroking Diamond, who is rustling around, pawing at me, and wanting a bottle. I reach for a bottle, stick it in his mouth, and Koree and I laugh as he guzzles the nutrients greedily. I stretch my arms – the carrier is making my shoulders sore, but I don't mind.

"Are you ready to fly solo?" Koree asks, raising his eyebrows. His eyes are sparkling with hints of gold in the yellowish light that casts down on us.

"Oh, yes," I exhale.

I slip Diamond into his pouch, grab two more bottles, and stand up, facing Koree, who has his hands resting in the pockets of his pants. He doesn't move, his eyes boring through me as if I really were a ghost. I bite my lower lip, not sure what he is staring at, but somersaults turn over in my stomach…in such an exciting way I think I might just jump out of my skin. He cocks his head to the side then steps closer to me, takes each of my hands in his, and pulls me toward him so that our faces are about an inch apart. He rests his forehead on mine for a minute, and it seems like the most natural thing in the world, to be in this position with a baby dragon nestled between us. He pulls his forehead back, whispers throatily, "Teak…."

I am speechless as he leans his mouth to mine while at the same time holding the back of my head tenderly with his hand. Our mouths connect, as if they have been waiting a million life times to find each other.

The kisses becomes deeper, stronger – a sort of probing or searching. I match his movements, tingling everywhere as my heart races, and all I know is that I want more of it. More kisses. More Koree.

My head is swirling out of control, and I push back away from him, panting, my lips almost raw. I find his eyes and know I have to tell him the truth. My words are a whisper. "Koree....I have never....you know....kissed a boy before."

He smirks at me, his golden-green eyes twinkling. "Hmmmm, this is interesting news." He cocks his head to the side, his lips turning up ever so slightly. "On a scale of one to ten...I think you scored a solid...eight"

"Eight? That is it?" I shove him playfully.

"I think you need more practice."

"Well, let me see if River is up for it," I quip, surprised at my quick response.

"Oh, no you don't." Koree reaches for me again, stroking my cheek with his finger. He kisses me again. Over and over his lips take control of mine. Then each kiss becomes deeper, longer. Suddenly, he pulls back from me and I struggle to catch my breath. Every nerve in my body is screaming…in the most pleasant way. I lick my lips, tasting remnants of Koree.

He peers into my eyes, his chest rising and falling. "I have something I need to tell you." His voice is serious and somber and dark. I freeze as my heart sinks into my stomach, grinding in agony. I must have done something wrong. Diamond squirms against my chest – pushing against it with his tiny claws.

Koree's words interrupt my thoughts. "I've never kissed anyone before, either," he grins wickedly. "I think we both need more practice."

I breathe out and a laugh erupts from the same lips he was just kissing. He reaches for me, kissing me again. I am dizzy, my head spinning so pleasantly I never want it to end.

Out of the blue, Koree yowls, his lips parting quickly from mine.

"Ouch!" he yells. I instantly open my eyes, wondering why he is shouting.

"What did I do?" I am afraid that I bit his tongue or accidently hurt him somehow while we were kissing. I scan his eyes first and move to his face. Then I notice a red mark on his chin.

"You didn't do anything…. Diamond's first flame….on my chin!"

We both look down at Diamond, whose indigo eyes are wide and alert. He hisses at Koree and shoots another tiny flame, no bigger than a candle's…directly at Koree.

"You little bagger," Koree laughs at him. "If you were bigger you'd get a halter and some discipline." Diamond continues to stare at Koree with his deep blue eyes, as if he is sizing him up.

"I think he is jealous of you," I tell Koree.

"You think?" he sarcastically answers. Then we both burst into laughter. "We need to get going anyway. It's your big night." Koree grabs my hand and we cautiously thread our way to the back of the building where two ebony dragons are waiting for us. One I recognize as Onyx and the other is a smaller version of him.

"Okay, here's the deal," Koree explains. "I'll tie your legs to the stirrups so you won't fall."

"Stirrups?" I ask, almost insulted. "I thought we rode without saddles in the air."

"These are specially designed, light weight saddles that have stirrups. You also will have reins, but you won't really be steering her. She'll follow Onyx...they're mated.

"Mated?"

"Yeah, like married, only in dragon language."

"Got it!" I flash a grin at him, check on Diamond, and jump onto the smaller Ebony. "What's her name?"

He rolls his eyes in an exaggerated fashion. "Raven, if you must know."

"I must. And I like it," I call out to him. Koree digs in his pants pockets and pulls out some small strips of cord. He ties my legs to the stirrups then ties Diamond's tail to the carrier. Diamond hisses at him, puffing up like he could actually be a menace to Koree. I smile down at him, patting his head in an effort to calm him.

"I'm beginning to feel a bit threatened," Koree teases, petting Diamond's head along with me. "Are you all settled?" he asks me.

"Yes," I answer.

"Here's how this will go down. I'll lead on Onyx, and you're just going to ride tonight, to get the feel of it – you know, by yourself." He takes my hand, opens it, and places an object in it – a small silver whistle. "If you get scared…or get in a situation, just blow this whistle, and I'll circle around and help you."

"Okay?" It comes out as a question as I wonder what kind of situations I can get into.

"Are you nervous?"

"No….well, maybe just a little."

"You'll do just fine." He struts over to Onyx, and hops on his back. Onyx takes flight quickly, and right behind him Raven spreads her giant wings, following her mate. She catches air and the wind blows against my face. A thrill runs through me at the weightlessness of being off the ground – the pure freedom of flying. Diamond is sound asleep, nestled against my chest, his little breaths a song of harmony and contentment.

Koree takes Onyx higher, and we circle around Harcourt Stables. I do some experiments with Raven. First, I press my leg into her right side a bit, and she moves to the right. I then press my left leg into her left side, and she moves to the left. I want to whoop with delight at my discovery, but I am afraid of waking Diamond.

All too soon Koree lands Onyx and Raven follows, landing directly behind him in a field behind the dormitories. Koree hops off of the larger dragon and strides over to me, a huge smile on his face. He unties the rest of the cords as I dismount easily, scratching Raven behind her sleek ears.

"What did you think?"

"It was fantastic! When can we go again?"

"Tomorrow night," Koree laughs, tugging me next to him. He holds me in an embrace, Diamond tucked between us. I nestle into the crook of his shoulder. After a few moments, he pulls away and gently kisses my forehead.

"You'd better get some sleep."

"Yes," I say grudgingly, not wanting to leave him. We stare at each other for a few minutes, the warm air wrapping us tightly in our own cocoon. Then Koree and I walk, hand in hand toward the Incubation Room, the dragons obediently following us.

When we arrive, Koree stops by the door. "Later?" he asks, his voice throaty and deep. He reaches in and kisses me, a tender tickle on my lips.

"Later," I breathe into him. He leans back, pats Diamond on the head then gently pulls some of my hair behind my ear, staring at me for a minute. He turns from me then, leading Onyx and Raven away, his outline disappearing in the dark night followed by two almost invisible black dragons.

Chapter 27

The next day I am in Thann's riding group. Since Echo doesn't need much practice, she is tending to Diamond, and he doesn't seem to mind. Thann immediately has us lope the dragons, something I have never done, but I catch on quickly, and I enjoy the gentle rhythm, the swaying back and forth on the huge Emerald dragon I am riding…glistening green scales, almost the same color as Koree's eyes.

"Line up now," Thann orders, his voice blasting across the arena. I turn the Emerald around by pushing my boot gently into his right side and pulling at the reins.

Thann strides up to us and hands us each a duck egg and a large wooden spoon, grinning the entire time. "Okay, we're having our first race. The first one to cross this line – he points to a line in the sand – with the egg still on the spoon wins fifty merits."

"Ready?" he asks.

We all nod our heads. I hold the spoon out in front of me like everyone else. "Go," Thann shouts, and we all take off.

I decide that winning isn't my goal. I just want to keep my egg intact. All of the other riders take off, leaving me breathing their dust. I am so focused on the egg in my spoon that I am afraid to look up, hearing rather than seeing egg after egg hitting the ground with a splat. I even hear a few curse words as I cross the finish line, sure that I am in last place, still gripping my spoon and egg.

"Fifty merits for Teak," Thann calls out, smiling radiantly. Shock overtakes me when I realize I am the only one in the group with an egg that didn't fall. Thann lines us up again, and his tone becomes serious. "I didn't tell you this, because I wanted you to figure it out on your own, like Teak did, but a large part of dragon riding is based on precision and control, not speed." He collects our spoons and my egg, which I hesitantly hand over to him. For some odd reason, I want to keep it, a trophy more meaningful to me than the useless golden sword I won in Weapons.

We spend the afternoon going through precision drills. I take several turns tending to Diamond so that Echo can get in some practice. Then Thann announces that we are all to go to our dormitories before we eat dinner. Koree appears, strolling casually up to

Thann. I am not sure where to go…the dormitory or the Incubation Room, but I decide to follow everyone to the girl's dorm. Thann opens the door, and we all enter. Flame, Loris, and Celerie sit on Flame's bed, and I plop down on Echo's bed next to her.

"We are performing a room inspection. We have reason to believe someone might be in possession of illegal weapons here," Koree announces, his voice like the commander of an army. He and Thann search methodically through all of the girls' belongings, even Echo's. They rifle around for a while, pulling out clothes, hair brushes, and other assorted items from the dressers. Then Thann gets down on his hands and knees and feels around under Flame's bed. He pulls out my bow and arrows along with the blades that Entho packed for me. He stands up, displaying the weapons. My weapons.

"Care to explain this?" Koree asks Flame, his voice ice. "Maybe your grandmother gave them to you?

She flips her long dark hair with her hand. "I don't know whose they are…I've never seen them before."

"Hmmm…" It is Thann. "They're under your bed, so that means they're in your possession. One hundred demerits." Thann hands Koree the weapons, grabs Flame by the arm and escorts her out of the dorm.

"You're free to leave," Koree tells the rest of us, walking out of the room with my weapons. I gaze longingly at his broad shoulders and thin waist, catching my breath as he strides away.

"Looks like you have it bad," Echo whispers to me.

"What do you mean?" I ask, just as Diamond lets out a squeal. I reach for a bottle.

"You know, a thing for Koree….snock, it's written all over your face."

"Well, I am glad you finally learned to read," I whisper back to her. We both break into laughter as we stand up and walk out of the dorm.

The sun is setting on our way to the cafeteria and a feeling of happiness washes over me. Friends. Who knew it would be this wonderful? I think of all the years I spent at Weapons – the loneliness and humiliation – of being called "Teak the Freak" on a regular basis. Of going home on the weekends to Entho, who was always working. I gave up on ever thinking I would have a friend again after Canto was destroyed and Reese turned against me. Or a boyfriend. *Is Koree my boyfriend?* I let out a deep sigh thinking of him as Echo babbles on about something Gunter said to her. I try to listen, but her words just seem to blend together into a sort of verbal mush the more I think about Koree.

Echo interrupts my thoughts, poking me on the shoulder. "Yooo hooo? Anybody home?"

"Oh, I am sorry, what were you saying?"

"That I killed Koree and buried him behind the barn. Holy snock balls."

"What!" I stand still in my tracks, as if what she said could possibly be true.

"Dirty dragon tits. I was kidding!" She grins widely. I shoot her a nasty look, which only causes her to snicker.

We sit next to Gunter and River in the cafeteria. They both want to hold Diamond and I pass him across the table, watching like a nervous mother as they handle him. Kebb told me it is good to have others handle him as long as it is for short periods of time. He needs the human interaction to become a trainable dragon.

"We're galloping dragons like crazy," River tells us. He winks at me, and I am not sure what to do, so I look away, fiddling with one of Diamond's bottles.

"Yeah, well, we're carrying eggs on spoons. Beat that!" Gunter pipes up, shoving a piece of bread in his mouth. I catch sight of Reese, eating by himself at a table. I still don't trust him, but he hasn't bothered me lately. Two other boys are eating together at the table next to ours.

"Who are they?" I ask, noticing that they are as huge as River, maybe even bigger.

"Um," Gunter begins, chewing food between words, "That's Shagg and Flenn. They're really good riders, almost as good as River. They're brothers."

"Aww, come on," River interjects. "I'm not that good."

"Right," Gunter mumbles as he stuffs more bread in his mouth.

After we eat, I give Echo her lesson on reading in the library but find it difficult to focus, because I spy Koree at a table doing his best to pretend to study. He keeps looking up at me, his green eyes glistening in the light like two small oceans I could easily drown in. To make matters worse, I keep remembering what his lips feel like on mine. How I want to kiss him again and again and again.

Finally Echo says, "Snock, I'll leave you two love birds alone. I think I'm getting it and can practice on my own for a while. Besides, I'm sick of watching you two make goober eyes at each other." She stands up, gathers her papers in a huff.

"Are you sure?" I ask, feeling like a terrible.

"I'm sure," she giggles. "I'll go see what Gunter is doing."

Koree immediately sits down beside me and reaches for my hand under the table.

"Same time tonight?" he whispers.

I nod my head, a smile creeping up on my lips. Anticipation filters

through my body, and I find it hard to focus, thinking of another

night flying on dragons…another night with Koree.

Chapter 28

The days and nights disappear like a setting sun that is spinning out of control. I take care of Diamond, who appears to grow by the minute, learn to ride dragons, both on land and in the air, meet with Koree, Thann, and Kesper, and somehow help refine Echo's reading skills. Occasionally I am called upon to act as a healer, but fortunately the fevers have stopped.

I didn't know that I could function on so little sleep, but I seem to be managing. Each night I fall into my bed in the Incubation Room with Diamond snuggled up with me until Koree comes for us.

In a little over two weeks, I have mastered galloping a dragon. We have a final race before I am moved to Research. Thann lines us all up, and I am dismayed to find Reese ride up next to me on a sleek Metallic. We are racing against Persia's group.

"The first one across the line wins fifty merits," Thann calls out. "One, two, three, go."

I immediately launch Pebble into a full gallop, my hair flying behind me like a fierce wind. It is one of the wildest, most free feelings I have had, except for flying on dragons, which I am able to do without straps or stirrups now. I pass River easily and am approaching Shagg, who is in first place. I glance to my right and Reese is gaining on me; I had no idea he could go so fast. I squeeze my legs and Pebble drives forward. Dust flies all around me as I struggle to stay seated. Still, I am not about to let Reese win.

I lean forward, and Pebble gains more speed. I can spot the finish line ahead of me, a solid white line in the sand as I pass Shagg. But Reese is right beside me, thundering along on the Metallic. I know the glimmering dragon is faster than Pebble, but I decide to give it my all. I bend further over Pebble's neck, and she rockets forward. I am slightly ahead of Reese, and a grin overtakes my face as the finish line leaps before my eyes. Just then I catch sight of Reese's leg shooting out from his stirrup, furiously kicking at me.

I am immediately thrown off balance and my left foot flies out of the stirrup. I cast my eyes toward Reese as he places his leg back in his stirrup and crosses the finish line. Rage like I have never known overtakes me. I am seething, anger pouring out of me as I struggle to put my foot back into the stirrup. We have passed the finish line in second place, but Pebble thunders forward.

I wobble as Pebble gallops along, trying desperately to stay in the saddle. In a matter of seconds, I fall completely off of Pebble, hitting the ground with a solid thump. Pebble seems to gain speed as I dangle from the saddle, my right foot caught in the stirrup. It takes only an instant for me to figure out I am being drug behind her, my head bouncing against the ground like a stone skipping across water. Still, Pebble plows doggedly forward.

Pain engulfs every part of my body, especially my right leg, which is twisting violently in the stirrup. My head is spinning, each time it hits the ground with a thump I think it might explode as dirt and sand seep into my mouth and ears. I don't know how to make Pebble stop…I don't even know if she will stop if I am not on her. Pebble turns sharply to the right, and my head strikes the fence. I scream out in pain and fury.

Somewhere in the distance, I recognize a voice as it blasts across the arena. "Ho." It is Koree. Pebble immediately stops at his command, her hind end digging into the ground. My body bounces a few more times and then plops like a dead fish on the ground, my leg still caught in the stirrup. I can't seem to move or gather my bearings, as Koree jogs up to me, untangles my leg from the stirrup, and lays me on the ground.

He cradles my head in his hands. "Are you okay?" he asks, his eyes filled with concern.

"I…think…so," I groan.

Koree runs his hand up and down my leg. "Not broken." He stands up quickly, his body full of purpose, his green eyes now blazing with anger. "Thann, get her to the Infirmary."

Thann rushes over to my side, lifts me gently into his gigantic arms and starts walking away from the arena. I turn my head back toward Koree, curious why he would delegate this job to Thann. My entire body pounds in pain, which only adds to my confusion.

I peek over Thann's shoulder as Koree storms up to Reese, pulls back his arm, and punches Reese directly in the nose. Blood gushes as Reese falls to the ground screaming, holding his nose between his hands. "Five hundred demerits for kicking the stirrup out of a galloping rider." Koree seethes. "You could have killed her."

I am not sure, but I think I hear Reese say, "I will get you for this," as Koree picks him up by the arm and leads him out of the arena.

Chapter 29

Footsteps, recognizable boots, pad against the slick tile floor, a steady rhythm that sends my heart soaring. The doorknob opens and Koree enters, swiftly pulling a chair up by the side of my bed in the Infirmary. It has been two days and I haven't seen him until now. I still ache everywhere, even though I have been given medicine, but seeing him takes all of my pain away. I flash him a brilliant smile, unable to contain myself.

He tenderly takes my hand, rubs his thumb across it. His eyes lock onto mine. "Are you okay?"

"Yes, just multiple contusions and lacerations."

He furrows his brow. "What's that?"

"Healer language for lots of cuts and bruises," I smile.

"Oh, thank the Angels," Koree exhales. Then he grins, flashing white teeth and a distracting dimple at me. Relief floods over his face and his features soften, but just as suddenly, his eyes become serious. "I've been stripped of all my pins and have been demoted to Level 1 instead of 10. I'll be in isolation for a month."

"What for?" I gasp.

"Striking a cadet instead of going through proper protocol."

I sit up quickly, "Oh, Koree, no…it is all my fault." But my head swims with dizziness, and I have to lie back down on the pillow. Koree stands then and leans his head down toward mine. He puts his mouth close to my ear, nibbles on it playfully, then whispers, "Shhh. I won't be in isolation…I'll be at the tree houses." My lips curve up, making the connection. Of course…the Rebellion.

"Totally worth it," he says, a little too loudly. He reaches his hand toward my cheek, as if to stroke it but I take his hand in mine, noticing his knuckles, which are swollen and bruised. I softly swivel my fingers over the bruises. I rub them gently and then kiss them without thought.

"You didn't hold your fist right," I scold, moving my eyes up toward his.

Koree smiles weakly at me and the moment freezes with us staring at each other.

"I'll miss you." His words are soft, and he bends down closer, his mouth next to my ear again.

"With you in *Research*, we'll be spending a lot of time together… I've gotta go…I just wanted to say good-bye…and that I'll see you… later."

"Later…" I whisper back, soaking up his essence as if I were a dry cloth. Koree kisses me on the forehead, turns around swiftly and leaves. My eyes become heavy as the steady rhythm of his footsteps dissipating down the hall lulls me to sleep.

I awake just as one of the healers brings in Diamond. "He's been missing you," she formally intones. She's the tall one with skunk hair. I reach out, grab my little white dragon and stroke his tiny head. "Pretty soon he'll be running around…getting into all kinds of trouble." She sets him on my stomach, and he hops up on all four legs, bouncing in small circles while spitting little red and yellow flames out of his mouth. I can't help but laugh at him.

I turn my face up to the healer. "How long will I be here?"

"Just until tomorrow. If you promise to take your medicine."

"I will," I tell her, lying back on my pillow while Diamond frolics on my lap. I play with him for a while until he settles on my chest in a little ball and falls asleep.

The next day I am released from the Infirmary and am allowed to go back to the Incubation Room. Kebb brings me a large box for Diamond. "He's going to start needing exercise now. You'll be spending less and less time with him in his carrier." He hands me a leash and collar to put on Diamond. The dragon training has begun. I slip the collar over his neck and he tries to dig it off with his foot, twisting and turning at all kinds of angles. I place him in the box, and he squeals, wanting me to pick him up, his indigo eyes pleading with me like grey clouds on a rainy day begging for sun.

"Stay firm," Kebb warns. Pretty soon Diamond is skipping around the box, almost turning somersaults. After a while he yawns, gets tired, and curls into a ball, falling asleep instantly. I reach down to pick him up so he can sleep with me, but Kebb interrupts.

"Let the little guy be. He needs to learn to sleep on his own. He'll be fine." I draw my hand back, but I feel a sense of loss without him against my chest. Then I do a double take...it is not so bad having a little bit of freedom.

Kebb speaks again, but this time it is not about Diamond. "You'll need to clean up for the ceremony tonight."

"What ceremony?"

"The Assigning Ceremony."

"Oh...." So this is it. This is the night we all get our Assignments. I choke on my saliva thinking about it. I have wanted nothing more than to be a dragon trainer since I was a child, but I already know my assignment...Research. Disappointment floods over me, then I think of Koree...losing all of his pins and not even seeming concerned about it. "What time is the ceremony?" I ask Kebb.

"Seven o'clock sharp." He waddles away just as Echo and Gunter barge through the door.

"Hey, we brought you some Dragon Cards," Gunter tells me.
Finally, my own deck of dragon cards! I snatch the deck out of his hands and turn every card over, examining each dragon.

"Let's play a game," Echo offers. She grabs the deck from me and deals out the cards. I try to concentrate on the cards as I sit on my bed, but I can't stop thinking about Koree...wishing he was here with us. Naturally, Echo wins.

"It's from all that time in the Infirmary, I swear," she explains, I am sure in an effort to make me feel better about always losing.

"Yeah, you swear..."Gunter adds with a smile. "A lot."

Echo lifts her head. "I can't help it if I was raised with five brothers. Snock, I do the best I can."

"It's okay. I think it's kinda cute." Gunter takes Echo's hand in his and holds it in a tight grip. Watching them makes me think of Koree, and I miss him so much my heart feels like it might squeeze into two pieces. Just then Thann barges in, his gigantic body barely fitting through the doorway.

"Hey, is there a party here without me?" he barks.

"No, Golden Boy, we were just leaving," Echo answers.

"Don't let me chase you off."

"Oh, we have some things to do," Gunter answers, raising his eyebrows up and down as he gazes at Echo with dreamy eyes. They say good-bye and walk hand in hand out of the room.

Thann sits down beside me, taking a chair by my bed. "So, how are you feeling?" he asks, staring into my eyes, a perpetual smile plastered on his face.

"Fine."

"Are you up to a meeting… you know…"

I think about it. The walk. The steps down into the damp tunnels. Diamond. It overwhelms me. "I...I am not sure."

"Even if I can get you there from here…really quickly"

"How?"

"Different tunnels."

"Okay," I hesitantly answer as Thann snags Diamond from his box, wraps him in a blanket and retrieves the carrier.

Thann holds out his humongous hand and I place mine in his, following him to the doorway. After so much time with Thann, escaping Destroyers, running in the tunnels, and just struggling to survive, it seems more than natural to hold his hand.

But as I firmly clasp it, at a level I don't yet understand, I viscerally long for a different hand to hold.

Chapter 30

I am lost in thought as Thann guides me through a series of underground tunnels that lead to the room where we always meet. I shiver from the dampness, checking on Diamond to make sure he is warm. Thann opens the door and we find Kesper sitting at the large table in the middle of the room. Alone.

"Hey, Mom," Thann states in his typical easy going manner. He reaches down and kisses Kesper on the cheek. For a moment sadness washes over me like a thick dark cloud as I think of Entho. How much I miss him, and a huge helping of regret accompanies it, remembering how many opportunities I had to kiss his cheek and didn't.

"Koree will be here soon," she says absentmindedly as she rifles through some papers. "Yaren can't make it."

"Okay," Thann answers. "Got any food here?"

"Teenage boys," Kesper says, tilting her head up. "There's some fruit in the bowl over there. And some bread and cheese on the counter."

Thann finds the food, offers me some. I take some bread and cheese, my favorite, wishing Koree would hurry up and get here. Thann and I sit next to Kesper on the hard wooden chairs. Kesper is concentrating on the papers. "I'm doing a weapons inventory," she tells us without looking up.

Just then the door opens and Koree strolls in. He plops down next to me at the big wooden table, reaching for my hand with one swift movement. Instantly, I relax, the hand I was longing for fitting perfectly around my own.

Thann speaks first. "I want to start with something."

Kesper's head flies up, her eyes golden eyes flashing. I am not sure if she is insulted or angry. She always leads the meetings.

"Go ahead." Her voice drips with ice. I wonder if Thann has stepped on her toes.

"Koree and I are going on a mission….to Bay City."

"What are you talking about?" she spits out. If her eyes were flashing before, now they are exploding.

She launches a steely glare to both Koree and Thann. "It's way too dangerous there. Especially for you, Thann." She sighs two or three times, rubs the back of her neck. Fidgets. Pulls on her necklace, lowering her voice. "I almost lost you when I sent you for the cadets. With the new Purity Law enacted, it's a suicide mission."

"Would you please listen for once?" It is Thann, and his voice is almost whiny.

Kesper nods her head, but she is definitely not portraying a look of defeat.

"Koree and I are going to an orphanage in Bay City. There are about 100 children in it. They need our help." My head leaps up. Winter. I told Koree about Winter and now they are going there?

"We're bringing them here…to the tree houses," Koree interjects.

"One hundred children? What are we to do with one hundred children? It's all we can do to care for the ones we have…the children with parents who work for their food." She is almost yelling, out of control. I have never seen her this way. "And how do you plan on doing this?"

"With the Lavs." Koree's voice is solemn, serious. Like when I first met him. I can't believe he didn't tell me about this plan. Part of me is angry about it but the other part is swelling with love and pride. To think that he and Thann would do this…bring Winter here. Is it all just for me? Or are they crazy?

"The Lavs? Have you lost your minds? You're just going to travel into the city on illegal dragons and bring one hundred children home with you?"

"That's pretty much it," Thann answers with a grin on his face. He seems to be enjoying this.

"We've got a plan." Koree interrupts. "We had some people at the tree houses make us red uniforms just like Siv Gareth's elite army. And, of course, we all know that Siv Gareth is the only one with Lavs." He grins at Kesper, his lips slowly curling up.

Thann takes over. "We're going to fly the Lavs in close, then walk them into the orphanage and tell the Guardians we're moving the children to a different location. It will be done at night."

"Then we'll walk them out, hit the air once we're out of the city, and land them here, where they're safe…take them to the tree houses. We've talked to everyone there. They're willing to take on these kids." Koree explains.

"You talked to them without talking to me first? I'm not happy to say the least. And what about you, Thann, your Light Skin? Have you taken the Purity Law into consideration?" She turns to her son, concern overshadowing her amber eyes. Anger flaring behind the concern.

"Got it covered…" Koree speaks up. "It was Teak who gave us the idea on the way here from Bay City. We're dying his skin and hair dark. Right now we're experimenting now with different substances."

Thann pulls up his tunic and reveals an assortment of colored spots all over his firm, muscled stomach. He looks bruised with the odd colored marks contrasting against his fair skin.

"We like this one best," he smiles, pointing to a dark spot. "Berries, iodine, charcoal…and what else?" He turns to Koree.

"I don't remember…we wrote it down on the…"

Kesper interrupts. "No, you're not going. It's too dangerous."

"Yes we are." Thann and Koree, say at once.

Thann's eyes become serious, reminding me of Koree's. "Mom, I'm almost seventeen. This is important to me. You can't keep me from going…or Koree."

I finally speak up. "It is because of me. It was my idea. I was the one who wanted to save Winter. I am going, too."

"Over my dead body." Koree's voice is loud and firm as he turns his head toward me, his green eyes blazing in the shadowed light of the room.

"I'll lock you up before I let you go," Kesper adds.

"Well, she is good with weapons," Thann contributes. I lift my head up and offer him a smile.

"Thann and I can handle this…we've done this kind of thing before," Koree stubbornly states.

Kesper's voice is strained, rising like a shrill whistle. "When?"

"Never mind, Mom. You don't want to know." Thann is grinning again, and a smile breaks out on Koree's face. I wonder what they have done in the past.

"That's enough of this nonsense," Kesper firmly states, shaking her head at the boys. She expertly changes the subject, and we discuss plans on how to start weapons training for the soldiers at the tree houses. We learn that more Light Skinned people are being filtered in, probably the final wave, and that will increase our need for supplies as well as training.

"Teak, are you ready to start?" Kesper asks me.

"Sure, when?"

"Tomorrow. We're having the Assigning Ceremony tonight. It's earlier than usual. I'm going to say that we have an extremely talented group of cadets, which overall is correct."

"Okay," I answer. "But I am going to need a lot of targets for practice."

"Koree, can you get on to that today? Get with Teak after the meeting...in private...and see what she needs."

"Yeah, no sweat."

The meeting ends abruptly. Koree and Thann stand up, and I stretch my sore body, checking on Diamond. He is fast asleep. Thann, Koree, and I turn to leave.

"I need to talk to you, Teak...alone," Kesper announces as she looks up from the papers she is still inspecting.

"Okay," I answer slowly, curious about why she would want to talk to me alone. "But I don't know my way back. Thann brought me here using a different route." I wonder if I will ever get used to traveling in the creepy underground tunnels.

"Thann, will you wait outside for her?"

"Sure." He and Koree leave the room, deep in discussion about the best mixture to use to dye Thann's skin and hair. Kesper and I sit alone at the table.

She doesn't waste any time getting to the point. "I didn't want to say this now…didn't want to have to tell anyone this." A tear forms in the corner of one of her eyes, misting it over like a golden pool. My stomach tightens into a knot. I have no idea what she is going to say, but a terrible feeling settles in the pit of my stomach.

"Bello has been destroyed….she…she's dead."

A jolt runs through me, as if I have been kicked. I find it hard to breathe. Bello? My Weapons Instructor…dead? Destroyed? It seems unthinkable. I stare straight ahead, trying to process it. The room is still and quiet, but somehow spinning at the same time. Sounds creep into my ears like they are amplified; I can almost hear the flame burning from the candle. I sniff once or twice, trying to tamp down tears I know won't help, that won't bring Bello back. I think of her skin, so light and her Power, so, well…powerful. It seems impossible that she could be gone. I want to know specifics, how, who, when, but then again I really don't want to know.

"It is a mistake," I croak to Kesper. "She has Power." But deep down I know the truth.

"And so do the Destroyers," Kesper answers. "Strong Power. Dark Power."

I gulp at the air like a fish out of water, thinking of the times I hated Bello, regretting those moments, guilt creeping into my body like a slow moving poison. I feel myself shrinking, pulling away. *She can't be dead...not Bello...Bello. She was an unstoppable force in every way.* I am slowly shaking my head back and forth, as if by doing so I can make Kesper stop – bring Bello back to life.

"And there's more." Kesper wrinkles her forehead. She is hunched over as if a hundred years of sadness washed over her, aging her into an old woman. She stands up, wanders to a bookshelf and returns with a large brown envelope. I instantly recognize it...the package that Thann and Koree came to the clinic for. The package for Kesper.

"It is from Entho." She hesitantly hands the envelope to me. My hands are trembling as I take it from her. What could be in the envelope that is so important Entho would have sent it to Kesper weeks ago?

She speaks again, her voice wavering. Her golden eyes meet mine, sadness and pain erupting from them. "I was to give it to you if anything ever happened to him." A solitary tear spills out of one of her eyes, leaking down her face like a small stream trying to find its way to the ocean.

"No," I gasp. I pull my hand to my mouth, as if by covering it I can place a shield in front of myself, protecting me from what I know I am about to hear.

She nods her head, and the single tear turns into a steady stream of tears leaking down her cheeks like shameless raindrops. Her voice becomes hoarse, harsh, rasping in my ears.

"I have just gotten word from my scouts that Entho is either dead or in prison.

Chapter 31

Bello dead...Entho...dead or in prison. I let out a scream that is primal, visceral. I feel it all the way through to my bones... fall to my knees and cry, deep endless sobs. I clutch the envelope to my heart, as if it could bring Entho back. Diamond lets out a piercing yowl, joining in my pain. He is in front of my heart, where he belongs, but I can't seem to process who he is, why he is there. Gentle hands reach for him, take him away. I can't fight it. In my mind I think that, no, I can take care of him. He is mine. Diamond belongs to me. But everything is murky. I feel Kesper's hand patting my back, hear her saying some words, something like, dear, dear... and Diamond wailing in the background.

A door crashes open, and Thann and Koree are instantly next to me. Koree wraps me in his arms, lifts me up. They are strong arms and I need them more than the breath I am somehow taking in. I hear Kesper tell them about Bello...about Entho... but it is as if the words are far away, at the end of a tunnel. Tears are streaming down my face like a torrential rain as my heart explodes into a thousand, perhaps a million pieces that can never be put back together again.

Entho…I wail in my heart…in my mind…Entho…Bello…Entho…

Over and over again, as if saying their names will bring them back to me.

Their faces flash before me – haunting memories and images. I sniff, refusing to believe they are both gone. And yet know somewhere deep inside me that they are. That I will never see them again. Never hear their voices. Never kiss Entho on the cheek…never tell him I love him. *Why didn't I tell him I loved him the last time I saw him?*

I don't know how long we stay that way, the four of us. It might be minutes and it might be hours, but I finally stop crying. I am totally spent. Koree is holding me up and Thann has one of my hands. I hiccup, swallowing hard. There is nothing left inside me except a dull ache and an empty hole.

"I'll take her to the tree houses," Koree states, taking charge as usual. I am still sniffling, gulping giant rattling breaths in and out of me. I try to think of other things, but waves of knowledge crash over me, knowledge of death and prison and never seeing Entho again.

Knowledge of living without Entho and his healing and Bello and her weapons, her Power that wasn't powerful enough. Knowledge that Entho couldn't heal himself, even though he could heal everyone else. Then it becomes raw once more, making me want to scream over and over again…to let the entire cycle of pain spin out of control. *When will it stop?*

Kesper's voice is low, but it echoes loudly in my ears. "Take the back way," she tells Koree, handing Diamond over to him. He places Diamond in the carrier and I watch like a lifeless statue, feeling the little dragon snuggle next to me but unable to attach any emotion to it. I do manage to stroke his little head, but the movement is slow, as if it were someone else's hand moving against his sleek leathery skin.

"You might need an excuse as to why she won't be at the Assigning Ceremony," Koree tells her. "I doubt if she'll be up to it."

"Yes, yes, I will come up with something."

Koree leads me through the tunnels. I follow obediently, holding his hand as if it were the only thing that is keeping me alive. Koree doesn't speak, asking nothing of me, and it seems like decades that we twist and turn in the dank darkness, me putting one heavy foot in front of the other.

I am dead inside. I can feel Diamond's tiny heartbeat against the beat of my own heart that I wish wasn't beating at all. I trail after Koree, obediently, up a ladder that leads us outside. My eyes blink as more tears flush down my cheeks. I try to adjust to the painful light outside.

"Onyx is waiting," Koree tells me, squeezing my hand, pressing against the small of my back with his other hand.

"Are we flying?" I ask, my voice expressionless.

"No, we can't risk it in the day." Koree tenderly lifts me onto Onyx, mounts the dragon as well, and we walk at a brisk pace for quite some time. My head bobs up and down, and I feel the dragon's movements as if they are in slow motion. At the same time, it feels as if I am a spectator watching from somewhere up high...my body is on the beautiful black dragon but I am floating above me, looking down at myself. At Koree and Onyx. I am two people, split distinctly in half.

I hold onto Koree's waist and it is the only thing that feels right. I fight back another wave of tears when Diamond wriggles in his carrier and lets out a giant squeal. A squeal of life. Life goes on, he seems to be telling me. I stroke his pale head, and his indigo eyes find mine and latch onto them. I gulp sweet air into my lungs as I pull him tighter to my chest.

At last we reach the tree houses, which I realize I have never seen in the light of day. Almost every giant tree in the orchard has a camouflaged wooden house tucked neatly into it, hidden by the massive branches of the trees, painted to blend in. If I didn't know they were there, I might not even see them in the daylight. People are outside…Light Skinned people, so many that it takes my breath away.

There are crops of food spanning for what must be miles and a beautiful river flowing nearby. The orchard is nestled into a valley with green rolling hills surrounding it. I immediately understand that it is the perfect place to hide people…and dragons. I spot a gigantic

pasture on the other side of the river, brimming with purple dragons

– Lavs – glistening in the sunlight.

I turn to Koree. "They are beautiful."

"The people or the dragons?" he asks, his voice husky.

"Both," I murmur, gazing out at the idyllic scene before me. Still, I

feel as if someone has cast a spell on me as we dismount Onyx. I am

going through the motions of life, but it feels as if deep inside of me

there is nothing there. I am completely empty.

Koree laces his fingers through mine, guides me to the empty tree

house. We climb up, enter the usual way. He settles me on the

couch and slides next to me in one fluid motion. He takes Diamond

and a bottle from the carrier, tips the little dragon back and feeds

him. A part of me wants to snatch Diamond away, to take charge

and say he is mine and I can handle his care, but I let out a giant

breath instead. I am actually grateful that Koree has him.

Koree turns to me with wide eyes as he holds the bottle for

Diamond. Sad, soulful, green eyes that see right into the very center of me. Of who I am…the best of me and the worst. When he

speaks, his words are low and deep, as soulful as his eyes. "I am so

sorry….I know what you're feeling." The muscles in his square jaw

flex as he clenches his teeth.

Anger erupts inside me for a moment as I wonder how he could

possibly know what I am feeling. Then I realize that if anyone

knows how I feel, it is Koree. My eyes, red rimmed tarnished coins,

find his. "They are gone," I answer, my voice hoarse from crying.

"Maybe…not your dad…" He meets my gaze with intense green

eyes. Emerelds seeking gold. "I will find him for you…if he's in

prison. I'll figure out a way."

At that moment, gazing at Koree in the faded orange tree house light,

I feel two things that are new to me. A wave of love crashes through

me, a deep love like I have never known…for this boy who is

willing to risk his life to help me find my father. And a deeper

resolve…a resolve to find Entho if he is alive, to quit wallowing in

my sadness…to take action. If he is dead, I will deal with it on the other end, but as long as there is a chance he is alive…I will hold onto that hope like a lifeline that is thrown to a drowning person.

I muster a half-hearted smile, and Koree strokes my hair, gently brushing his hand over the tangled mess. He kisses me tenderly on the lips, a kiss that holds at least a hundred secret messages that I can't seem to understand at the moment.

Then, like waves crashing against a rugged shoreline, I remember it.

The envelope.

Chapter 32

Tenatively, I pull the crumpled brown envelope out of my tunic. I have no idea how it got there, but I hold it in my hands, thinking of it as a precious gem. I stare at Entho's handwriting, and I am afraid I might start sobbing again, that my world will stop spinning, that I will fall off that cliff of knowledge time and again and drown in an endless depth of sorrow. Yet I know I need to read it, that whatever is in the envelope might hold the last strings that bind me to Entho.

Koree's voice saves me from falling off the cliff. "You don't have to read that now…if you're not ready."

I choke back tears that threaten to spill out again. "I know." I take a huge breath and turn my eyes to his. "Just stay here with me?"

"Always."

My hands shake as I gingerly open the envelope and pull out two thick pieces of paper. Entho's personal stationary. Before I read it, I thumb through the pages, imagining him writing the words in his humble office – the only room in the mansion that spoke of the true

Entho. I devour his words, my stomach clenched into a knot of despair riddled with curiosity.

My Darling Teak,

If you receive this letter, then you know something has happened to me. Most likely I'm just imprisoned. My knowledge and Power as a healer make me valuable to the Alliance.

Because of this, I have a lot of explaining to do, and I hope you don't end up hating me for what I say. I should have told you this long before, but I could never find the words or the right time. However, I think you're old enough now to understand.

First, I want to apologize for not always being there for you. After your mom died, I was lost. In some ways I still am. But part of Pana's death forced me into action. For years, I have been smuggling Light Skinned people out of the city to safety – most of them to Harcourt. When you told Bello you wanted to train dragons, I was angry. I wouldn't allow you to die like Pana did. But Bello talked sense into me, and I realized it was a perfect opportunity – that you would be safer around dragons than

Destroyers. Bello and I contacted Kesper, who was happy to have you, especially after seeing your Assessment scores. However, there is more as to why she would want you at Harcourt.

Which brings me to the real purpose of this letter. I love you. You are my daughter and always will be. But it is time you learned the truth about your birth and heritage.

Pana and I were childless. It was the one thing she wanted more than anything, to have a child. But year after year, we were left disappointed. At the time, we lived at Harcourt. I was the resident healer, and Pana was a dragon trainer. The Purification Law had not passed yet, but the killings had already begun. Light Skinned people with the Mark of Power were usually left alone, though.

Kesper lost her husband this way. He was a good man, and they were expecting their first child, but Strom was unmarked. He was slaughtered on his way back to Harcourt from the city, only because he had Light Skin. Kesper went into labor within hours of his death. Two babies were born, twins, a boy and a girl, both Light Skinned The boy had the Mark of Power on his right cheek, but the girl had no mark. Kesper despaired that the girl would be destroyed like her father.

I offered to take you, the unmarked baby, to raise as our own in Bay City where it was safer at that time. I most likely wouldn't be bothered because of my standing as a healer. Kesper agreed grudgingly. She couldn't bear the thought of losing you like she lost Strom.

I made two birth entries that night – one male, the other female. The female entry listed Pana and me as your parents. It was easy enough, since I was the resident healer at Harcourt. We left with you in the night, before anyone could see you. We loaded you safely onto Emory and flew back to the city. No two parents could have been happier.

You might be wondering about the mark on your cheek – the Mark of Power. I put it there when you were a toddler. I don't know why it didn't occur to me to do this when you were born, but you were almost three when the idea came to me. I had found a discarded book on tattoos. I bought some ink, mixed the colors, and formed a tattoo on your cheek, trying to match Kesper's. That Mark has kept you alive...more than you will ever know.

Teak, I want you to know that you are loved and that Kesper only did what she had to do to keep you alive. Please don't hate her. You are my true daughter and I will always love you.

All my love,

Dad

Chapter 33

I drop the letter and envelope to the ground, staring into space. Kesper is my real mother? Thann is my brother? I hear Koree in the background, asking me if I am okay. But once again I am in a tunnel, wading through water that is up to my stomach and I can't seem to move or think. Everything is muffled, wrong, distorted.

Koree shakes me, just like I shook Thann when the Destroyers cast a spell on him. I want to stay this way, just go away inside myself. The pain and confusion are too great.

But Koree's voice…it beckons.

"Teak….Teak…."

I turn to him, speak words that sound like they belong to someone else. "Read it."

He hesitates. "Are you sure?" All I can do is nod my head, my jaw slack.

He reaches down, picks up the letter and envelope, and reads the pages silently. Diamond is playing in the tree house, his little feet padding against the wooden floor like falling marbles. I wait like a statue for Koree to finish reading the letter.

"Oh, Teak," Koree reaches for me, holds me in a deep embrace until Diamond squawks, wanting to be picked up. Koree grabs him and sets him on the bed. He turns back to me, his eyes searching mine for answers or maybe for questions. I can't be sure.

"They lied...all of them," he flatly states.

"I know." Once again, I think if anyone knows about being lied to, it is Koree. He rubs his fingers up and down my arm. The feeling is pleasant, but it is a direct contrast to the numbness inside of me. Then it all washes over me again and I let out a wail of misery, stemming from the deepest part of me, the unhealed wound of my mother's death, Bello, Entho, and now the knowledge of deceit on a level I could never have imagined. Tears fall again like an endless rainstorm and I wonder if they will ever stop.

Eventually Koree takes me by the shoulders, lays me down on the couch, puts my head in his lap and runs his fingers through my hair, over and over again, like the wave of pain that keeps overtaking me.

"Sleep," he simply states. "I am here."

I close my eyes, exhaustion taking over. I feel heavy, tired, and old. Koree tenderly runs his hand up and down my arms and then travels to my hair. He gently strokes my cheek until I finally fall into a fitful, dreamless sleep.

Sometime later I jerk up, panic coursing through my body. "Entho," I shout.

"Shhh...." Koree holds me, draws me toward him. The sun is fading, forming shadows on his face. I reach for his cheek, feeling soft stubble as I move my hand up and down it. I lean toward him, find his lips. His lips brush against mine, and I am suddenly greedy for him, for the taste of him, for all of him. We kiss deeply, and he reaches under my tunic, stroking my back, moving his hands toward my stomach. And then higher. Tingles run up and down my body everywhere he touches me.

He stops abruptly, jerks himself away from me, breathing heavily. "Teak, we have to stop."

"I know," I murmur, disappointed and relieved at once as my chest heaves and I let out short, ragged breaths.

He peers into my eyes. "I love you, Teak." It is a raw whisper, his jade eyes searing into the very center of me. I am suddenly more afraid than I have ever been. At this point I am not sure if I can ever love anyone again. Loving someone…it can only end in loss.

"You don't have to answer. I just wanted you to know."

I nod my head slowly. "I am just so empty right now…and afraid…to love you."

He reaches for my hand, rubs his thumb in tiny slow circles on it. "I understand." He pauses, his green eyes soulful. "I won't lie to you, and I won't leave you." He breathes deeply. "Ever."

"Do you promise?"

"Yes."

Koree wraps his arms safely around me, holding me in a tight embrace. I nestle into the crook of his neck, draw in a deep breath, and a few pieces of my shattered heart fall back into place.

Chapter 34

After a while I wrench myself away from Koree, staring straight into his eyes. "I am going to the Assigning Ceremony," I tell him firmly.

His eyebrows furrow and his eyes flash with concern. "Are you up to that?"

"Yes. I want to go." I let out a giant breath. "Are you supposed to be there, or are you in isolation?"

"Well, it can go either way for me." He grins slowly. "I can show up in uniform without my pins. Or just not show. You know, since I am in isolation."

I bite my lower lip. "That reminds me," I ask him. "Why didn't you use your Power on Reese instead of hitting him? I have seen you use it before."

"I don't know. I just got so mad at him that I didn't think." He curls his lips downward. "You could have been seriously hurt…or worse."

"I know." I think for a few seconds. "Did you really get in trouble?"

"Naw, Kesper's sweet on me. It's all just for show. The Rebellion is what we all want and are working toward. What are a few dragon pins, when there's so much more at stake?"

"She is my mother…" My voice trails off. "And Thann is my brother…" I think back to my early attraction to Thann – that odd connection I never understood. Could it be because we are twins? Twins…I have a twin brother. The realization of this pelts into me like a relentless hailstorm.

"Yeah, pretty weird, huh?" He breathes deeply and fastens his eyes on mine. "Kesper saved me…in more ways than one. Don't be too hard on her, okay?"

"I can't promise that right now. I am pretty mad at all of them."

He sighs. "I bet…but I think that's a pretty normal response."

"I have another question for you." I tell him. "How do you have Power? How did you get it? Are you Marked?"

He throws back his head and laughs, and I am suddenly embarrassed. I feel my face flush, heat overtaking it like red, hot ocean waves. I worry that my Mark will turn bright red, repulse him.

"That was more than one question. And that's just an old wives tale." He stops laughing, peers into my eyes, and gently traces the outline of my Mark with his finger. "Anyone can have Power. You just learn to develop it."

"How? Who taught you?"

He pauses. "Kesper mostly. But I practiced a lot on my own."

"Do you think I could get Power? Can you teach me?"

"Sure, if you teach me how to shoot a bow and arrow. And how to kiss a little better." He kisses me tenderly then, and I fall into his lips like I just fell off of a cliff.

Koree opens his eyes. "If you're serious about going, we'd better hurry. I need to get cleaned up, and so do you."

"I must be a mess."

Koree's eyes are green misty pools. "No. You look beautiful."

I meet his eyes with mine. I can never seem to hear him say that enough, yet I don't know how to respond. I smile weakly at him as I scoop Diamond up.

We scramble out of the tree house, mount Onyx, and gallop toward Harcourt. I hold on tightly, my hands around Koree's waist and rocking to the rhythm of the dragon moving up and down. Diamond's head is bobbing on my chest with each stride the dragon takes, and a feeling of contentment washes through me, cleansing me of so much of this horrible day. I breathe it out like the last wind of the winter…when you know that spring is coming. Still, other emotions rumble deep inside of me…those of fury and anger and the deepest despair I have ever know. I tamp them down for the moment as the dragon skids to a stop and Koree and I dismount.

I race into the Incubation Room and am relieved to find it empty. I place Diamond in his box and he scampers around happily, spitting out tiny flames. Shadows line the room as the sun begins to set, the eggs humming in harmony with something I can't seem to hear or understand at the moment. I hurry to Kebb's sink to clean up. I splash water over my face time and again, washing the salty tear stains away, watching with fascination as they splash into the copper

sink, as if by this one act all of my pain and confusion can disappear.

I find a towel, dry off and quickly brush my hair. Then I put on a

fresh tunic, place my pins on them and mix two bottles. I tuck them

into the carrier, hook Diamond back up to my chest, and bolt out the

door.

Koree is waiting outside. I gasp at the sight of him, clean shaven,

hair combed, and wearing the golden tunic without any dragon pins.

I want to freeze this moment, the sight of him. I can only think of

how he looks, how the air seems to go out of me, how I get that

feeling in my stomach like something is fluttering around in it. As I

gaze at Koree, I think about how much I have lost…Entho,

Bello…my mom. But another thought strikes me. I have gained a

lot along the way, too…Koree, Diamond, my friends…a brother.

Could it be that you have to lose something to gain something?

"You look beautiful," Koree tells me again, interrupting my

thoughts. He kisses me lightly on the cheek and entwines his hand

with mine. We jog toward the arena, Diamond bobbing up and

down in his carrier.

When we arrive the crowd has gathered but nobody is on the stage yet. "Gotta run," Koree tells me, squeezing my hand lightly. "I'll see you later."

"Later," I answer, a hitch in my breath, as he disappears in a flash of gold, scurrying off behind the stage. I suddenly feel alone as I fight back tears and sadness. Bello is dead. For five days a week she was the closest thing to a mother that I had since I was six years old. And Entho. Oh Angels…Entho…Entho…Entho…A small tear drips down my cheek and lands on Diamond's resting head, leaking out onto his pale white skin like ink spreading on paper. He opens one vivid blue eye, tilts his little head and seems to be telling me it will be okay.

I shake my head rapidly back and forth. This isn't the time to fall apart. I search for Echo, Gunter, or even River, but I can't seem to find them. Then a fluttering hand catches my attention. It is Echo, and I thread my way toward her. She is standing next to Gunter.

"Holy dragon tits, where have you been?" she barks at me. "I've been looking all over for you."

"I just had some bad news…about my dad. I needed to be alone."

"Is everything okay?" she asks, concern filling her icy blue eyes.

"Yes, it is fine." I flash her a weak smile, as she reaches for a bottle and Diamond. I let her feed him as Kesper, Thann, Koree, and Persia walk out on the stage holding hands.

Kesper gives a speech about how talented this group of cadets is, how we have progressed faster than any other group she has had. She is quite convincing. Persia struts over to a podium and picks up a stack of papers. She and Koree then back away. My attention is focused on Kesper…my mother. My birth mother. I swallow back tears of frustration and anger as I study her face…so much like mine I should have figured it out right away.

Thann is holding a box and stands near Kesper. I gawk at him…my brother. I have a brother. The realization of it sends me into a tailspin. I have a brother and a mother I didn't even know about until a few hours ago.

Kesper and Thann are huddled together on the stage, deep in muted conversation. I lose track of time as I study them, cocking my head to one side. Something is missing, I think, but I can't seem to pinpoint what it is. As I continue to focus on them, I suddenly realize what it is. That something is me.

What if Entho never took me? What if I had been raised by Kesper with my twin brother? I would be up on the stage…probably wearing gold. I would be a Master Trainer. I wouldn't have had to go to Weapons. But then, I wouldn't have Entho for a father...or my mother. My stomach twists into knots.

My thoughts are interrupted by Kesper's voice. "Now we will give Assignments. I want to remind you all that each and every Assignment here has equal importance." Thann hands her a paper, she takes it, holds it up to her face. It is quiet as everyone strains to listen.

"River Coan. You are assigned as Dragon Trainer." Everybody claps and cheers. It is the most coveted position…what we all came here hoping to attain. River jogs to the stage, his huge body more limber than I would ever imagine. Kesper reaches into the box, pulls out a dragon pin, and places it on the neckline of his tunic. His grin is wide as he travels to the back stairs where Koree and Persia each shake his hand and present him with a diploma.

"Shagg Rester. You are assigned as Dragon Trainer." More clapping and cheers. He receives his dragon pin and diploma, smiling, and departs down the steps.

"Gunter Longbird. You are assigned as Dragon Trainer." Echo yells loudly as Gunter makes his way to the stage. All I can muster is a clap, but I am very happy for him. His eyes have completely disappeared into his face as Kesper places the pin on his tunic and he reaches for his diploma. Echo turns to me, "Hot dragon buns, isn't he smash?"

"Koree? Of course," I answer.

"No, Gunter!"

"Mmmm....sure," I respond, smiling at her. "Look who's all goober eyed now," I tease. She smiles widely and hands Diamond back to me. I gently put him back in his carrier. With a full stomach, he nods off to sleep in spite of all the noise.

"Echo Ovale. You are assigned as Hatchery Apprentice." Echo lets out a loud whoop and almost runs to the stage. I picture her with all of the eggs and hatchlings, working with Kebb, nodding my head in agreement to her Assignment. She stands tall as she receives her pin, grabs her diploma, shakes hands with Koree and Persia, and almost leaps off the stage.

"Reese Blevins. You are assigned to Dragon Maintenance." A silence falls over the crowd. Everybody knows what Dragon Maintenance is…scooping dragon poop…cleaning pens… grooming dragons for the trainers. No matter what Kesper says, nobody wants this position. "Reese?" Kesper asks. "Is Reese here?" Apparently the cadets in isolation must have been let out for the ceremony. Kesper clears her throat. "We'll move on."

"Flame Gardener. You are assigned to Dragon Maintenance." The silence lingers. Flame trudges up to the stage, receives her pin as if it is hot and she doesn't want it near her, snatches her diploma and storms past Koree and Persia, refusing to shake their hands.

"Teak Frain. You achieved the highest assessment score of any cadet…ever in the history of Harcourt. You are assigned to Dragon Research." I try to act surprised as I travel to the stage. I hear clapping and cheering, a few hoots and whoops from my friends, most likely Echo and Gunter. As it quiets, I reach Kesper, and she places a dragon pin on my tunic.

"Congratulations," she smiles, as if I were any other student here, as if I weren't her daughter. I stare into my mirror eyes for just a moment too long.

"Thanks, Mom," I say, ice dripping from my voice.

Chapter 35

To Kesper's credit, she holds the smile on her face, as if it were glued there and stuck in place. I move along, shake Koree's hand and then Persia's. Koree's brow furrows and his eyes follow my every movement, green guards working overtime. I take my diploma and trudge down the steps and wait by Echo.

The Assigning Ceremony finishes in a blur. I hadn't realized that being close to Kesper would bother me so much. Her face reels in my mind over and over. Was there pain on it? Or does she even care? And Thann. Did he hear what I said? A large heap of regret pours over me. I wouldn't want to hurt Thann. Ever.

After all of the Assignments, Koree finds me. "How are you holding up," he asks, his eyes glistening with specks of gold in the candle light.

"Fine," I answer. Koree's eyes continue to bore through me, and then he tenderly pulls my head toward him, and right there in front of everybody gives me a long, deep kiss. He draws back slightly, whispers in my ear. "Now that I'm not your trainer I can be your boyfriend." He grins all lopsided at me.

"Are you sure I want to be your girlfriend?"

"Oh, I'm sure." He kisses me again, longer and deeper. When he pulls away from me, his lips are swollen. He strokes the back of my head with his hand. "We need to go…you know…the dinner."

"Okay," I agree, but it is the last place I want to be. We venture toward the cafeteria, following the crowd of people ahead of us. I spy Gunter and Echo among the horde of people, holding hands, deep in conversation with Thann.

When we arrive, Koree has me sit with the Master Trainers at the front of the room. I manage somehow to eat the food without tasting it, talk to Koree and Persia, and tend to Diamond. He starts squirming and squealing and I know he wants out of his carrier. I put his leash on him, stand up to take him for a walk. I feel Koree's hand on my back.

"I'll go with you."

I smile up at him. "I can handle it myself."

"I know." But he walks outside with me anyway. I set Diamond on the ground. "He's getting scales."

"Who?"

"Diamond, can't you see them?"

I squint my eyes in the dim light, and sure enough, I see the beginnings of pearly white scales erupting from his soft baby skin. I am both delighted and dismayed about it. "Wow," I breathe out.

Koree reaches his head toward mine, and I think he is going to kiss me, but instead, he leans toward my ear.

"Reese has escaped," he whispers.

"Oh no." Reese. Why is it always Reese, I wonder.

"I am staying with you all the time," Koree announces, puffing up his chest just the slightest.

"Okay. You won't get an argument out of me. Do you have permission…from Kesper?"

"Don't care." He kisses me then, long and slow. I close my eyes, tasting mint and sweetness, smelling the leathery, musky Koree smell that sets every nerve of mine on fire. When he stops, I open my eyes to find a disgruntled face glaring at us. It is Kesper.

"I need to speak with you in my office, Teak. Alone. Now."

I stick out my chin, sending her a look bleeding of hate and indignation. "Fine," I answer, in the snarky voice I had once reserved only for Bello. My chest tightens at the thought of Bello and of how badly I treated her the past few years. I tuck Diamond back into his carrier and try not to lose patience with him as he hisses and kicks against me.

"I'll walk you there." Koree leaves no room for discussion as he grasps my hand firmly in his. The three of us walk silently to Kesper's office. Anger builds in my chest like a volcano about to erupt…anger at Kesper and Entho, and even my real mother, Pana. Fury rises up in my chest at being lied to by the people I trusted the most, and I want to lash out at somebody. Right now, Kesper is that somebody. When we reach Kepser's office, she unlocks the door, and lights a candle. Koree and I follow her in and he reaches for Diamond.

"This little guy could use some exercise," he tells me. I nod my head absentmindedly.

Koree takes Diamond and leaves me alone with Kesper. I cross my arms over my chest and glare defiantly at her, shadows from the candle light waving across her face, washing it in colors of orange and yellow. We are squared off – enemies about to wage war. She stands silently before me like a soldier waiting for orders, and I promise myself that this is a battle I will win.

At all costs.

Chapter 36

Dreadful silence lingers, as Kesper and I face each other, golden eyes blazing at each other. I wonder why she brought me here just to stare at me. My chest heaves and I grip my hands into tight balls. I shoot Kesper my nastiest glare. Still, she says nothing. Her eyes, though, are soft, unlike mine. I wait for her to take charge, but she remains infuriatingly silent, just watching me intently.

At some point something inside of me explodes. "You abandoned me," I irrationally shout at her. "You gave me away and kept Thann." The words that roll off of my lips sound childish...selfish. But I don't care as more as anger bubbles to the surface. I cross my arms over my chest, and it occurs to me that I am trembling, and I can't seem to stop.

"I didn't want to," she chokes out, an answer somewhere in those words. Tears fill her eyes and her voice wanes. "But I didn't want them to kill you, either." She hangs her head, and blonde hair tumbles down to her shoulders. "I was wrong...I wasn't thinking clearly…your father…Strom…your birth father had just been killed."

"Not good enough," I seethe, refusing to take my eyes off of her.

"Come with me," she commands, and I am instantly irritated.

"Why should I go anywhere with you?" I ask, sticking out my chin in defiance. "I don't owe you anything."

"I…I know. I just want to show you something." She turns from me, bends down and pulls the rug back, and opens the trap door on the floor.

The tunnels. She wants me down in the tunnels, and I wonder why. It is the last place I want to go. She steps down onto the ladder, her blonde head disappearing from view almost immediately.

I am left alone in Kesper's office. I could just leave, find Koree and continue as before, ignoring Kesper as much as possible. It isn't like I see that much of her anyway. But questions and confusion burn in my brain. What does she want to show me? How could she just give her baby away? Why me? What was so wrong with me that my own mother would give me to someone else?

I gaze around Kesper's dimly lit office. The answers I seek are not in this room. Kesper is the only one with those answers – the only one who can put the lid on the pressure cooker inside of me that is about to explode. As much as I despise her at this moment, and as much as I despair at the thought of going down into the tunnels, I take a deep breath, my decision made.

I step foot onto the rickety ladder and descend into the depths of the tunnel, not knowing what to expect. It is cold when my feet hit the solid ground, but Kesper meets me with a torch, the yellow-ish red flame outlining her pale face. She looks regal, wrapped in her golden cloak, as if she were a real a queen. Thann is right, that *would* make me a princess. My lips curve up at the thought.

"Come," Kesper tells me.

I follow her through the winding tunnel until we reach a room I have never been in before. She unlocks the door, opens it for me.

I tentatively step in, not sure if I should trust her. She brings the torch into the room, sets it in a holder on the cold stone wall. The light flickers against the wall ahead of me where paintings are hung – perhaps thirty or forty. They are all large canvases of a tiny, pale baby with tufts of almost white hair on her head. Huge golden-brown eyes stare back at me, as if I should know who she is. The baby is wrapped in a pink blanket in most of the paintings. In some of them she is wearing a light maroon gown and matching bonnet.

"The paintings…they are all of you," Kesper states simply.

"Me?" I can't help but ask. I gaze around the room – at all the babies – an eerie shrine of infants. "Who painted them?"

"I did."

"How did you know what I looked like?"

Kesper clears her throat and hesitates for a minute. When she finally speaks, her voice is catching with emotion. "You…you were burned in my memory. I held you for hours and memorized every feature on your tiny body. I etched you into my heart and then had to let you go. I knew…that someone would kill you for being unmarked.

Entho convinced me that he could keep you safe." She lets out a deep sigh, staring straight into my eyes. "Obviously, he did."

I bite my lip, thinking, moving my eyes from one painting of the baby to the next, her dark amber eyes staring back at me all the while.

"Painting you…it has kept you close to me. It has been the only way." She smiles tenderly at me, like a mother might smile at her daughter. Her real daughter. I am stone faced, sober. I dart my eyes back to the paintings. At this moment I want to stop hating her. I want to trust her. I just don't know how.

"You lied. All of you lied." I flatly state, still staring at myself on the wall.

"I know. It was wrong. But I have never stopped loving you. I was so afraid they would kill you…like they did Strom. Thann was Marked. I always thought he'd be safe. Until now…"

It feels as if a giant hole has been bored through me, and nothing will ever fill it. I have no words to respond to her confession as I slowly turn my head away from my infant self and toward Kesper. Toward my mother.

She doesn't seem to notice, or maybe she doesn't care. She continues rattling on, and part of me is registering every word she says and the other part of me is holding her at bay, as if she were a scorpion about to bite me. "I was so excited to have you come here. But I felt I owed it to Entho not to divulge any information....about your birth." She is stammering now and fidgeting with her dragon necklace, obviously uncomfortable. I refuse to make this easy for her.

"I was happy just to have you here. That I got you back for a while... at least I could watch you...know you were here...were near me." She smiles weakly at me and continues with her solitary dialogue.

"When I gave you Entho's letter, I wondered if he would tell you the truth in it. I was ready for it...or so I thought." She sighs deeply. Then suddenly, as if I hadn't just found out she is my mother, she changes the subject. "You're wearing her bracelet...Pana's?"

I glance down at my dragon bracelet, nod my head, but refuse to answer.

"She adored that bracelet." Kesper takes a deep breath, her chest heaving. "I knew she would love you, and I can tell she did." Then Kesper does an odd thing. She reaches behind her neck, unclasps her diamond dragon necklace, and walks behind me.

Instantly I am at alert, not knowing what she is doing. I stiffen, a statue frozen in place in an eerie tunnel room where the infant ghost of myself is staring back at me in a multitude of poses. Kesper gently lifts my long unruly hair out of place and fastens the necklace around my neck.

"I want you to have this as well. I have treasured it always, but not as much as I treasure you." Kesper is in front of me now, and tears stream down her cheeks, splashing silently onto the cold, dark floor.

"They loved each other so much."

I finally speak, curiosity overriding my oath of silence. "Who?"

"Entho and Pana." She swipes a tear from her cheek. "They had one of those special loves….maybe that kind of love just can't last. I don't know." She takes a deep, ragged breath.

"Pana…she was engaged to Siv Gareth, did you know that?"

"What? Siv Gareth. THE Siv Gareth? My mom was engaged to Siv Gareth?" It comes out as one string of words without a pause. I wonder what other surprises are in store for me.

"Yes. She and Entho grew up together, and he came to Harcourt after Healing Academy. Pana fell off of a dragon and twisted her ankle. Entho treated her and after a while she broke it off with Siv."

"And Entho and my mom…they fell in love, got married?"

"Yes, they did. But Siv never got over it. That is actually what started the killings, the slaughtering of the Light Skinned people. He hated Entho…for taking Pana away from him and pretty soon he started hating all Light Skinned people." She breathes deeply in and out, sadness seeping out of her like a swirling dark cloud. I have been so caught up in my own pain I hadn't stopped to think of anybody else's – my parents, Kesper's, or even Bello's.

Kesper returns to her usual self. "Siv's Power is strong…and very dark. We must stop him. No matter what. When the New Alliance first started, it was a good thing. There had been many wars and devastating destruction. People were starving…dying in the streets. There was rioting. The world had gone mad. We had to rebuild." She pauses, her face falling like hot, dripping syrup. "Strom, and I, Siv, and Koree's parents were all instrumental in structuring the New Alliance." She finds my eyes and a chill runs down my spine when she continues. "And then Siv…he just went crazy…after Pana left him. He slowly took command of the New Alliance. Now it is just the Alliance and as you know, Siv is the sole leader." She pauses. "An extremely brutal leader."

I think back to that day in the school yard. Siv Gareth standing in the middle of it, calmly speaking to us…loading us onto Lavs to be slaughtered. If Entho hadn't saved me…if he hadn't tattooed my cheek with the Mark of Power…I would be dead. Like Canto and the others.

"Siv Gareth killed Strom, your husband, didn't he?"

She nods her head, swallows, her golden eyes still bleeding tears.

"And Koree's dad? And mom?

"Yes, he was responsible for their deaths."

I tilt my chin up. "Siv Gareth killed my mother, too."

"I don't think he would ever hurt Pana. He never got over her."

"I saw it. I was there." In that moment I am certain. Any lingering doubts I might have had filter away like ocean waves lightly pushing against sand.

Kesper reaches for me, pulls me toward her, and holds me, just like any mother would hold her distressed teenage daughter. My first reaction is to push her away. "You're not my mother," I tell her, my voice flat as I shove her away from me.

Her face falls, and I instantly feel terrible for hurting her. "I know," she simply states. "Pana was your mother. But I can be your friend."

Just then a bomb explodes inside of me and tears that have been locked away since I was four years old spew out of me like an erupting volcano. I know the truth now…it is what I always wanted. Kesper reaches her arms around me again and holds me as I cry…bottomless, raging sobs. Endless tears stream out of my eyes – for my mother and Entho – for this woman I barely know who gave birth to me and then gave me away to someone else.

This time I don't push her away.

We stay like this for a long time and the sweet aroma of lemons and violets swirls around me. I can feel her chest rising and falling against mine. I came from her, I think. I have the same face and hair and eyes. Eventually, I reach my arms up and wrap them around her. The hate and anger I have been holding onto for so long slowly dissipates, leaking out of me like a slowly deflating balloon.

When the tears stop, when I am spent and sucked dry like a used lemon, I turn my face up toward Kesper's. My lips curve up slightly, because I know Koree would roll his eyes at what I am about to ask, but it is a burning question, and I need to know the answer more than anything else in the world right now.

"Who named me?" I ask Kesper. Her golden eyes shift downward – toward mine.

She wastes no time. "Strom and I did. We didn't know we were having twins, although I was as big as an elephant we should have guessed." She smiles tenderly at me then. "If it was a boy his name would be Thann…that is my father's name. If it was a girl her name would be Teak…like the wood…strong, resilient, and golden. I think you are named properly."

I numbly nod my head. Strong. Resilient. Golden. Someone put thought into my name. Small pieces of me come together then, an elixir of knowledge and relief and satisfaction. I remember asking Entho about my name…the meaning of it. Of course he wouldn't know how I got my name. He always said that he and my mom just liked the name. But my name has *meaning.* In that thought, I feel strong and powerful. *I* have meaning.

A face cascades into my thoughts then. "What about Thann?" I ask as I pull away from Kesper. "Does he know?"

She reaches for a spot on her neck, as if she is about to fiddle with the dragon necklace, only it is gone. "No…that's entirely up to you. I'll respect any decision you make."

I stare at the baby pictures again, going from one to another, stopping at each one. I can't help but feel like there is something missing in each painting…the same feeling I had when I watched Kesper and Thann on the stage without me. It finally occurs to me what it is. A baby boy. To go with the baby girl.

My voice is throaty, but confident when I answer. "I want him to know."

Chapter 37

I wake in the tree house, snuggled up to Diamond and Koree. I remember flying here late at night, emotionally spent...of Koree leading me to the bed, tending to Diamond...of falling into the deepest sleep I can remember having.

Koree opens his eyes, slowly. "Good morning, Princess," he grins.

"Hey, who got you started on that?" I ask.

"Thann, who else?" He reaches for me, kisses me lightly on the lips. I worry about morning breath, of looking like a mess.

"Mmm...you taste good," Koree tells me.

"Really?"

"Mmmhmmm..." He kisses me again, slowly and I revel in it. Then he yanks himself away from me abruptly. "I'd love to stay here all day, maybe figure out what comes next." His green eyes sparkle with mischief. "But we have a Rebellion that needs our attention."

I jump out of bed, find his eyes. "Is everything ready?"

"Yeah, I've got it covered. Let's go eat. I guess since you slept in your clothes you won't have to get dressed."

I follow Koree out of the tree house, Diamond perched on my shoulder, swishing his tail happily against my back. We land on the soft dirt and I am engulfed with the smell of cooking food – eggs, bacon, sausage. My stomach immediately rumbles. "I am starving," I tell Koree.

"That's good, because you'll probably work it off today." Koree grabs my hand and leads me to the Lindens tree house for breakfast. He introduces me to them and their three teenage boys, Foxx, Hawkk, and Wolff. The boys fire question after question at me.

"How did you learn about weapons?" Foxx asks, his brown, droopy eyes serious.

"I have been in Weapons Training since I was six years old."

Foxx gasps. "So you're rich?"

I laugh at him. "No, but I guess my dad is."

Wolff interrupts. "Did you really kill a Destroyer?"

"No, two," I answer, not sure if I should be telling him this.

"How do you hold a bow and arrow?"

"I'll show you real soon, okay?" I tell Hawkk, the youngest of the three.

"Can you teach us how to throw blades, too?" he adds.

"Yes, blades, too."

"Wow…you are so smash!" Foxx tells me. His brown eyes are sparkling and he looks at me like he is a puppy and I am his owner.

"Uh…thanks," I answer. Koree hands me a plate of steaming food, and I dig into it with gusto.

"Can we play with your dragon?" Hawkk asks, almost shyly.

"Sure," I answer, handing Diamond over to him. "Just be gentle with him." Diamond screeches in the boy's hands and spits flames at him. His brothers laugh at him, but I show him how to pet Diamond and in a few minutes he settles down.

Thann arrives a short while later. "Hey, love birds," he teases, reaching for some bacon, popping it into his mouth – he chews and swallows. "Let's get rolling." He turns to Koree, reaches his hand out flat, spits on it. Koree spits on his hand, holds it face down, and they connect their palms together. "From the Mountain to the Moon," they yell in unison, grinning at each other, then breaking their hands apart.

My eyebrows leap up, curious what that was all about. But I don't have time to ask. People are assembling in a wide field. Koree nods in their direction and Thann quickly stands. I fetch Diamond from Hawkk, and the three of us head in the direction of the field, Koree and Thann bantering back and forth.

"I hate being odd man out." Thann quips.

"Find your own woman. This one's taken."

"Geez, she looks too much like me for that. It would be like kissing my sister or something."

Koree and I gawk at each other. Has Kesper talked to Thann? Should I tell him now? I let the moment pass.

Thann laughs out loud. "It's okay. Mom told me this morning. I was just messing around." He reaches for me, pulls me into a great big bear hug and almost squishes me to pieces. "I'm happy to have a sister." He kisses the top of my head and releases me to Koree.

"Me, too," I tell him. "Only, you know, a brother."

He suddenly becomes serious. "Did you ever feel like something was missing in your life?" he asks me, his amber eyes fixed on mine.

"Always," I answer. "More than just a brother, though."

Koree puts an arm loosely around my shoulder and another over Thann's. We all start walking together, Diamond perched on my other shoulder.

"It's weird, having a sudden sister," Thann continues.

I can't help but laugh. "So, can I be called sudden sister instead of Princess?"

He acts as if he is in deep thought. "No. Princess overrides everything."

"But I am not a Princess!" I argue.

Just then we reach the massive line of targets that Koree has somehow arranged to have built and erected. My jaw drops as I stop in my tracks. There must be over one hundred people waiting for us, lined up holding bows with quivers of arrows on their backs.

"That was fast," I tell Koree. "How did you get this done so quickly?"

"Everybody here pitched in. They've been working night and day to get this ready."

Koree and Thann lead me to the center of the targets. They both hold up their hands, and it instantly becomes silent. I am suddenly nervous, and I fidget with Kesper's necklace, biting my lower lip. I have never spoken in front of so many people. Diamond screeches and playfully swishes his tail against my back. He seems to think that everyone is gathered for his personal amusement. I nervously pat his head.

"This is Teak," Thann announces, his voice roaring. "I just found out she's my sister." He grins at the crowd. I can tell he is enjoying this. "So be nice to her and listen, 'cause she's going to show you how to shoot." He gives me a little push, hands me my bow and some of my arrows. I grab my bow – an old friend I thought I would never see again.

I clear my throat, stare intently at the row of pale faced people all around me. Their eyes, mostly blues and greens and light shades of grey, are trained directly on me, waiting for instructions. I gawk at them…so many in one place. It is an eerie feeling. For most of my life, I have been one of the only Light Skinned people in a crowd – to see so many people like me gathered together in one place sends goose bumps up and down my arms and back.

As my eyes move from one pale face to the next, I think, "These are my people. They are just like me." My nervousness dissipates, and I find strength from inside myself that I didn't know I had. I set Diamond on the ground so that I can properly hold my bow.

"Okay," I start. "Hold the bow like this." I lift up my bow and demonstrate exactly where to put it on my shoulder. I show them how to hold to hold up their elbows while pulling back on the string.

"Aim at where you want the arrow to go," I announce as they awkwardly handle their bows. "And breathe…breathe deeply."

I glance down the row of people holding their bows, elbows at all sorts of odd angles, and a river of disappointment creeps through me. This is our army? To top it off, Koree and Thann seem to be the most awkward of all. I arch my eyebrows as I walk over to them, letting a huge stream of air out of my lungs. Diamond frolics by my feet.

I reposition both of their bows, bend their elbows at the proper angle. Then I show everybody how to hold the bow properly again. It takes most of the morning just to get everybody holding their bows somewhat correctly.

I demonstrate how to nock an arrow and order them to try it. This is like watching clowns at a carnival. Arrows fall to the ground, fling upward, fly behind the shooter, and bounce off of the strings in a multitude of directions. I travel up and down the line, helping each person nock the arrow correctly.

Finally, everyone can hold their bows and the nocked arrows in place. At this point I am ready to show them how to pull back, aim, and shoot. "When you shoot an arrow, before aiming, you must slow your breathing, calm yourself…become one with the target." I walk to the line, take several deep breaths, focus on the target and let the string go, hearing the familiar "ping" as it flies through the air, watching as it lands directly in the middle of the target. A bull's eye – of course. Diamond, by my feet, lets out a pint sized roar, strutting around my feet as if he were personally responsible for it.

"I will count to three, and you do the same," I tell the crowd in the loudest voice I can muster. I count to three and my face scrunches up in frustration as arrows fly all over the field, like crazed dancers gyrating out of beat – not one arrow even making contact with the target. I groan out loud.

I demonstrate time and again. With each effort, arrows line the field like flat, dead soldiers. I breathe deeply, trying to remember my first lesson, but the memories are misty. I remember Bello complimenting me and telling me I was a natural, but I was young, and these are teens and adults who have never held a bow in their lives. How will I ever get them ready for battle? Sighing, I travel from person to person, showing the proper hold, how to nock an arrow, how to aim. Koree was right. I am already tired. Diamond has already given up on keeping up with me and is curled up on my quiver of unused arrows, fast asleep.

We take a short break for lunch and then continue with practicing. A few arrows have managed to make contact with the targets, but that is it. I am so discouraged I want to cry, and by the time night falls, I am beyond exhausted. Thann, Koree and I eat with the Lindens, and I barely make it into the tree house before I fall asleep, Diamond nestled beside me.

I wake the next morning to find Koree gone. I get up, wash my face and change into clean clothes. I am feeding Diamond his bottle when Koree's copper curls appear from the tree house ladder. I smile, my heart fluttering in rapid beats at the sight of him.

"I brought you breakfast. This way we can eat alone," he grins, dimple and all. He hands me a plate of food.

"Thanks. I was wondering where you were." I take a bite of sausage, chew thoughtfully then look up at him, troubled. His brilliant green eyes meet mine, and he furrows his brow.

"What's the matter," he asks, gently stroking my cheek with his finger.

"We will *never* get them ready," I complain. "They are *so* bad!"

"Sure we will. We have time."

"I hope you are right."

"I'm always right."

"Right," I answer, sarcasm dripping from my voice.

"I'm going to have to silence you for that little remark, Princess." Koree pulls my body next to his chest, runs his fingers through my hair and kisses me, and it feels as if I am meeting the other half of myself for the first time.

He does, indeed silence me.

Chapter 38

The days pass in a blur. I have new respect for Bello. I never knew instructing students could be so demanding. Most nights I fall into bed too exhausted to even talk to Koree or play with Diamond. Disappointment is my overriding emotion as each day my students show little improvement. I start to see some progress after about a week, though. At around three weeks, most of the soldiers are hitting the targets, if not making bull's eyes. This gives me the reprieve I need.

After practice Koree and I eat then fall asleep for several hours. We wake and then my lessons start – flying dragons at night. Soon it becomes natural for me to soar through the air on one of the well trained Lavs, and I can't seem to get enough of it. We make the transition to shooting bows and arrows off of flying dragons at about week five.

At this point we split into three groups. Koree has one group, I have another, and Thann takes a third. I am restless all day, relieved of my daytime instructor duties. I am supposed to rest, because I am taking my group flying at night. I miss Koree, who is outside with his group practicing blades and spears. Diamond is playing in the tree house, getting into trouble, hopping from bed to bed, spilling cups of water and almost anything he comes into contact with. I laugh at him as I follow him around cleaning up his messes.

When night finally arrives, Koree climbs up into the tree house. "Your turn," he says, lightly kissing my forehead and wrapping me in his arms. His chestnut curls droop into his eyes, and his face is flushed, tired. Tonight he smells of the woods and fire and leather.

After a few minutes I gaze up at him. "I have to go. My group is waiting."

"Later?" he asks in a husky whisper.

"Later," I answer, standing on my tip toes and kissing his cheek. I open the door, climb down the ladder with an ease I never thought I would have and land on the soft dirt.

I venture toward the Lav pen in the darkness. I open the gate and choose one of the huge dragons, halter her, and lead her out to the field.

I mount the purple dragon, and squeeze my legs. She takes off easily, gigantic wings flapping almost silently as we soar into the starless night sky. My group follows me, and I circle around the targets in the field, which have been laid flat for flying practice.

I pull an arrow out of the quiver on my back, balance on the soaring dragon, and load it into my bow. I lean forward, and the well trained dragon flies toward the targets, swooping low enough for me to focus on one. I nock the arrow, pull back my string, aim, and let go. I lean back, feeling weightless as the dragon quickly speeds upward.

Curious, I glance over my shoulder to see where my arrow has landed. I am dismayed to see that I missed the target completely and watch in fascination as my students, one by one, circle around and hit the target or come closer to it than I did. I let out a groan of frustration.

I circle around again, determined to hit the target. I relax a little, feel the purple of the dragon encompass me, swoop down and release my arrow. As I pull the Lav back up into the air, I glance over my shoulder to see where the arrow landed. A bull's eye. I let out a whoop of joy.

We make pass after pass and I don't want to stop when the first glimmers of sun start peeking through the sky. I know it is our last round, that we will need to land the dragons so that we won't be seen in the morning light. I circle around the target, aim, let my arrow fly and then pull up.

It is becoming easy now, natural, as if the dragon and I have one mind. She listens to my body movements and responds, taking me where I want to go. I gain some air, wondering how Koree does spins and loops. *Can I make her do a big loop on my own?*

I push into the dragon's flank, and she moves with grace, turning her body in a sideways, upward motion, not quite a loop, but the start of one. A thrill rushes through my body as we start to turn in a circle. As the gigantic purple dragon pivots, a flash of silver catches my eye. I turn my head, shocked at the sight of a red cloaked rider who streaks by on a glistening Metallic - so fast I can't even tell who it is.

Just then a sickening thud carries across the wind, and my ears are filled with the loudest piercing scream I have ever heard. The Lav – she is screaming. Terrible, loud, piercing screams that pulse in my eardrums like recurring explosions.

I lean over the Lav's long neck and let out a gasp. A spear is sticking out of her chest and an arrow has penetrated her neck. The red-cloaked rider. It had to be him. Or her. But why?

I shoot my head up. Arrows, one after the other, are firing at her enormous lavender body…and at me. I scan the countryside but the rider is nowhere to be found.

More arrows batter ruthlessly at us, and I squeeze my head down into her neck as we begin to plummet toward the ground like a heavy stone falling from a cliff.

As we slowly descend, a deadly rainstorm of arrows continues to pound at us, just as the purple Lav launches into an awkward spin – faltering left and right, over and under – a slow motion, out of control gyration.

I wobble on her back, squeezing her neck with each horrid movement and dodging as many arrows as I can.

I dare not look down.

Chapter 39

I hug myself tightly to the enormous dragon's neck, pull an arrow out of my quiver and nock it into my bow. I search the ground now for whoever is shooting at us. Arrow after arrow races by us, and another hits the Lav. She screams – tormenting noises that squeeze at my heart as if they were actually hitting me instead of her. She falters as we spin, her great wings wobbling as the ground looms before us in gigantic, swirling circles.

I wonder what the odds of surviving a dragon crash are. Images of my mom's neck hitting the ground as she fell off of Emory swirl in my brain. I almost choke with fear. My fate...the same as my mom's. Entho's words echo in my mind. "Stay away from purple dragons." How could he have known?

I bring my head up slightly, searching for something, anything to help us. I start reaching for the whistle in my pants pocket when I spot the slightest movement in the woods. I turn my head to see who it is when an arrow is launched from that very spot. I quickly move to the side in an attempt to avoid it, but the Lav leans in the opposite direction. The arrow slams into my right hand, pinning it to the Lav's neck. I let out a yelp of pain as I look down. The arrow has pierced through both of us at once like a giant needle. Instinctively, I try to pull my hand free, but it is stuck to the dragon's neck, my blood now spilling out and mixing with her own spurting river of blood.

At that moment, she spews a violent flame from her mouth that singes my hair, heat wafting over my face. Blood sprays over me, and I don't know if it is the Lav's or mine.

I bite my lower lip as we propel downward. I don't have a lot of time. Another arrow flies at us, and anger explodes through my entire body. There is only one thing to do, and the thought of it makes my stomach churn.

I bear down, yanking my hand free from the arrow as fast as I can. I know I will need that hand for what I am planning to do…injured or not. Hot, searing pain shoots through my hand as my flesh rips apart from the arrow embedded in the Lav's neck. I shout into the air, surely matching the Lav's screams with volume, pain, and absolute rage.

I wish I could shoot flames from my mouth, because surely I would right now. My entire body shakes from the pain, and for just a minute I am dizzy and everything turns black. I rest my head against the dragon's long neck, her scales scratching my cheek. I breathe deeply, sucking air into my lungs as blood drenches my face. I wipe my eyes with my left hand. The ground is getting closer and closer, and I realize I must act…act or die.

I lean back a little, inspecting my injured hand. The arrow penetrated the palm of it…near my little finger. It is mangled and bloody, and I tentatively wiggle my fingers, fighting back the urge to cry out in pain. But they move…my fingers all move except my pinky, and I can still pull the string of my arrow without it. I tear the bottom of my tunic with my left hand, balancing precariously on the plummeting dragon, and with a loud rip, a long strip of cloth breaks free. Quickly, I wrap it around my hand. Then, I try to turn the spiraling, screaming Lav in the direction of the shooter. Naturally, she refuses.

"Please…it is our only chance," I beg her, my words floating out on the early morning breeze. "Please, please, please," I plead, but the shimmering, bleeding dragon continues to fall.

"Pleeeaaaeeeessssseeee," I cry out to her. More blood sprays into my face, and I wipe my eyes with my left hand. I pull on the reins and move my boot into her flank. "Turn, turn…tuuuuurrrrrnnnnnnn."

At last, I think she understands as she pins back her ears and begins shooting flame after flame into the air ahead of us. But she turns, thankfully, she turns.

"Good girl," I tell her, stroking her neck with my good hand as I lean forward. She shrieks, splitting the morning air into a thousand pieces, as we approach the running figure on the ground. I pull an arrow from my quiver, breathe deeply, aim, and let the lonesome arrow fly, fighting to ignore the pain in my right hand. I shoot again. And again. Aiming at someone I don't know…someone. A person who is trying to kill me.

The realization of this paralyzes me and I stop shooting as the man falls to the ground. Why is he trying to kill me? I can tell it is a man, but that is all. I am too far away to make out the details of his face. But I seem to recognize something about him. Another piercing scream turns my attention to the Lav.

She lets out an enormous shriek and a giant red flame, as if she understands what has just happened. Just then the ground starts approaching…closer and closer. Fast. Way too fast. I rub her neck, squeeze my legs together in an effort to make her rise.

"Please…please….please…" I beg her again, over and over. Because I know that it is our only chance. We cannot hit the earth or we will both be dead. Her blood continues to spurt, drenching me like a red fountain in the wind. It is acrid and metallic and sweet. And thick. Very thick. I swipe at my eyes so I can see.

But, thankfully, gloriously, as blood drenches my body, we slowly…very slowly…begin to rise into the early morning sky.

"Thank you…thank you…thank you," I tell her, rubbing her bloody neck, purple mixing with bright red on my left hand as a huge breath escapes my lungs, trapped there for what seems like a life time.

Suddenly I am paralyzed with fear. My entire body turns to stone, and I can't seem move, clutching the Lav's long neck like a life preserver. I can't seem to think past wondering if this is how I will die. Because I know she can't fly forever. With the spear and all of the arrows in her body, she certainly can't land on the hard surface of the ground.

I shake my head, images of Koree and Thann…Entho, my mom, and even Kesper dancing in front of me….and my new friends…Echo and Gunter. No…there has to be a way…a way out of this. I have been trained to think in situations like this since I was six years old. I scan the dragon's body. There is a spear is in her chest, an arrow in her neck, and two arrows sticking out of her hind legs. The arrows aren't that big…but big enough. She can probably still fly… for a while… but it is the spear that disturbs me.

I am thinking about Koree's whistle; maybe I can blow it and someone will hear it and help us. But how? Nobody can help us land. Then, suddenly, out of the blue, a thought sneaks into my brain. It is a long shot, but maybe it will work.

I stroke the dragon's bloody neck, and lean over her as blood splashes my face, some actually spilling into my mouth. I purse my lips and wipe my mouth with my sleeve as I push my left leg into her flank so we can turn around.

"To the water…to the river," I tell her, shivering now, my teeth chattering uncontrollably. "We will land there. You will be okay." I continue to steer her with my legs in the direction of the water. I know that dragons don't like water, that it is instinctive to avoid it because water quenches their flames. If I can gain her trust, maybe…just maybe…the water could break our fall. But will she trust me enough to land in the river?

The giant Lav spreads her wings and soars gracefully downward, screeching and squealing. At more than one point I join her, matching her pitch with my own wails of pain and fury until we near the river.

I start taking her down…telling her over and over again to trust me, to take it slowly. I keep stroking her neck…telling her it will be okay. Buckets of blood continue to pour out of her giant body, drenching me like a red flash flood. I keep wiping at my eyes so that I can see.

The blue green river fills my vision too quickly, and I sense that we are going too fast to land in the river. I turn her in a circle around the river and try to slow her down. She responds with ease, as if she can read my thoughts.

I tell her, "This is it…down we go…into the water." She stops screaming, seems to concentrate on landing, and gradually the greenish blue river slowly looms before us. She seems to fatigue at that very moment and we drop with a loud splash into the water.

That is when it occurs to me that I don't know how to swim.

Chapter 40

I hang on tightly to the Lav's neck, a windstorm of relief steaming
out of me. I am alive...she is alive, and I realize soon enough that I
don't need to swim.

She paddles her legs – even the ones with arrows – toward shore,
each stroke rippling water beside us, a whirling scarlet tidal wave.
Loud flapping noises from above startle me. I tilt my head back and
look up. Dragons – about twenty Lavs – are speeding toward us. I
breathe out in relief when they land on the shore, sandy dirt flying up
around them like an angry dust devil. The tree house people
dismount and race toward us, seemingly in one fluid motion, their
Lavs painting everything before us a light shade of purple. The giant
Lav limps out of the river.

"Are you okay?" Kord, a tall man with reddish blonde hair asks as
he reaches for the Lav.

"I...I am fine. But the Lav...she needs help. I can help her," I
answer, my teeth still chattering as I jump off of her and shakily feel
the ground beneath my feet. Huge red streaks of blood furiously

ooze out of the Lav's wounds, forming a scarlet trail on the once beige sand. Kord quickly puts a halter on the Lav, leading her ashore.

He wrinkles his brow as he glances over at me. "Your hand…" I look down at my hand, and the make shift bandage has fallen off. It is mangled mess of bloody flesh.

Ziff, one of the men from my group rumbles toward me. His hair is so light it is almost white, his blue eyes like ice storms. "Get Koree for me, I tell him. "Have him bring my healing case." By now my teeth are chattering so hard that I am not sure if Ziff can even understand what I am saying.

He stops in front of me, a statue on the shore of the river. "What happened to your hand?"

"Hit with an arrow," I sputter.

"Yaren is coming," he says, in a matter of fact tone, reaching for my wounded hand. He pulls a cloth out of his tunic and gently wraps it around my hand. Blood leaks onto the white cloth, staining it bright red. I am covered in more blood than I ever thought possible, my hand feels like someone has ripped half of it off, and I am freezing, shivering uncontrollably. But my lips curve up, ever so slightly when I spot Yaren thundering toward us on his small mottled dragon.

The diminutive figure stops his dragon, kicking up a cloud of dust, and he dismounts in one solid movement. He races toward me, incredibly agile for a man who appears to be about one hundred years old.

Memories of Yaren fill my mind – how he saved Thann and me from the Destroyers, flew us to Mount Gareth, and told us to run in the tunnels to Harcourt where we would be safe. At the moment, though, I don't feel very safe. I cross my arms over my bloody chest, images of arrows and spears shooting at me the only prevailing thoughts I can conjure up.

Yaren is by my side so fast that I don't even see him move. He is carrying a large brown bag; it almost looks like a suitcase. He reaches into the bag and pulls out a clean bandage and a vial of medicine.

"Dis be hurtin'," he tells me as he pours the medicine over my hand. I stifle a scream and look away, biting my cheek so hard I can taste blood. He then wraps my hand in a clean bandage, and in a few minutes the pain begins to ease.

Yaren turns to Ziff. "I be needin' blankets. Bein' for de girl and de dragon," he orders in his strange accent. Immediately Ziff runs off. "I be takin' care of de dragon," he tells me. "You be sittin' and restin'." I obey him without complaint, sitting on the bank of the river and wrapping my arms around myself tightly.

Yaren gently strokes the Lav, talking in his soothing lyrical voice as he mixes a potion from some large bottles and puts it in a tube that looks like a long water bag. He then trickles it down the dragon's throat. She spits in protest, but most of the medicine stays down.

"Gulf, Shander, you be standin' by her side. You be holdin' her up. She be goin' down." Two large men I have never seen before approach the dragon, each grabbing onto one of her sides. In a few minutes the dragon's head starts to wobble. "Don' be lettin' her fall," Yaren calls out to them. They hold her steady, muscles quivering against the enormous weight of the dragon. Another man jumps in to help. And another.

Perched in the background, I continue to shiver and chatter like an antique mechanical monkey toy. Soaked with water and blood, I wonder where Koree is, why he hasn't come. But my attention is drawn to the dragon, to Yaren and what he is doing.

He grabs a tool from his bag, opens it and places it around the spear in her chest. He quickly yanks on the tool, and the spear grudgingly follows along. Blood gushes out of her chest, first one large spurt, then smaller ones, over and over again, like the wound in her neck. I know this isn't good, that she will bleed to death if something isn't done. Instinctively, I stand up, wanting to help.

But Yaren quickly puts pressure on the wound, slowing the flow of blood. He places a bucket under the wound and begins stitching it closed. It seems like gallons of blood have spilled over him, over the ground, and into the bucket, as if a red pond has exploded. I sigh in relief when the blood slows to a trickle and the chest wound is closed.

As I watch, a warm, fuzzy blanket wraps around my shoulders, and I turn to thank someone. It is Zif, but he moves past me so quickly, racing toward the bleeding dragon, that I don't have a chance to say a word. I pull the blanket tightly around my shoulders, the warmth soaking in to my bones. Zif places several blankets on the dragon, and I watch, horrified, as the seeping blood immediately stains them red.

Yaren pays no attention but travels to the dragon's hind leg, uses a sharp blade and cuts into the flesh. He easily pulls out the arrow and stitches up the wound. Then he repeats the process with the other hind leg. Next, he moves to her neck. "Dis be de most danger." He seems to be talking to himself, as if he is in a trance. He delicately makes a cut into her neck, encases it with a bandage and pulls the arrow out with his hand. Blood gushes out, a red downpour. Yaren pushes hard on the wound, slowing the flow of blood, then begins stitching it up. Finally, he finishes, his small chest heaving in exhaustion.

"We be puttin' her on de groun' now. We be doin' it slow." Yaren is talking almost in a daze. The large men lay the dragon down slowly, and she rests on her side. Her belly moves up and down with each slow breath, her giant wings tucked neatly to her side. They cover her with more blankets and Yaren bandages her wounds.

He stands up then and shakes his hands, spraying droplets of blood against the already blood drenched earth. Then he strolls to the river, washes off his hands and body, splashing water over his bloody face, and returns to the sleeping Lav. Yaren checks on her again, and then ambles toward me. I tense at his expression, afraid I have done something wrong.

"You be brillant'... you be smart." He tells me quietly, grinning through an almost toothless mouth.

"Wh...what?" I ask between chattering teeth.

"You be landin' in de water. You be savin' de dragon's life. She be trustin' you good, girl, trustin' you good."

I nod my head, still shivering. It is quiet for a minute as Yaren turns his attention back to the sleeping dragon.

"What is her name?" I ask him.

He turns back toward me, his black eyes boring into me.

"Amethyst." He says her name slowly, as if it is actually three names. Am. E. Thist. Then, "We jus' be callin' her Ami."

Amethyst, I think, a purple gemstone…to go with a diamond. Nothing could be more perfect. I can't help asking another question, although I am afraid of the answer. "Who is she bonded with?"

Yaren smiles widely, toothlessly, his black eyes twinkling. "I be thinkin' she be yourn dragon now, girl. She be bondin' wit' you."

I slowly walk to the sleeping Lav and kneel down next to her, stroking her tucked in wings, joy spreading throughout my entire body. Two dragons. I am now bonded with two dragons. And one is a Lav. Unbelievable.

I memorize every feature of Ami – her deep purple scales, her small ears, her long tail and magnificent wings. I wonder if Diamond will like her. Probably not, I think.

I am tenderly petting her head when a voice thunders across the cool morning wind. Words that send chills up my spine and more fear in my heart than I ever thought possible.

"Teak…Teak…come quickly. Koree's been hit!"

Chapter 41

Thann's voice is a sharp edge slicing through my ears. He thunders toward me on Raven, stirring up dust and the worst fear that I can imagine. My heart hammers in my chest. Koree...hit. I can't fathom it. Tears burn in my eyes, and my throat is on fire as I race toward Thann as fast as I can, the soft blanket flying off of my shoulders. Time slows down, and it feels as if I am running through a lake, surely about to drown. Koree...hit. Koree...Koree...Koree. Not Koree, no...not Koree.

It feels like a year has passed when Thann pulls the Ebony to a stop, her hind end digging into the sandy earth next to me.

"What happened?" I sputter.

Thann looks down at me, terror frozen into his amber eyes. "It was Reese." He does a double take. "You're covered in blood...are you bleeding?"

"It is mostly dragon blood."

His voice is a haunted whisper. "Are you okay?"

"Yes. I took an arrow in my hand, but it will be fine." I feel air move in and out of my lungs, but I don't know how it is happening. I don't care about my hand – I would surely give it up to know that Koree is okay.

"How is Koree?" I stammer, the words spewing from my mouth. I am so afraid of the answer I can actually hear them float away, as if they were spinning tensely through a shattered glass tube.

"Took an arrow. Reese got him." Thann's words speak of finality.

"Where?"

"In the woods."

"No, where is he hit?" I am shaking, not from being drenched with water and blood in the chill of the morning but from pure dread in my stomach.

"In the shoulder."

I breathe a thousand lifetimes of relief. Thank the Angels – it isn't a lethal spot. "Is he bleeding a lot?"

Thann answers quickly. "What do you think? Of course he is."

I can't help but scream at him. "Did you take him to the healers?"

Thann doesn't answer right away and when he does, I can barely hear his voice. "No. And you know why." I don't need an explanation. The Rebellion. Of course.

Anger seethes through my entire body, the thought of Koree lying alone in the woods with an arrow in his shoulder, blood spilling out of him. I glare at Thann. "I am going to take him to a healer. Now." I turn away from him and take off running.

My feet are pounding the earth and I can only think of one thing – helping Koree – when I am literally tackled from behind, my face and body slamming ruthlessly into the sandy dirt. I twist my head to see who it is, but I already know. Of course, it is Thann, and his enormous body has me pinned tightly to the ground. Fury steams through me like a train out of control as I futilely struggle to break free from him.

I sharply…desperately…elbow him in his side, somehow forgetting all of my training. He doesn't even flinch. Then he grabs my arms and presses me fast to the ground. I am kicking at him now, furiously acting like a silly girl instead of a trained soldier. I can't seem to shake this monstrous brother from my back.

A firm voice interrupts our melee. "Thann!"

I stop kicking and twist my head around. It is Yaren.

"She said she was going to get a healer," Thann shouts, breathing heavily. He sounds like a little boy tattling on his sister.

"Be getting' a healer for who?" Yaren asks him.

"Koree. He took an arrow in his shoulder."

"De boy be needin' help. I help de boy." Yaren's usually lyrical voice is more of a monotone at the moment.

"NO!" I scream, kicking at Thann again.

"You're wasting time," Thann yells at me. "Yaren can help him. Stop fighting and let's go."

It takes me a few minutes to shift gears. Obviously, Thann isn't going to let me go until I agree. I feel helpless and angry, but thoughts of Koree lying hurt on the ground override everything else.

"Okay," I sputter. "Okay." I am breathing heavily.

"If you run again, I swear I'll tackle you," Thann seethes into my ear. He slowly lets go of my hands and lifts his mammoth body off of mine. I spit sand out of my mouth as I gingerly stand up, facing Thann square on.

"I won't run," I seethe. Then I swiftly stand up, pull my hand into a fist, and punch Thann squarely in the stomach. It barely fazes him.

"What was that for?" he groans, his golden eyes slashing through mine

"For tackling me." I am glaring back at him, my fists clenched into tight balls. It is all I can do to fight back the desire to hit him again.

"You be stoppin' dis fightin' now." Yaren scolds us again, his voice rising. "You be takin' me to de boy. I be takin' de arrow out."

"Yaren's right. Let's go," Thann spits at me, his golden eyes narrowed.

"Okay," I agree grudgingly. Thann grabs my arm and leads me to Raven. I stumble along, an unwilling prisoner. Yaren has already disappeared.

I mount the black dragon and Thann hops on in front of me. The dragon spins around so quickly I have to hold onto Thann's waist to keep from falling, which is the last thing I want to do.

Raven rockets forward and in a few minutes Yaren pulls up beside us on his small dragon.

I hang onto Thann as thoughts of an injured and hurting Koree shatter through my head and my heart.

More than anything right now, I wish I had the Power to make Koree all right.

At any cost.

Chapter 42

Thann lands Raven at the edge of the woods and leaps off of her in one swift movement. I instinctively follow Thann's lead, grasping his hand somewhat unwillingly. Yaren has somehow landed and is silently trailing behind us.

I am not as experienced as Thann at hurdling over logs and rocks. Leaves crumble under my feet and birds howl in protest at us. Frogs croak somewhere. Tree limbs snap at my face, but I can't seem to feel anything. My mind is focused on one thing – finding Koree. In a small clearing surrounded by trees, Thann slows down, dropping my hand. He runs ahead of me.

When I spot Koree lying on the ground, all alone with an arrow sticking out of his shoulder and blood pouring relentlessly onto the ground like a scarlet leaking fountain, my heart skips a beat. "Koree," I faintly mutter. I am glued to the earth, unable to move or think.

Yaren wastes no time and is immediately by Koree's side. He opens his bag and pulls out an assortment of large bottles. He mixes precise amounts in a bowl and then gently lifts Koree's head up.

"You be drinkin' dis now, boy. It be makin' you sleep."

I watch, a spectator, too afraid to move. But when Koree moans and thrives, it shakes me out of my trance. I sprint over to him and fall down next to him..

"Teak," he croaks, opening his eyes, groggily finding mine. He licks his dry lips.

I answer hoarsely. "You are going to be okay…it…it isn't in a lethal spot."

He swallows. "I know." He finds my eyes again. "It hurts. Bad.

"Oh, Koree," I stammer. "We need to get you to a healer."

"No healer," he slurs. Then he opens his faded green eyes wide. "You're covered in blood."

"I am fine," I answer in a low voice. "It is mostly dragon blood."

"Hmmmmm....magical."

I raise my eyebrows, confused at what he said. Magical? I turn toward Thann. "What is he talking about?"

"Some people think that dragon blood is magical. They'll even kill dragons for their blood."

"That's horrible," I cry out. *Killing a dragon for its blood?* I turn my attention back to Koree, putting the thought of killing dragons out of my mind.

Yaren digs in his bag and pulls out an odd knife, one like I have never seen before. The blade is thin and narrow with a small green handle. He pours something over it and immediately cuts into Koree's shoulder where the arrow is sticking out. I have seen Entho do this sort of thing many times and it never bothered me, but with Koree I look away, biting down hard on my cheek. Thann's giant hand tenderly squeezes my shoulder.

I pinch my eyes shut when Yaren announces that the arrow is removed from Koree's shoulder, a huge blast of air escaping my lips. I dare to look down at Koree now as Yaren methodically brings out

362

a needle and thick thread that almost looks like cord or twine and starts painstakingly sewing up the gaping hole in Koree's shoulder.

 The arrow lays by Koree's side, drenched in blood but definitely bearing the unmistakable carved stamp of Reese's family – the Blevins Buzzard.

Apparently I wasn't the only one who brought weapons to Dragon Academy.

Chapter 43

If I had any doubts about Reese's involvement before, they are gone now. I turn to Thann. "Where is Reese?" I ask him.

"Dead."

"You are sure?"

"I'm sure."

"You saw the body. His body?"

His face is pale, grave. "I saw the body. It was him." He clears his throat. "And I saw Flame's body, too."

"Flame's?"

"They must have been working together."

I feel a life time of tension fade from me like a rainbow after a storm. A violent storm. I think back to when we were children. Reese was once my friend. I should at least feel some remorse for that. But I don't. All I feel is an enormous reprieve. Ten years of torture has been enough for me. And Flame…I don't feel any remorse about her, either. From the moment I met her all she did was cause problems and strife in my life. Still, shouldn't I at least feel bad?

I cast my eyes down toward Koree. Yaren is sprinkling something a dried substance on the stitched wound.

"What is that?" I inquire, curious.

"Dried dragon blood. It be magical." I turn to Thann, raising my eyebrows. Entho would be having a fit over sprinkling dried dragon blood on a wound. Thann just nods his head, as if telling me everything is alright.

Just then Gulf and Shander silently creep up on us. They are carrying a makeshift stretcher – a blanket wrapped tightly around small logs. I wonder how they knew where we were – how they would know Koree would need transportation back to the tree houses.

"You be puttin' de boy on dere real easy," Yaren orders. He wipes his bloody hands on a rag. Koree's blood, I think, not just anybody's blood, but Koree's. I shiver as the men cautiously move Koree onto the stretcher. They lift it up easily, each man taking a side.

The men disappear with Koree and I am left with my jaw hanging open, all that has happened crashing over me like a brutal waterfall.

"I be tendin' to yourn hand." It is Yaren, shaking me out of my stupor. He reaches for my injured hand and unwraps the existing bandage. My hand is throbbing now, so deeply that I can feel my heartbeat pulsing though it.

"Dis be for de pain in yourn hand," he says, handing me the same bowl he used on Koree. I take the brew willingly and gulp it down. Yaren pours a solution over my hand. Then he sprinkles the same dried dragon blood over it before I even have time to balk. He bandages it tightly.

"You not be needin' de stitches," he tells me. "You jus' be changin' de band-age."

I nod my head. "How is Ami?" I ask him.

"She be jus' fine. De dragons be healin' fast."

I breathe out a sigh of relief. "Oh, good."

Yaren meticulously packs his supplies, stooping over his bag like the old man that we all know he is,

"We'll meet you at the tree house," Thann quietly instructs Yaren, his voice a throaty whisper.

Yaren simply nods his head as we turn away. We find Raven waiting patiently for us and we both hop on her back without saying a word. In what seems like no time at all we are at the tree houses.

I jump off of Raven and rapidly scale the tree house ladder, exhaling at the sight of Koree tucked cozily in bed, his russet curls dangling down onto his forehead. Gulf and Shander are standing over him. Thann's flaxen head appears, and suddenly it is very crowded. Diamond is squawking in his box, and I wonder how I could have forgotten about him. I pick him up and he leaps onto my shoulder, scolding me as he swishes his tail fiercely in my face.

"We'll be leaving now," Gulf mumbles, nodding his head. He is short and stocky and looks to be about thirty years old. His blue eyes are storms of worry and concern.

"Thanks, guys," Thann tells them. He pats each man on the back as they leave the tree house. I bring up a chair and prop myself next to Koree. Thann does the same. Diamond soars off of my shoulder and lands next to Koree, tilting his head. He lets out a squeal and settles down into a little ball by Koree's legs, as if he is watching over him. Entho would have a fit about a dragon in bed with one of his patients, too, I think. But, sadly, Entho isn't here, and I am not going to disturb Diamond or Koree.

Thann and I sit silently watching Koree's chest rise and fall. I take Koree's hand in mine. It is both rough and smooth, and I wonder how that can be as I lace my fingers through his.

Finally Thann speaks. "You love him, don't you?" he asks.

I don't hesitate, nodding my head. "Yes, I do."

Just then Koree stirs, opening his glazed green eyes. "I heard that," he slurs.

Chapter 44

The days pass and Koree seems to gain strength by the hour. Thann is in and out of the tree house, and we sometimes play Dragon Cards to pass the time. Yaren checks on Koree several times each day, but I am able to change his bandages and tend to his basic first aid needs. People are constantly visiting, and it seems like I rarely have a moment alone with Koree. Kesper comes almost every day.

She doesn't bother knocking on the door but just enters with a flourish that only she can possess. She is lemons and sugar and business all tied up in one. Her golden eyes move over Koree's prone body with a mother's concern and she tenderly strokes his cheek. He grins up at her foolishly, like a little boy. She never stays long, though, leaving in a flurry. But before she leaves, she always embraces me, holding me tightly to her – just like a real mother would.

After about two weeks, Koree is up and about, and his wound is healing nicely. Yaren has given me permission to take the bandage off of my hand, but it is still tender. I stretch it out as often as I can and move my pinky to exercise it.

Thann and I have taken over Koree's group and continue to train for the Rebellion. I have just arrived at our tree house, and it is dusk. Koree and I eat dinner as night sneaks up on us like a thief. For once we are alone, and Diamond is at my feet, chasing his tail and turning somersaults.

Koree is antsy, as if he has been caged up for years. "I'm going out of my mind," he tells me, his emerald eyes glistening. He is sitting in a chair, bouncing his leg up and down with nervous energy. "Let's go for a quick spin on the dragons."

"Your shoulder," I snip so quickly I even startle myself.

"Feels fine. I've gotta get out of here...do something."

I think about it for a minute. "Okay," I answer. "But do you promise to be careful?"

"I promise," he replies with a lopsided grin.

We slip out of the tree house like naughty children and gather Raven and Onyx. Diamond is balanced on my shoulder, swishing his tail and turning his head around in anticipation.

"Koree?" I ask.

"Hmmm?"

"Did you bring the straps to tie Diamond down?"

"No, just set him down in front of you. He can fly now if he has to."

"Really?" I ask. "He can fly?" I reach up and stroke Diamond, and he twists his head around, his blue eyes blazing into mine.

Koree laughs. "Look how big his wings are getting. It is natural for dragons to fly."

I pull Diamond down from my shoulder and inspect his wings, pulling one out from his side. Koree is right. They are growing. "Okay," I agree grumpily.

We mount the dragons, and I set Diamond down in front of me. He nestles between my legs, twisting his head around, a general in charge of his ranks. Koree takes off on Onyx and Raven soars

upward gracefully, the dark sky rushing by me in a blur.

I spin around until I am beside Koree. "Are you okay?" I shout

across to him.

"Yeah," he roars back. "Never better!"

We fly the dragons in gigantic circles, soaring through the darkness

and looping around Harcourt, the tree houses, even the stream.

Koree speeds ahead of me, and I wildly chase after him. The wind

blasts over me, under me, and what feels like through me. Diamond

lets out a squeal of joy. I catch up to Koree, turn my head toward

him, and rocket forward. Now he is chasing me. We go back and

forth like this several times until Koree slows Onyx down. I circle

around him.

"We better land," Koree sensibly shouts. I am disappointed, feeling

like I was just let out of prison and could ride all night long.

"Yes," I agree, my voice smoking away on the wind.

We land the dragons in the field behind the tree houses. Koree leaps off of Onyx and strides over to me. Diamond leaps onto my shoulder from his place on the bigger dragon.

Koree's face is a backdrop against the dark sky. "Thanks. I needed that," he throatily tells me as I dismount Raven and we put the Ebonies in their corral.

"No problem," I answer. I bite my lip, thinking. "I want to see Ami."

"Sure," he answers as he wraps his good arm around my shoulder. We walk for a while, the swishing of Diamond's tail the only conversation between us. When we reach the Lav pen Ami lithely steps toward me and snuggles her enormous head against my chest. I pet her lovingly. Then Ami slowly moves from me to Diamond, her nostrils flaring.

I turn to Koree, "Is she..." But I stop when he motions me to be quiet. Ami gently noses Diamond, and I wait for him to protest, but he leans in close to her, and they gently touch noses with each other. Then Ami does an odd thing. Her forked tongue leaps out of her mouth, and she begins to lick Diamond, like a mother cat cleaning her kittens.

"Ami is acting like a mother dragon to Diamond," Koree whispers. "That is odd."

"What do you mean?"

"Usually a dragon won't have anything to do with another mother's dragonling. It is taboo for them."

"Why is she doing it?" I ask as Ami continues to lick Diamond.

"I don't know." Koree's brow is wrinkled and he seems to be thinking. I wait for a response, curious.

"It must be you," he finally says.

"Me?"

"They have both bonded with you. They must be bonding with each other."

Just then Diamond's little tongue pokes out, and he licks Ami's cheek. She placidly closes her eyelids, seemingly content to let him do it. Ami's tongue scrapes the side of my left cheek and Diamond's little tongue tickles my right cheek. I can't help but reach out and touch Ami's neck, stroking her as both dragons continue to lick me.

I never want this moment to end as a ball of warm, loving fire fills my chest.

Chapter 45

Morning arrives too soon, the orange light spilling through the cracks of the tree house. I stretch and rise up out of bed, then shimmy down the rope ladder on my way to the cleaning room. Diamond follows closely behind me, and sometimes he actually catches air. I laugh at him as I open the door. Three other women are cleaning up, and they bristle at the sight of Diamond following me into the room.

"He won't bother you," I tell them.

"He belongs in a pen with the others," a woman with platinum blonde hair and green eyes tells me. She is beautiful, but she contorts her face in such a way that she suddenly appears to be ugly.

"He is my dragonling. I have raised him since he hatched. He belongs with me." I respond with finality. Diamond is not going in a pen.

The woman glares at me but turns away. I rush to the very back of the room and quickly clean up. Diamond perches at the side of the tub I am in, his blue eyes watching me intently. When I finish, I put on a clean tunic and pants. Diamond leaps onto my shoulder, and we walk back to the tree house.

Koree is awake by now. "I'm starving, how about you?"

"I guess so," I mutter grumpily.

"What's the matter?"

"This woman…she told me Diamond belongs in a pen."

Koree laughs out loud. "He can be with you as long as he behaves. It's not her business."

I let out a sigh of relief as Koree wraps his long arms around me. Diamond jumps up on my shoulder and licks Koree's cheek and then mine. Back and forth his raspy little tongue laps at us. We both bust up laughing at him.

"Is he trying to include you in our bond?" I ask Koree.

"Perhaps…" he answers mysteriously. "Maybe he learned it from Ami. I have never seen a dragonling lick people. It's kinda weird."

"Well, he is a special dragonling," I respond proudly.

"That he is," Koree answers, his green eyes falling on the small white dragon. Koree's eyes shift to meet mine. "Are you ready for breakfast?"

"That I am," I answer, smiling at Koree.

We stroll hand in hand toward the Linden's camp with Diamond following close behind. Thann is already there, shoveling food into his mouth like he can't get enough of it. We take plates from Mrs. Linden, thank her and sit down next to Thann.

"You might want to save some food for the rest of us," Koree snips at him.

"Growing boy…you know."

"If you grow any more, you'll be a giant, and we'll have to exile you to the woods," Koree quips.

"Might not be bad…maybe there'll be some large women for me." Thann takes another huge bite of eggs.

Koree stiffens, then, his eyes blazing into Thann's. His voice turns to a whisper. "We need to get going…the orphanage."

"You read my mind, sleeping beauty." Thann stops eating for a moment. "I hope you're rested enough."

"I think I'll make it." Koree flashes a grin at Thann.

"You give him an okay to fly, doc?"

"Doc?" I question, raising my eyebrows. I have never heard that term before.

"It's what they used to call healers…short for doctors."

"I am no healer. I have told you that. Maybe a million times."

"Looks like you healed this hammer head. And a few others." He points to Koree.

"Yaren really healed him, but okay," I laugh. "Yes, this hammer head is fine to fly."

"Then this is the plan," Thann's voice changes…deep and serious. "We've lost a lot of time. We'll train for a few days, and if you're ready we'll go."

"I'll be ready," Koree answers.

I know what they are talking about and fear rushes through my body.

I had forgotten about their plan to rescue the children from the

orphanage. Winter, I think. I had forgotten about Winter.

I bite the side of my cheek as I move my eyes from Koree to Thann.

But I say nothing.

Chapter 46

It is the last day of training with our groups before Koree and Thann leave. I race to the Lav pen and Ami thunders toward me. I open the gate and she leaps out at me. I pat her head and she strokes my face. I jump on her back and find my group. I don't need to say anything to them. By now they know the drill.

With barely a sound, each member of my group soars into the cloudless sable sky, a train of lavender dragons lined up nose to tail, giant pairs of wings spread wide and tails swishing against the thick night air. I wait my turn, the last member of the dragon train, and tentatively nudge Ami to take off. We hit the air immediately and soar into the chilly night sky, the quarter moon teasing us with a sliver of light.

I grip Ami's neck, her thick scales scratching against my hands, the cool wind splashing against my face like a gentle rainstorm. Just then, Ami leans her enormous body to the side, and as she docs so, a voice muffles across the sky. It is definitely a female.

"You are a warrior." She speaks like me, as if she has been trained in Weapons for years. But it is an adult voice, of that I am sure. I twist my head all around me, searching for the owner of the voice. Is it one of my students? Then I realize that it can't be…they are all male. Did I just imagine the voice?

"Who are you?" I ask, my teeth suddenly chattering. I look all around me again.

She giggles in reply, almost girl-like. "It is me…Ami."

"Ami," I ask, dumbfounded. I don't know if I say it out loud or just in my mind.

"Yes."

It takes me a while to respond. "How…how are you talking to me?" For some reason I am not afraid any more.

"It is in our minds. We are bonded."

"What!" I shriek. I let go of her neck and pull my body straight up. I wobble, and for a minute I think I might fall off of her, but she adjusts her weight against mine. It is as if glue is holding me to her.

"How…how?" I sputter.

"It just happens…especially when our blood has blended." She giggles again. I suppose it is just in my brain, but it sounds so real that I turn my head all around me again, searching for a face to go with the voice.

Realizing that nobody is there, I answer her. "Oh, Ami," I breathe out. "This is the most wonderful thing in the world."

"It is," she answers. For a while we just fly, an easiness between us, like when I am with Koree or Thann. Then a streak of jealousy runs through me, as if I were watching Koree kiss another girl.

"Ami," I shout.

"What?"

"Are there…others? Do you talk to other people?"

"Just you."

"Oh. Good."

Holding onto Ami's neck and speeding through the thick night air, I feel more free and alive than ever. We are bonded…and we can talk to each other.

I throw my fist up in the air and let out a hoot of absolute delight.

Chapter 47

My students swoop down and make shots at the targets, most of them making their mark. I take a turn, ask Ami to take me close to the ground, reach for an arrow and nock it, pull back my string, aim, and let go. I squeeze my legs out of habit, but Ami is already bulleting upward, and a thrill of confidence fires through me when I glance over my shoulder to see I have made a bull's eye. I shake my fist into the air again as the cool wind kisses my cheeks.

When night fades away from us, the Lavs begin to land in the training field. I want to stay in the sky and talk with Ami forever, but memories of the last time I stayed out too long haunt me. Ami lands on the field, and I don't even feel a jolt, tucking in her enormous wings as we follow the others toward the Lav pens. When we get close, I hop off of her back. As we approach the Lav pen she stops and turns to me. She closes her eyelids contentedly, and it almost appears like she is smiling.

"Good-night, young warrior."

"Warrior?" I ask. "Why do you keep calling me that?"

"You have a warrior's heart."

"I am not a warrior. And besides, how would you know?" I can't believe I am arguing with a dragon.

"I just know."

I want to pressure her, push her into telling me how she could know something like this. I hated Weapons – despised the training. I know my heart, and it is anything but a warrior's. Instead, I simply agree with her.

"Okay," I tell her. "I trust you. Good-night." I stroke her long neck lovingly. She lumbers back into the pen, and I suddenly miss her.

"Warrior?"

I answer without thinking. "Yes?"

"I love you."

Once again, I reply without thought or fear or reserve.

"I love you, too."

Ami settles contentedly into the pen, snuggling up beside another Lav, somewhat bigger than her. I wonder if they are mated.

I race to the tree house, scale the rope ladder, and burst into the room. Koree is awake, sitting in a chair and reading a book, Diamond fast asleep on his lap. I don't even stop to ask him about the book – what it is and where he got it.

"She talked to me," I blurt out.

"Who?" He has a puzzled look on his face. Diamond lifts his head and tilts it to the side, yawning.

"Ami! Ami talked to me, and I talked back. We communicated in our minds."

Koree's lips curl up, a bit of a smirk on his face. "It happens," he says nonchalantly.

"With everybody?" I pull up a chair beside him and reach for Diamond.

He takes a while to answer. "No. Only those with Power."

"What? I have no Power. Everybody knows that."

"Apparently you do."

"Me. Power?" It is unthinkable.

Koree pulls me onto his lap and kisses me gently, his lips soft and sweet. 'Yes, you," he tells me, taking a long strand of my hair and tucking it behind my left ear. He seems to be examining my Mark of Power.

"It is just a tattoo. You know that."

"No. It is more." His lips curve up.

"But."

"Sssshhhh." He kisses me again, and I am dizzy with Koree and Ami and what feels like real Power flowing through my veins for the first time in my life.

Chapter 48

The next two days pass this way. Whenever I fly on Ami we have conversations, and I get to know who she is. Sometimes I take Diamond with me. I wonder if I will ever be able to talk to Diamond. Koree can talk to several dragons, but he warned me that most people can't do this., and with each outing I gain more confidence.

Koree and I are eating alone in our tree house when a familiar flaxen head pops up. Thann.

"Don't you know how to knock?" Koree quips between bites of food.

"Nope," Thann closes the door. "Hey, little sis, how goes it?" He grabs a piece of bread and chews it, deep in thought.

"*Little* sis?" I counter. "We're twins."

"Yeah, well I asked Mom, and she said I was born first, so that makes me older and you the little sis. Get used to it. Besides, I'm taller."

I laugh at him and he turns to Koree, his pale golden eyes serious. "Are you ready to go get those kids?"

Koree nods his head.

"From the mountain to the moon?" Koree asks.

"Yep," Thann answers, fixing his eyes on Thann while grinning crookedly.

"What is that all about?" I butt in. They both stop and stare at me, as if I have intruded on their private world. Diamond stops chasing his tail at that very moment and stares back and forth between the two of them with curious, indigo eyes.

Koree links his eyes to Thann's, and for a minute they just stare at each other. Finally, Koree speaks. "Should we tell her?"

"Well, she is my sister. Why not?"

"Okay," Koree agrees. He rolls his eyes up, as if he is trying to remember something, then reaches for my hand, lacing his long fingers with mine. His voice is deep and serious. "When Thann and I were about ten years old..." he begins, "...we begged Kesper for a tree house. She had one built for us in the orchard. Whenever we could, we would sneak away and hide out there, which is really here – this very tree house."

Thann joins in. "Yeah, it was right when all of the dragons' wings had to be clipped 'cause of the new law. They sent men out to check, to make sure all of our dragons had clipped wings, but Koree and I wanted to keep flying, so we snuck Onyx and Raven out here to the tree house, built a pen for them and kept them hidden. We didn't know then that Mom had tricked the men who came and had all our dragons' wings clipped incorrectly…so it wouldn't interfere with their flying."

"We took Onyx and Raven," because they're black and we could fly them at night without being seen," Koree adds. "We'd sneak out at night or tell Kesper we were sleeping in the tree house, and we'd get the dragons, walk them up to that hill." Koree points to a hill behind the tree house. I can't see it through the thick tree house walls, but I know which one he is talking about. "We thought it was a mountain back then, remember?"

Thann laughs. "Yeah, we were pretty little. It's no more than a hill. Anyway, we'd take Onyx and Raven up to the top of that hill and we'd yell, 'From the mountain to the moon!' as loud as we could. And we'd take off flying on the dragons." Thann pauses for a moment, his giant foot tapping on the wooden floor. "Then we added our secret handshake, which is kind of disgusting now that I know Koree has been kissing on you. Yuck, my sister's spit on my hand." Thann scrunches his face up, exaggerating his disgust.

Koree and I laugh. "So, whenever we start an adventure, that's what we yell – from the mountain, to the moon."

"I like it," I say, imagining what they both must have looked like as little boys, wishing I could have been involved in their adventures.

Koree's eyes turn serious as he makes eye contact with Thann. "We leave tonight?"

Thann nods his head. "That's the plan. And I've been thinking," Thann's eyes match Koree's with seriousness now. "I've been listening to Mom, and things are rough in the city. I think we'd better take Teak. She knows the city better than we do, and she knows the kids. She's better with weapons, too. It's our best shot."

Koree turns from Thann and stares at the wall of the tree house – at nothing for the longest time. Silence enfolds us like a vicious captor. His eyebrows furrow and he clamps down on his jaw, grinding his teeth. Eventually he nods his head, so slowly it can barely be seen.

"Okay," he mutters, his voice gravelly and deep. "But I'm not happy about it."

"Are you in?" Thann asks me.

"I am in….from the mountain to the moon," I answer.

Then, without discussion we all three spit on our hands, hold them palm up, and place them one on top of the other. First Koree's, then mine, and Thann's on top, a sandwich of spitty palms… mine in the middle.

Chapter 49

Koree has left to gather some supplies, and I am still reeling from my involvement with the mission. Winter's face swims before my eyes. Winter...we will be bringing Winter here. She will be loved and safe.

Thann is working on something at the table. I am not sure what it is, but his head is bent over and his tongue is sticking out of the corner of his mouth. I stare at Thann for the longest time, imagining what it would be like to grow up with him. Thann says something, but I don't even hear him, his voice humming in the background along with the flickering candle.

"Hey."

Thann's voice pulls me out of my thoughts, just like when we were in the tunnels.

"What?" I search for his golden eyes.

"You okay?"

"Yes." I sigh deeply. "I have been meaning to ask you something."

"What?" The candlelight flickers, forming a perfect shadow of Thann on the wall. By now he is tipping back on a chair, his long legs stretched before him.

I stare at Thann, trying to imagine him as a boy, viscerally missing the brother I should have had as a child. Desolation runs through me like a swiftly running river I am about to drown in. "Do you ever, you know, think about what it would be like to grow up together?"

He throws his head back and laughs, like a lion roaring. "Yes, every day, every moment. I wanted a brother or a sister more than anything."

"Well, you had Koree. I didn't have any sibs."

"I guess." Thann pauses, his broad chest heaving. He narrows his eyes, and the light seems to disappear from the tiny tree house. He sighs deeply. "Koree was in rough shape when he came. It took a couple years...for him to...for us to be okay."

"What do you mean, rough shape?"

Thann's amber eyes remain somber as his voice lowers. "I hated him at first."

"You hated Koree?" It seems hard to believe.

"Yeah, my mom….our mom gave him a lot of attention. I guess he needed it after all that happened. But I was jealous of all the attention she gave him."

"He told me...about his parents. And Siv Gareth."

Thann is quiet, pensive and his words come out a soft whisper. "He didn't talk."

I am confused. "Who didn't talk?"

"Koree. He didn't talk for over a year. Not a word."

"Koree?" I am flabbergasted. "He didn't talk?"

"Yep. You should have seen him. His eyes were empty. He walked around, did his chores, ate…but he wouldn't talk to anyone." Thann sighs deeply. "And I wanted a brother…or a sister…I didn't care. I wanted a playmate. It was lonely here. There were no kids to play with, and Mom kept me under a tight reign. She's a bit overprotective."

"I know that feeling all too well. So what happened…he obviously talks now."

Thann's golden eyes lock onto mine. "Koree's Power is really strong. Especially with the dragons."

"Is that why he has so many dragon pins?"

"Partly, but he has some real Power. He just reins it in most of the time."

"How do you know?"

"We're brothers now, we have no secrets." Thann stands up, stretches, grabs an apple and takes a bite out of it, chews slowly, thoughtfully. He leans casually against the table and continues with his story.

"One day he was doing chores and he was in a dragon pen. He had been with us for over a year. He found a hatchling…a Crimson, smashed up against a rock. Someone or something had deliberately tried to kill her, had sliced her throat. He picked her up and came running toward the barn…she was bleeding everywhere. I was in the barn…farting around instead of doing chores, so I was the only one around. I was furious with him for hurting the hatchling." Thann stops for a minute, his eyes half closed.

"I yelled at him. I accused him of hurting the hatchling."

"Poor Koree," I breathe out.

Thann bristles. "Yeah, well, he doesn't want your pity, that's for sure."

"I know. I just feel real bad for all he has been through. So, what happened to the little hatchling?"

"Koree laid the hatchling down on the ground, and I was sure she was dead. Blood was pouring out of her neck." He breathes in deeply like it hurts to draw air into his lungs. "She was really small…too small to have hatched. She didn't stand a chance."

I can't help myself, interrupting Thann. "Did the hatchling live?"

Thann nods his head and continues. "Koree held his hands over her, and I swear to this day I could see the Power go out of his hands and right into the little hatchling. After a few minutes the blood just stopped…she quit bleeding. I had never seen anything like it."

"Oh," I gasp, trying to picture Koree and Thann as little boys.

"The hatchling didn't move for the longest time. Koree kept petting her and after a while she was breathing normally and just stood up."

"Wow," I exhale.

"I couldn't hate him after that," Thann concludes.

"Is the dragonling still alive?"

Thann smiles, his lips spreading apart into a wide grin. "Yeah, you've ridden her a lot…Pebble."

"Pebble?" I ask, astonished. I remember asking Koree about her name…how touchy he was about it.

"It was the first word he spoke. He looked me in the eye and just said, 'Pebble'."

"Pebble," I whisper, back to Thann, like it is a holy name. "That explains the huge scar on her neck." I bite my lower lip, thinking, Thann's breathing matching my own.

I wait a while before asking the question that is burning in my mind. I am not sure if I should, but I can't resist. "Can they talk to each other?"

Thann's head snaps up and his eyes narrow. "What do you know about that?"

"Ami and I…we…talk to each other."

Thann straightens his body, almost jumping up. "No snocking way."

I am suddenly embarrassed. I nod my head and then stare at the ground.

"Do you know there are only a few people in the world who can do that?"

I slowly lift my head up. "No," I answer. Every day I am brutally aware of all that I don't know about dragons. Another thought pops into my head. "Can you?" I ask Thann, curiosity overriding all else.

Thann lets out a deep breath, shaking his head slightly. "No."

"Oh." Thann is unusually quiet. Then I realize he didn't answer my question. "So, can Koree and Pebble talk to each other?"

It takes a while for Thann to answer. "Yes. With Pebble and almost every dragon he comes into contact with."

Chapter 50

The day passes slowly, like wading through heavy water. Koree,

Thann, and I meet, spending most of the day firming up plans. We

have agree to leave Diamond with the Linden boys while we are

gone. It would be too dangerous to take him. I pull him off of my

shoulder and snuggle him tightly to my chest, like I did when he was

just born. I wonder if I we will be able to talk to each other one day.

After lunch, Thann leaves, and Koree is somber, quiet, reminding me

of when I first met him. He is sitting at the table fiddling with a

small dragon figurine. It is carved from purple stone, probably

amethyst, and it looks exactly like a miniature Lav.

"Are you scared?" I ask, sitting down next to him. Diamond curls

up in my lap.

"I'd be stupid not to be," he answers.

"We don't have to do this. There will be other times."

He jerks his head up, finding my eyes with his own – tortured

emeralds that are bursting with fire. "No, we have to. I keep thinking of those kids. What you said. I got lucky when Kesper took me in. They have nobody."

"I know. Every day I think of Winter. And Entho. Do you think he is alive?

"I have a feeling he is," Koree confidently replies.

I relax, his words comforting me. "Koree?"

"Hmmm?" He raises an eyebrow.

"Thann said you had a lot of Power."

"The rat," Koree answers, but he is smiling as he turns his attention back to the figurine.

"Did you always have it? Were you born with a gift or something?"

"No." Koree turns his soulful eyes away from the tiny dragon toward mine. He breathes deeply, sucking in the stagnant air. "When I first came here, I was so deep inside myself, from all the pain and anger, it just slowly developed…as a way to cope, I guess." He breathes in and out again, and I feel the wind of his breath on my face.

"I did horrible things at first."

"You?" I am shocked, the thought of Koree doing something horrible is unfathomable to me. "Like what?"

Koree hangs his head, his voice so low I can barely hear it. "I would smash the eggs…with my Power." He stops there, and I think that is all he is going to reveal, but he continues. "I would find a dragon egg out in one of the pens, before anyone else could take it to the Incubation Room, and I would lift it up and hurl it against something… with my Power. Somehow it made me feel better to watch the egg crack, to see the yolk dripping down. I was so full of hate. Until this one day I smashed a hatchling. It was Pebble."

He stops talking, and almost chokes, his throat constricting, his body tense. "I watched her tiny body smash against a rock, and I realized I did it." He lifts his head and turns toward me. "She cut her throat on the sharp rock. It was so clean that it looked like someone had slit it on purpose. Seeing what I did to her… I flashed back to my mom, to watching her head…"

"Shhh." I stop him, running my hand up and down his back, the need to comfort him strong. "You were just a child."

"It doesn't make it right." His voice is raw. "I realized I was no different than the Destroyers who killed my parents. I stood over Pebble, shocked and disgusted with myself. At what I had done. And then Thann came and accused me of doing it... of killing her."

"I was watching Pebble die, knowing it was my fault, that I did it to her. So I turned my Power around, focused on loving her like I loved my parents. I just really focused on healing her wound. And it worked." Koree wipes his brow with the back of his hand, as if he had just done a full day of chores.

"I've never done anything like that again. I'd rather die than hurt a dragon."

I think of what Thann told me, how he made me think that Koree didn't harm Pebble, how it was someone else. "Does Thann know you hurt Pebble?"

"Yeah, I told him. Later when we were older." I nod my head, thinking of Thann – how protective he is of Koree. It all fits together now.

"Well, Pebble lived, and you learned. Don't beat yourself up about it."

"Easy for you to say," he tells me, but I see a hint of a smile and he pulls me into his lap, kissing me – slow, tender kisses that make me tingle everywhere. He runs his hands up my back, sending every nerve ending I have on edge.

Koree leans back, then, his eyes searching mine.

"What," I ask him. "What is the matter?

"Stay here tonight. Let Thann and me do this alone."

"Not an option."

"I know."

Just then Thann's golden head appears. He is toting a large black bag and plops it on the floor of the tree house. He promptly reaches into it and pulls out a stack of thick lavender colored paper and a bottle of ink. "Who has the best handwriting?" he asks. Without discussion, Koree and Thann both look at me.

"Okay, okay. What do you want done?" I can't help but smile at Thann.

"Papers…orders from Lord Gareth himself." He shoves a different piece of paper at me. "Here, it's an official order I snagged from Mom's office. It's from our *brilliant* leader. I thought we could copy it, make it official for when we get those kids tonight."

"Okay," I say tentatively.

"Just do your best. Koree and I are going to go get some more things ready."

"Sure," I answer, but then a thought creeps into my mind. "Hey Thann, Koree? Did Kesper agree to this?"

Both boys look at each other and guilt is written all over their faces. "Oh no…" I begin.

"What she doesn't know won't hurt her," Thann tells me, busting up.

"I'll handle it when we get back. She never gets mad at me," Koree adds.

Thann continues, his voice exaggerated. "Because he's nothing but a big suck up, that's why."

They banter back and forth for a while as if this is nothing but a big game for them. I glare at both of them, which only makes them laugh harder.

"We gotta go. See ya, sis," Thann smirks and kisses me on top of my head. He is out of the tree house in an instant. Koree enfolds me in his arms and kisses me quite differently. I never want the kiss to end, cling to it and to Koree a little too tightly. His lips stop moving and we both open our eyes.

"Later?" he whispers as his eyes burn into mine, two sparkling green fires.

"Later," I breathe out, licking my swollen lips, the taste of Koree lingering on them.

Koree disappears behind Thann, conversation flowing between them easily, the ghost of their voices wafting up at me, an early afternoon gift.

When it is finally quiet, I set to work creating the false document. It takes me several hours. I keep making mistakes, crumpling up papers and starting over. I finally finish and am pleased with the outcome. The document is a direct order from Siv Gareth requesting that the children be moved from the Bay City Orphanage to the West End Orphanage. I made up the name of the other orphanage, delighted at how official it sounds.

Just when I finish, Thann and Koree return with a flourish. I hold out the document for them to inspect, hoping it meets their approval.

Thann whistles. "Not bad."

I furrow my eyebrows. "It needs an official seal," I tell him.

"Got it covered." He pulls out a stamp, squeezes it on the document, and a seal forms on the thick lavender paper.

"Where did you get that?"

"Had one of our blacksmiths here at the tree houses make it. I pilfered what he needed from the stores."

"Wow, you are good."

"That's right, little sister."

"Oh, please," Koree butts in, rolling his eyes slightly.

Thann is all business, though, so much like Kesper at a meeting that I can't help but smile. He reaches into his bag and pulls out some amber bottles.

"Okay, little sis, it's time to become dark." My jaw drops. I had completely forgotten about this part of the mission, how somewhere else in the world people with Light Skin are being slaughtered by Destroyers. If there are even any Light Skinned people left.

"I'll help," Koree offers. He takes a soft white cloth from the bag, turns one of the bottles over and dabs it on the cloth. Gently, he takes my arm in his hand and starts rubbing the liquid on.

"Yikes, that stings!" I let out, a natural reaction. Instantly he pulls the cloth away.

Koree turns to Thann. "You didn't tell me it stings…I don't want to hurt her."

"Aw, buck up Princess, it quits stinging in a minute." Thann has a cloth in his hand and is already rubbing the mixture on his arms without complaint. "It beats the alternative. Like getting your head chopped off.

"He is right. I can take it," I answer with determination as a burning sensation travels up my arm.

"You sure?" Koree's green eyes bore into mine.

"Yes. I can take it. If you don't want to do it, I will."

"Okay." Koree pauses then tenderly dabs the stain on my arms. Next, he moves to my face. He is taking his time, as if he is painting a picture, his head tilted to the side and his tongue sticking out of the corner of his mouth. Thann is already finished and has dyed his blonde hair a deep brown. I am shocked at how real it appears.

Thann's now dark body shadows over us. "This is going to take forever, lover boy," he complains. "We haven't even gotten to that mess of hair."

He grabs a bottle from his bag and sets to work on my hair. I remember the mud we piled in our hair on our way to Harcourt after just finding out about the Purity Law. This concoction can't be any worse than that.

Thann and Koree finish at about the same time. My long hair is wet and slimy. It smells terrible, like onions and vinegar. I can't help but gag.

"What a light weight," Thann jokes.

"We will see about that," I quip back. He laughs again, as if this is all just a childhood adventure.

Koree finds a mirror and hands it to me. I have never liked looking in the mirror, and I am especially afraid now of what I might see. When I stare at my reflection I barely recognize who I see. The girl staring back at me has my eyes and nose and face.

But this girl is definitely *not* a Ghost. She is dark and she is beautiful.

Teak the Freak has disappeared.

Chapter 51

Koree nudges me, and I wake to thick, black darkness, startled and confused. He takes me by the shoulders, gently wrapping me into his arms and kisses me. My heart beats quickly, and I greedily kiss him back. "This is it," he murmurs. I place my hands on his cheeks, feel the bit of stubble on his firm jaw, and I kiss him back again and again, knowing I might not get the chance for a while. He holds me for what seems like too short of a time. "Not too late to back out," he whispers into my ear.

"I know. But I am going."

"You sure? Thann and I can handle it."

"I am going. And that is final."

"Okay," he whispers, but I notice he is clenching his jaw.

"Do I still stink?" I ask him.

"Mmmm…maybe just a little." He wrinkles his nose, and then we both laugh and it breaks the tension, if only for a moment.

I step into the red soldier's uniform in the silence of the night. Koree does the same and then gathers what he needs for our journey to Bay City. A lump forms in my throat thinking about my home in Bay City – does anyone live there now, or is it empty? And Entho…is he even alive? Koree's voice interrupts my thoughts.

"I'm going to strap this to your leg." Koree is holding a dagger with a red handle, like those that the Destroyers use. He hands me some twine and I hold it while he ties the small knife to my calf. He reaches for another knife, just like the first and ties it to my other leg. I pull my tall boots over the calves of my legs and over the knives. At first they are uncomfortable when I move, but after a few minutes I forget they are even there.

Koree's eyes are serious, his voice matching them. "Use these if you have to."

"Did you and Thann do the same?"

"Of course." He pauses for a moment, looking directly in my eyes. "It's go time."

"Okay," I answer, as a disturbing feeling settles in the center of my chest. I shake it off as we grab our quivers of arrows and our bows, along with several spears.

We slip down the ladder and without talking thread our way to the Lav pen. Crickets chirp in the still night as our feet crunch on the crisp ground. Occasionally a dragon snorts. I think of what we are about to do, and my stomach creeps up into my throat. I swallow over and over. Koree must sense my discomfort and squeezes my hand.

He stops suddenly, the Lav pen not too far away. "It will all be okay. I promise," he whispers.

I don't respond but gaze into his eyes, pale green in the darkness. For just a moment the world is only Koree and me. But it ends too soon. His hand still enfolding mine, he leads the way to the Lav pen. Two quiet soldiers on a secret mission.

Thann is waiting there for us, dressed in his red soldier uniform. The night is still and cool with no breeze. The tree house settlement is tucked in for the night, unaware of our actions. I want to run to the

Linden's camp and wake Diamond up, tell him good-bye again. But I know I can't.

I follow Koree and Thann into the Lav pen and search for Ami. She immediately rumbles up to me, nestling her long head against my shoulder.

"Are you ready?" she asks me.

"I guess so."

"Remember, Warrior, I will be there. I will take care of you."

"I know." Hearing Ami's voice, I relax a bit as she follows me out of the gate.

Koree and Thann each halter a Lav and join me. Then together, we catch and halter eight more Lavs, bring them out of the pen and settle them beside the other three Lavs. Silently, we hook the eight Lavs together with ropes.

Koree and Thann place packs on some of the dragons. "Supplies," Koree tells me before I even get the chance to ask. He expertly ties our weapons to the dragons as well, except our bows and arrows, and some spears, which we are to keep with us. I am shocked when I discover three long swords with red handles strapped to one of the Lavs. Koree and Thann have been busier than I thought.

We lead the long row of purple dragons to the top of the hill. I am slightly out of breath by the time we reach the top. I look all around, thinking of Thann and Koree sneaking the Ebonies out when they were children, and my lips curve up at the thought. There are a few stars out but no sight of the moon. I pull the cool air into my lungs and wait for Koree and Thann. They arrive behind me with the Lavs, lined up in a straight row.

Thann begins. "Okay, if something goes wrong, anything, we take to the skies. It's our best bet."

Koree and I nod. "We need a signal," Koree adds. One all of us knows, in case we can't see each other."

"How about saying 'to the moon'," I offer, thinking about their childhood chant.

Thann answers first. "Sure, that's good. So if there's any problem, anything, one of us yells, 'to the moon', we hit the skies." His voice is deep and serious, almost ominous.

"Okay, when we get there, to the orphanage, who should do the talking?" Koree asks.

"I will. I'm the charmer of the bunch." Thann's dark face has disappeared into the black night, but his voice still belongs to him. "And we'll leave Teak out with the dragons, in case one of those kids recognizes her. You and I will go in, get the kids, load them up and walk them out until it's safe enough to fly."

"Perfect," Koree agrees. I nod my head, a little disappointed at my duty but understanding where Thann is coming from. I doubt if one of the children would recognize me with dark skin, but still if one of them did, it would ruin everything. Many of the children from the orphanage came to Entho's clinic while I worked there.

"And on the way home – with the children – what if something goes wrong then?" I ask.

"One of us needs to be in charge of getting those kids back safely." Koree scratches the back of his head, deep in thought. "Thann, you're the strongest, but I'm the best rider and Teak's best with weapons, what do you think?"

Thann doesn't wait to respond. "If something happens, you two cover me. I'll take the kids back."

Koree and I both agree. It is a logical decision.

For just a moment the three of us stand in a small circle and Thann's enormous arms reach around both of us. I breathe in the awful smell of the stain and the essence of my brother and my boyfriend. Then, without saying a word to each other we all spit into the palms of our hands. "From the mountain to the moon!" we yell at once, and I place my palm on Koree's. Thann's lands on top mine

When we pull our hands apart, Koree reaches for me, kisses me one last time, his lips meeting mine while he gently cradles the back of my head with his hands. For one last moment, I melt into him, his lips and touch all that I want or need for the moment.

"Come on you two, we have a mission. Holy snock!"

Koree moves his lips to my ear and whispers one word into it.
"Later."

"Later," I breathe out.

Koree turns his eyes away from mine and starts walking, grasping my hand in his. I move with him, Ami right behind me. "Hey, did you know about Thann and Persia?" I squeeze his hand, wishing I would never have to let it go.

"What about them?"

"Thann...he has a girlfriend. It's about time."

"Persia?" I ask. For some reason I can't picture Thann and Persia together in any other manner than training dragons and cadets.

"Yep, Persia alright." Koree reaches over and sneaks a quick kiss onto my cheek.

Thann's voice is animated. "You should talk. At least *I've* had other girlfriends before."

"I was waiting for the best," Koree answers, and I can't help but smile, a warm glowing feeling settling in my chest. Six months ago I would never have believed any of this could happen to me.

Koree and Thann banter back and forth, and I savor it like a last sip of wine. My brother. My boyfriend.

Then, on a clear black night with the two people I love most, we take off on a mission to bring back children who nobody loves or cares about. On three huge, illegal Lavs and eight others lined up behind us. We rise easily into the black sky and soar away from the safety of Harcourt toward Bay City.

First Thann.

Koree at the back.

And me in the middle.

Chapter 52

I begin to feel nervous as we approach the city. A million things that could go wrong rush through my head. To top it off, I feel the guilt of knowing this was my idea…to save a little girl and some other orphans that I barely know. A piece of me wants to scream at Thann and Koree – tell them we need to turn back. But another part of me knows that it is too late for that.

The eight Lavs are soaring, wings outstretched like flying dinosaurs, lodged between Thann and Koree. I follow close behind, the chilly wind rushing over my face, but I am too tense to enjoy it. I suddenly miss Echo. And Gunter. What are they doing now? Do they think about me? When I get back, I tell myself, I need to take some time to go see them.

"Relax. I will take care of you," Ami tells me, her voice soothing my nerves.

"It's just…"

"Your mind is tricky," she interrupts. "I will be with you every step of the way."

"But what about Koree? And Thann?" After all that Thann and I went through to get to Harcourt, I can't believe we are going back to Bay City. Back to the Destroyers.

"I am with them, too. Because you love them."

"Yes, I do." I start to feel better.

"Thank you, Ami."

"You are welcome." I reach down and pat her neck.

Ami is quiet, and part of me wants to keep talking to her to keep my mind off of what we are about to do. But, I have noticed that talking with Ami is on her terms. Her sleek neck is relaxed, and she doesn't seem stressed in the least. Just then, Thann lands his Lav in a small clearing. The eight Lavs and Koree follow suit. Ami lands without instruction or cues from me.

The boys have dismounted, and I immediately do, too, stretching my legs. Koree digs in one of the supplies bags and tosses us each a water bag. Then he hands us a snack. Apples and cheese. For strength.

I can't see him well in the darkness, but I sense his movement as he strides over to one of the Lavs and returns with the three swords and a belt for each of us. "Put these on," he quietly orders, handing Thann and me each one of the ruby handled swords. "Siv Gareth's soldiers always wear these." I nod my head in agreement. Thann and I obey without question and wrap the belts around our waists, inserting the swords in the sheaths on our belts. The last time someone inserted a sword in my sheath, it wasn't me. It was Siv Gareth himself. A shudder runs up my spine thinking about it.

But it is Koree by my side, and his hand is on my shoulder. He squeezes it gently. I turn to him, imagining his deep green eyes in the darkness.

"This is it," Thann tells us, chewing on his last bite of apple. He flings the core into the darkness.

We mount the Lavs again and walk them toward the city. This time I am in the lead because I know my way around. The city is a monster – one I had almost forgotten about. Stale, putrid odors greet us first as we silently plod along until the dirt roads turn into broken concrete streets. Large, black, crumbling buildings form a backdrop in the darkness. Although I can barely see them, I know they are dirty and slimy and covered with soot. An ancient trolley car, fallen to its side juts out into the road, and Ami leads the way around it, the boys and other dragons plodding along behind us.

Ami maneuvers around other obstacles, a few abandoned automobiles from a time I don't remember. Large rocks. Huge chunks of concrete. Eventually we make it to Chrissy Park, a place that brings back fond memories of Entho, of my mom. But now, in the shadow of darkness, the warehouses look like worn out boxes, and the flowers and grass from my childhood are replaced with fragments of stone, crumbling statues, litter. A few fires are burning in barrels outside the park, and they remind me of distant ships coming in to sea.

I search around, not sure which building to go to. There has to be an office or a place where we would go to give our orders. I squint my eyes in the darkness, scanning each building. I spot some signs, but it is difficult to decipher what they say.

"Take me closer," I tell Ami without even thinking about it. She doesn't answer but swiftly treks toward the box-like buildings. Then I spot a dilapidated sign. "Orphanage Office." That has to be it. Now, if only someone is on duty.

Ami stops next to the sign. I dismount, wanting to pat her on the neck, but I know that Siv Gareth's soldiers probably wouldn't be doing that. Koree and Thann pull up beside me and dismount. I look over at them, and if I didn't know better I would believe they were real soldiers. It is eerily quiet.

"Do you have the papers?" Thann asks out loud, his voice precinct and precise like we practiced – like a real soldier's. I dig in the coat my red uniform and pull out the forged documents. I hand them to him without comment. Koree hands me the rope that holds the dragons. I reach for it, making contact with his hand, feeling his familiar skin against mine.

Without a sound Koree swivels his body, back erect, and walks toward Thann. I am left with the feel of his skin still on mine and memories of kisses and laughter. Along with a deep fear I never thought possible. I try to control my breathing, knowing somebody could be watching.

Koree and Thann march toward the orphanage office, backs straight in strikingly red uniforms, their swords moving in rhythm to their long strides. By all appearances they are elite army soldiers and belong to Siv Gareth. They lithely climb up the stairs to the office, their feet thumping on stone steps, their backs disappearing into a small doorway.

In an instant they are gone, swallowed up by the enormous box building.

Chapter 53

I am alone now – left holding the dragons – who are antsy, snorting and pawing their feet restlessly. I doubt if they have ever been to the city. My heart is pounding in my chest like exploding thunder. I tell myself to breathe, to be calm. Ami nudges me with her huge head.

"Everything is fine." Her soothing voice calms me. I find her yellow eyes, and we stare at each other for a few moments. I let out a huge breath, my air blending with her snorting breaths.

I wait outside for what seems like a long time, walking from dragon to dragon. Up and down the row I go, glancing over my shoulder occasionally. Pretending to be a soldier is easy for me, but worrying about Koree and Thann takes its toll. Thoughts race through my head as I try to keep the Lavs calm, but they are anything but that. I have had enough training to know that Siv Gareth's dragons would be relaxed, better behaved in the city.

With each pass I make, the dragons become more agitated, swishing their tails, snorting, and pawing at the ground. One lets out a small flame. I bite my lower lip, worrying. Where are they? Where are Koree and Thann?

It has been too long. By now I am convinced that something has gone wrong, and I am about ready to tie the dragons up and enter the building myself – go in search of Thann and Koree. My stomach is clenched into a tight fist as I try to appear calm and aloof, my back erect and my gait that of a soldier. I am next to Ami, pulling on her halter and tying it onto a post when the front door of the building bangs open.

Koree, strutting like a soldier, leads the way out, and an enormous breath spews out of my lungs with a relief I didn't know possible. My lips curl up in a semi-smile. Children follow him, a row of small, silent captives.

One by one I start settling their tiny bodies on the dragons, tying their legs to the huge beasts.

"I am doing this so you won't fall off and get hurt," I tell them in a hushed voice, but their eyes are empty and not one of them even speaks. My first instinct is to reassure them, but that is definitely not what a soldier would do. I search for Winter, longingly, hoping to find her. But I don't.

Thann is out the door now. He and Koree help load the children onto the Lavs. Not one of the children fights us or offers resistance. No one questions why we would wake them and load them onto dragons in the middle of the night. I wonder if this has happened to them before.

We work quickly in the dark night, and nobody bothers us. I let out a deep breath, my stomach finally relaxing. I think we are going to make it. When all of the children are loaded, I untie Ami and hop onto her back, leading the way out. Koree is behind me, and Thann takes the rear, just as we planned.

We walk the dragons away from Chrissy Park…the orphanage…the city I hate…and a nearby prison where I know Entho might be. Mount Gareth shadows gloomily behind us, a backdrop of ugliness and beauty combined like water mixing with oil. Entho, I should be getting Entho, not these children. Entho. Entho. Entho. My heart squeezes, a vice of love and fear pressing it into a ball. Yet, I don't even know if Entho is alive.

Not one of us speaks, perched stoically on our Lavs. The only sounds are the occasional child sniffing or coughing. The padding of the dragon's feet on the broken concrete. A dragon snorting. Human voices from far away. Fires crackling in the distance.

At some point, the incessant humming of the city subsides, and it is eerily quiet for the longest time. Then, as if the city couldn't sustain the peace and quiet any longer, a strong wind blows all around us. My putrid hair flies crazily into my eyes as I balance precariously on Ami. I turn around to check on the children as a strong metallic, smell, like sharp acid, pervades my nostrils. The children are hanging on tightly to the Lavs, but the wind rocks against them, their hair flying wildly and their dirty brown cloaks flickering against the rushing air. I am relieved that we tied them down.

Just then, rain plummets from the sky. Not the gentle rain like we usually have in the city, but a fierce, pounding rain, bulleting water on us as if it were real ammunition. I think back to the night I found my invitation to Dragon Academy. The same storm pelted out of the skies that night. Were the Angels telling me something? Did I refuse to listen?

The stain we used to turn me dark streams from my hair and skin like burning blood, a fire in each of my eyes. I can't see an inch before me as I wipe at my eyes with my red sleeve. Stinging, biting pain stabs at my ears, even my mouth. My lips are on fire. I gag over and over, the stain trickling into my mouth, concern for Thann leaping into my brain. He must be experiencing the same thing.

The wind and rain, more ruthless than I could have imagined, won't let us alone. I worry about the children – they must be scared beyond reason. And cold. I begin shivering at that very moment, and my body goes numb. Just keep walking, I tell myself. We will walk until we can get out of this fierce rain and wind.

"Bend down into me," Ami tells me. I lean into her neck, and I find some relief, my face now somewhat protected from the merciless storm. I let out a breath. We can make it. Ami will lead us to safety.

Just then, words I never thought I would hear outside of a boyhood chant echo across the sodden, turbulent night air… terror filled words from a voice that is more familiar to me than my own.

Koree's voice. Of that I am sure.

"To the moon!" he shouts, and as if one time wasn't enough, he repeats it again. "To the moon!"

At that precise moment thunder and lightning perform a loud ominous dance with each other in the once darkened night, and as blinding light flashes across the sky, there is no doubt about what he is yelling and what it means.

Chapter 54

To the moon. No….no…it can't be. Thunder booms again, not only in the sky but in my chest as lightning crackles, filling the sky with more shattered fragments of light. Terror fills my heart and rain continues to bombard down on me. I scrape my sleeve over my eyes again and again, wishing I could see…know what is wrong…why Koree would want us to hit the skies. I turn my head all around, searching. Koree…where is he? And Thann? Does he have the children? I spin my head in all directions, but I see nothing but rain and darkness.

Without further hesitation, I reach for my bow, grab an arrow and nock it. "Up, Ami, to the skies," I shout at her in my mind. But she has somehow sensed what I need and is already flapping her enormous wings, battling against the strong wind. She teeters and wobbles and for an instant I wonder if she will actually be able to fly in the storm. The giant dragon rallies, though, raising us at first slowly and then with more speed upward. I lean into her, shivering from intense cold and fear and a terror – a death grip on her slippery neck. We rocket upward into the black sky. Into the unknown.

Wind beats against my face and body – joining in the miserable dance with thunder and lightning. As another lightning bolt careens across the sky, a picture is painted before me, and I no longer wonder why Koree yelled, "to the moon." There are about fifty Lavs circling around us in the storm. Siv Gareth's elite army - dressed in the same red uniforms that we are wearing.

True to Kesper's words, the soldiers mostly have swords, but some are toting arrows, knives, and spears. My first reaction is to turn Ami around and run. There is no way the three of us can take on so many trained soldiers. Especially with all of the children. Just then Koree's face flashes before my eyes. Even though I am not really seeing him, I know I can't leave him. Or Thann and the children. I am the only one of us with enough training to stand a chance at defeating this army. And I know those chances are slim. Very slim.

I set my sight on the first soldier I find, take aim, pull back on my string and watch as an arrow flies into the chest of a man. Or woman. I know that Siv Gareth takes women into his elite army, after all, wasn't that what I was being trained for? The soldier plummets to the ground, shrieking on the way down, rain bouncing off the falling body like a baptism gone wrong. I can't find it in me to hate him. Or her. Then I wonder…could one of them be Glendon or Pride? I thought I hated them at Weapons, but I certainly wouldn't want to kill them. I shake my head and push the thought from my mind.

I nock my bow again, at the same time searching for Koree and Thann through the pelting rain. Lightning flashes, now a friend, and I let out a sigh of relief when I spot Koree circling around the outskirts of the army, spinning, and looping and diving. My lips curve up for a split second. He is a difficult target with all of that movement. But I can't find Thann or the children.

Just then an arrow screams by me with a speed I never thought possible, so close I can feel the movement on my arm. Instinctively, I reach for where the arrow barely missed me only to find bare flesh. My sleeve is completely gone. As I reach again for Ami's neck, stapling my body against hers, a rage pours through me, a flash flood of anger I am not sure I know how to control.

In Weapons they trained us to make adjustments for weather and calculate the wind, the force of the rain. That is the easy part. But they taught us to hate…to hate our enemy. For the first time in my life I truly know who my real enemy is, and at the moment hate is a mild form of what I am feeling. I grit my teeth and reach back for another arrow. My battle with Siv Gareth has just begun.

Time after time, I squeeze my eyes against the rain and wind, find a moving target and shoot. Screams roar, competing against lighting and thunder and a sky that has gone mad as soldiers careen off of their dragons and plunge downward. Occasionally I dodge an arrow or spear, instinctively knowing when to move as Ami seems to read my mind. There is no time to talk or discuss strategies.

I take out soldier after soldier, knowing that it is either them or us, and I choose us. I choose Koree. I choose me. I choose Thann and the children.

Where is Thann? I search for him, ruthless rain blinding my eyes and a violent wind not just beating on my body, but beating in my heart. Thann. Thann. Memories of running in the tunnel with

Thann and being captured by Destroyers enter my mind. Of just finding out I have a brother and then losing him. His perpetual smile, constant shenanigans. Where can he be?

Quickly, as I duck down to avoid a dagger that is bulleting directly at me. I lean into Ami, but she turns in the opposite direction. She dips down, then, just enough to avoid a speeding arrow.

"Trust me." She tells me this again, and I have no choice but to do so. As I hang on to Ami's dripping neck, bobbing and weaving with burning eyes, a fierce wind and rain ruthlessly pelting down on me, complete desolation fills my heart. I have lost sight of Koree, and I have yet to see Thann and the children.

Chapter 55

A sword spins over my head, so close that some of my hair is yanked out with it. I let out a yelp, and Ami immediately darts forward. Flames shoot out of her mouth, flashing brilliantly in the night sky, lighting it up if only for a moment. The flame diminishes quickly, fizzling out from the fierce rain. But it is enough. For an instant, I can just barely make out the silhouette of Thann distinctly riding away from the battle, followed by the eight Lavs loaded with children. The outline is getting smaller and smaller in the black sky. For the slightest moment my lips curl up and relief floods through my body.

An arrow whizzes by my arm, and I instinctively move to the side, barely missing it. Ami screams in indignation. Flames shoot out of her mouth again, and she rages toward the soldier who shot at me. Before I can even shoot back at him, I watch as he catches fire, his red uniform disintegrating into oranges and yellows, flesh burning off his body like wax dripping off a candle. Then rain drizzles over him – popping and sizzling. The soldier releases a scream I will never forget.

Ami swings wide, rising higher and higher. Her plan must be to out fly them all, to get away, and my first reaction is to follow Thann and the children…to find safety. Then I think of Koree, left alone with what has to still be about thirty soldiers. Would he know to follow, or would he stay and fight? I can't leave him. Not Koree. Then, for a split second I wonder why he isn't shooting. Why isn't he fighting?

"No," I tell Ami. "No…I need Koree."

She pauses for a moment, but then her words are clear in my mind. "Very well," she tells me, descending back toward the battle, but a feeling washes over me, one of unhappiness and discontent. I can tell that Ami is definitely not happy about doing this.

I search for Koree as lighting crackles, illuminating the ebony sky. But a soldier is rocketing toward me, so close I can make out the long spear in her hand. Black hair flies wildly behind her, and I struggle to make out the features of her face. In one swift movement I pull an arrow out of my quiver, nock it, aim at her, and let the arrow fly. The arrow strikes her in the chest with enough force to send her flying off her dragon, cursing and roaring all the way down.

"Nice shot," Ami tells me.

"Thanks," I answer. "But I can't find Koree."

"We will find him."

"How?" I am almost crying. It is deathly dark, and I am surrounded by soldiers on dragons as tormenting rain and wind pelt down on me like wet, burning stars darting out of the sky. To top it off, I am hesitant to shoot at the soldiers. Koree is dressed just like them, and I don't know if I am shooting at him or a real soldier.

Ami suddenly soars upward as a spear careens by her. "I will call him to us."

"How?" I dumbly ask again, grabbing an arrow from my quiver. A Lav is charging toward us, and I let an arrow fly, hitting the rider in the shoulder. His Lav shoots out a flame, and I sink another arrow into the middle of his chest. The Lav dives down, perhaps in an effort to save the plummeting rider.

"He can hear me."

"Koree?"

"Yes, our blood has blended…just like yours."

"Are you bonded with him?"

"Almost every dragon is."

"Oh." I wait for Ami's words to call Koree, but I hear nothing. I am frantic, and I can't wait for Ami. "Koree," I scream as loudly as I can. "Koree." It becomes a mantra. Like in the tunnels, it keeps me going…focused. But I quit saying it out loud and just repeat his name over and over in my mind, reaching the point where I don't even care if I die. Because I don't want to live in a world without Koree in it. I cannot exist in that world.

A dagger swishes by my head, and I move just in time to avoid it. Ami screams again, protecting me. She chases after the knife wielding soldier, flames erupting like wildfire against the wind and rain. Her ears are pinned back behind her head, and all I can do is hold on tightly… she is moving that fast.

She continues to shoot flames against the dark sky as sweat from the heat mixes with cold rain, trickling down my back now, singeing my eyebrows and eyelashes. Hot and cold. Hot and cold. I begin to shiver, my teeth chattering in the stillness of the night. The stillness? Could it be over? Did we kill them all?

Ami lets out the biggest flame of all, lighting up the sky, and to the far right of me I spot movement. A lone rider is torpedoing through the sky, and I know the movements of the rider all too well. Koree, I breathe out. Koree. He is alive.

My heart feels like it has stopped beating and the sight of Koree has started it back up. Foolishly, I take a second to watch him…twirling, dipping, diving…looping and spinning…all at once. Koree…oh Koree. At first I don't even notice the dagger swirling straight toward my chest. Just when I sense it careening toward me, I push my body down toward Ami's neck and she propels us upward. But her giant body can't move fast enough, and as she streamlines upward, I feel a sharp pain in my calf. I scream out and Ami shoots a violent flame from her mouth. Without looking down I know the dagger has impaled my calf.

"Holy snock," I yell into the horrendous black sky. "You snocking baggers!" Anger rages through me again as I reach down, feeling for the dagger lodged in my calf.

"You are hit, Warrior." Ami's voice is full of concern as she tilts her body sideways and we continue to spiral upward. I move my fingers down my leg and in one quick movement pull the dagger out. I grit my teeth as a sharp pain shoots through my leg, but I know that my boot will act as a bandage.

"I am fine. Take us down," I tell Ami. She switches directions and dives down. I am more than ready for the fight that needs to take place now. If I had any doubts before, the burning sensation in my calf is a sharp reminder.

A rider speeds by us, a ruby handled sword held out before him. I waste no time. Just like with the Destroyer who was about to kill Thann, I aim the dagger from my calf and send it sailing. It zings through the wet air with a force I didn't know possible and lands directly in the center of the soldier's forehead with a sickening thud. Just like with Echo, I think, only this dagger sinks in much deeper. I am only satisfied when I hear a scream of agony and watch the sword slip out of hands. It will take a while for him to die, but at this point I am not concerned about suffering. He is one less soldier I have to worry about.

I pull back arrow after arrow, watch as soldier after soldier falls. I am a machine…there is no feeling attached to what I am doing. Ami glides through the air with determination, dipping and darting with ease, reading my mind where I want to be, helping me angle each shot correctly.

A strange feeling of exhilaration jolts through my body. We are invincible. Ami and I could take on the entire Alliance tonight, and I know we would win. Just then a soldier bullets toward us, barely visible in the dark sky. I narrow my eyes, breathe deeply, and reach back in my quiver to pull out an arrow.

For just an instant I swear my heart stops beating.

My quiver is empty.

Chapter 56

Ami shoots upward, avoiding a spiraling dagger, as I reach my hand back and grope blindly for the spears we packed. There are only seven spears. Lightning flashes just then. To my horror, there are about twenty dragons still flying around. Not good odds.

I grab a spear anyway, pull back my arm, and send it hurling forward and a soldier careens off a dragon, her Lav shooting flames across the sky and flying off in a rage. Six more times I launch spears at soldiers, only five of which make their mark. That still leaves about ten to fifteen soldiers…against Ami and me with no weapons and Koree, who isn't shooting. *Why isn't he shooting? He has plenty of arrows, is a decent shot.*

I search for Koree, and as lightning illuminates the sky again, I spot him, moving with tremendous speed. But he is so far away – numerous soldiers stand between us. I am not sure what to do now that I am out of weapons. I bite my lower lip, thinking how I can communicate with Koree, let him know I need him to start using his weapons, that mine are gone.

"I will tell him," Ami says. Was she reading my mind, or did I tell her that?

"Take me to Koree, please," I beg of her.

Ami pivots upward and then circles above the remaining soldiers. I spot Koree, dipping and diving, rolling and spinning on the huge Lav, and a thrill runs through me. We are going to make it. I just know it. My lips curl up in satisfaction as Ami veers to the left. I am certain that once Koree and I are together we can take out the rest of the soldiers, even if he has to give me his weapons.

We are soaring, gliding faster than I ever thought possible when I am almost launched off of Ami by a sudden impact. I struggle to find my seat, wrapping my legs tightly around the huge dragon, as the most intense pain I have ever felt sears through my arm. Shock and pain overtake me as I struggle to balance on Ami and find enough air to desperately suck into my lungs. A spear. A spear. Oh, Angels no, not a spear.

For a split second I stare at the spear poking through the upper portion of my left arm. My shooting arm. As if realizing what has just happened, Ami lets out a screech of anger, shooting flames out of her mouth as my head turns into a dizzy mush from the intense pain. A burning pain that throbs with each of my heart beats…and each beat seems to take a minute of my life away from me.

"Hold on," Ami yells. I have never heard her yell. My head is going to explode, her voice is so loud. "Hold on, Warrior," she tells me again, only this time her voice is pleading.

It becomes my new mantra. Hold on. Hold on. Hold on. I reach over for the spear, know that I have to pull it out, but I am not sure I can do it on a flying dragon, not sure even sure I can do it on the ground. My fingers wrap around it and I start to pull, but it is too much. I scream so loudly, I am sure the soldiers will find me.

My arm is paralyzed. Blood is oozing out of it – warm and thick – spurting out of my arm, a hot, red spewing furnace. It runs down my body, mixing with rain. Rain and blood. Rain and blood. Splashing into my face. In my eyes. Rain and blood. It must be pink, I think. Like in Entho's clinic when I would wash the blood off of my hands. Pink. Pink. Pink. I squint my eyes, try to wipe the blood away with my right hand as I shiver uncontrollably. My teeth chatter and I struggle to stay on Ami as my head becomes dizzier and dizzier as if thick syrup is moving through my brain.

Ami shoots a flame into the wet night, and it is squelched all too soon, but I see him. I know it is him. Koree is coming for me. He will save me. He will think of something. He always does.

I begin to lose my grip on Ami. I try to hold on with my right arm, but my strength is fading. "Koree…" I call for him, sure that he is getting closer to me. I feel it, feel him coming. I pull my head up, smiling. "I am here," I call to him. "Over here." An arrow shoots by my head, barely missing it. Ami ducks, shoots more flames, but I can't tell at who or at what.

Koree is flying toward me, his Lav's feet pulled back, wings spread wide. I can see his copper curls, only I can't really see the color, that is just from memory. I can feel them, though. I remember what they feel like. And I remember his kisses. And his dimple. And his strength. And how smart he is….

He is almost beside me. Maybe we can outrun the soldiers. Together. That is a thought. I smile over at him. "To the moon," I say, weakly, hoping he can hear it. But before I get a response, before I can process anything I hear movement, and even though my brain is foggy and my body is weak, my training overpowers all of that. I instinctively duck down, just the slightest. I turn my head toward Koree as a final lightning bolt streaks across the sky and a rebellious thunder claps so loudly, it almost deafens me. I pick my head up searching for Koree. But when I find him my heart pulls itself into a giant fist. The spear intended for me has penetrated Koree's chest.

"NOOOOOOOoooooooo," I scream, as he is thrust off his dragon, falling to the black earth below. I think, but I am not sure, but I think I hear him yelling "Laaaaaater."

"KOOOrrrrreeeeeeeee," I shriek.

"KOOORRRRREEEEEEcceee….." I try to tell Ami to dip down, to try to catch him. But I am sliding off of her, and all I can manage is to yell, "KOOOrrrreeeeeee."

Over. And. Over. Again.

Until. My. Voice. Is. Gone.

Until I don't care anymore.

Until the blackness engulfs me, and I am, falling, falling, falling.

Into the cold, rainy night sky.

Finis...

My eyes open slowly. To darkness. I blink them, adjusting to the miniscule shard of light creeping through a small, high window. Lines of faded yellow light. I am in a solid stone room encompassed by thick black bars. Obviously, it is a prison. The room is bare. No bed. No food or water. Just coldness, darkness, dampness. I am shivering, my teeth chattering back and forth uncontrollably.

I scan the room for a blanket, anything to keep me warm. Nothing. Just then, a memory crashes into my brain. Of a spear. In my arm. I rush my right hand to my left arm, searching for the spear, but it is gone, and I don't know how or who tended to my wound. It is clean, bandaged. But the pain remains. It throbs as if someone were pounding it with a hammer. Pound. Pound. Pound. My calf feels like it is on fire and my head hurts, is dizzy, and I can't seem to think. But I try, my thoughts swirling around in my brain like a slowly moving tornado.

What do I remember? In the whirling fog of my brain, I know I need to do something. I need to Remember.

Remember.

Remember.

Remember.

I Remember fighting on Ami, shooting my bow and arrows. Running out of arrows. And spears. I Remember Koree coming.

And.

Then.

I.

Remember.

Koree.

Koree falling.

Koree with a spear in his chest.

Koree falling off his Lav with a spear sticking out of the center of his chest. A spear intended for me.

A pain worse than any I have ever felt overtakes my body. Paralyzes me. Koree. Koree. Koree. Each time I think his name, a piece of me dies, dies with him. Koree. Koree. Koree. Tears stream down my face. Silent tears, an endless river flowing to nowhere. I am sure that I will never be able to stop them.

He is dead. He couldn't have survived that fall, much less the spear through his chest. There is a hole in my heart, in my own chest, as if the spear had penetrated me along with him. Penetrated my entire body. The emptiness engulfs me, overtakes me. And I want to die. More than anything else.

I.

Want.

To.

Die.

I sit up, settle my back in the corner of the room, stone becoming my only pillow. I perch my knees up and place my head between them. The cold dark floor becomes my only field of vision. Tears drop shamelessly onto the floor, eventually forming a small puddle. A lake of tears for Koree.

I will die here.

I don't care.

After a while, I hear footsteps. It sounds like two sets of footsteps. One is heavier than the other. They are getting closer to me. Then they stop.

Silence.

Eventually, I look up with what surely must be red rimmed eyes. A man and a woman stand in front of my cell. The woman is situated behind the man, as if she is his inferior. I recognize the man at once. Siv Gareth. I swallow poisonous bile as I sniff back tears and glare at him. He might as well have been the one who threw the spear at Koree.

Siv Gareth slowly pulls a black leather glove off his hand, his left hand. For an instant I stupidly wonder if he is left handed, like me. But I don't really care. All I feel is extreme coldness in the center of my chest so deep and strong, I doubt if I will ever be rid of it. I hate this man so deeply that I want to kill him. Bare handed. I envision my hands around his neck, choking the life out of him. Like the life was taken out of Koree. I quickly dry my tears, not wanting to give him the satisfaction of seeing me cry. I slowly pull my head up defiantly glaring into his black eyes.

He stretches his hand out, flexing his fingers, as if he is in pain, or maybe planning something. I have seen him do this before. He meets my gaze, unblinking.

Slowly I move my eyes toward the woman – there is something about her – something I recognize, but her face is hidden, concealed by the hood of a deep purple cloak. I tilt my head, as if waiting for the next move in this game, and she slowly, deliberately, pulls the hood on her cloak back, revealing long black hair and a face I never thought I would see again.

"Look, Pana, your little brat has arrived. The ugly little Ghost I should have destroyed a long time ago." Siv Gareth leers at me, his lips curving up in the torturous smile of a vulture.

He deliberately turns around, faces the woman. "Perhaps, Pana, we should have a little family reunion. What do you think?"

The woman doesn't respond, but I can make out every detail of her face now, and it is one I have memorized my entire life...a face I haven't seen since I was four years old.

The face of my mother.

A Special Gift for My Readers!

I hope that you enjoyed reading <u>To the Moon</u>, Book 2 in the Mark of Power Series. Book 3, <u>Into the Black Night</u>, will be released within a few months. You will be astonished and delighted with the characters' adventures and the twists and turns of the plot in Book 3!

I would love to give you a free copy of <u>Into the Black Night</u> when it is finished in thanks for posting an honest review on Amazon of either or both of the Mark of Powers Series books that have been published - <u>From the Mountain</u> and <u>To the Moon</u>.

It only takes a few minutes to do a simple review - a sentence or so about what you liked is enough, and this will help other readers find these books.

After you write a review, simply email me at

lisa@llcrane.com, and I will get <u>Into the Black Night</u> to

you before it comes out on Amazon for FREE!

With a grateful heart,

L.L. Crane

Excerpt from "Into the Black Sky"

Book 3, Mark of Power Series

The Mountain...

The seer was led to the Lord of the Mansion, his bare feet padding against the cold marble floor. Lanton held his arm tightly, not in fear that he would escape, but because he was blind. When they reached Siv Gareth, the seer was the one who stopped first. He sniffed the stagnant air like a stallion surrounded by mares.

Siv Gareth wasted no time. "What have you seen?"

"You don't want to know, my Lord."

For just a moment it was silent. Although he couldn't see Siv Gareth glaring at him with steely black eyes, the seer knew. But he wasn't afraid. Instead, he sighed deeply, the cheeks of his wrinkled face puffing out ever the slightest.

"Speak now of what you have seen, or I will cut your head off." The words came out of Siv Gareth's mouth like poisonous venom, the smallest speck of spittle landing on the ebony floor. Lanton tightened his grip on the old man's arm.

"Very well," the seer exhaled. "It were the Legend of the Twins that I seen, sir. It were the Legend all right."

"That old wives tale?" Siv Gareth laughed then, his deep voice rumbling through the amethyst mansion.

"It weren't the same, sir," the seer interjected. "It were different, all right. It were about them Light Skins with the yellow hair. I seen them, I did. They was the twins in the Legend. One were marked, the boy, he were. The girl, she were unmarked. One to be the warrior. The other to be the ruler." With that he swallowed noisily, as if it was a difficult process. Then, tilting his head to the side, he finished. "Only it were backward, sir. It were the girl who were the warrior and the boy who were the ruler. He were the new Lord, not you, and she were in the battles, not the boy. It were backward. But I seen it clear as could be. I seen it."

Lord Gareth leaped up from his purple throne, towering over the seer. "You are wrong," he shouted. "I am the one true ruler." And like a petulant child, he actually stamped his foot.

The seer didn't turn away, but he didn't answer, either. Ocean waves crashed against the mountain, echoing in the mansion as if they needed to have a say in the matter.

"Take his head off," Siv Gareth ordered Lanton. "And bring it to me when you are done. This, this…blind idiot will have no more of these foolish visions."

Lanton spoke firmly. "As you order, sir." He nodded to his superior, turned the seer around, and led him out of the doorway. Wordlessly, they weaved their way through the dark corridors that led them toward the prison.

When they reached an intersection in the halls, Lanton let out a huge sigh. He knew he would pay for what he was about to do, but he was to the point where he didn't care anymore. Instead of turning left, Lanton turned right.

The seer, of course, had no choice but to go with him. He knew they were going in the wrong direction, but he didn't say a word.

After a while, traversing the cavernous halls, orange fire light casting eerie shadows on the wall, Lanton stopped at a doorway. He opened it and poked his head out, turning from side to side. The only thing out there was the cold, salty ocean, crashing violently against the rocky mountain. The night was blissfully black, not a single star in the sky, which would give the seer the only edge he had – darkness.

"Go," Lanton whispered to the seer. "Don't stop. Go to Harcourt. It's your only chance."

He shoved the blind man out the door and with a thud closed it behind him. He breathed deeply, not sure of what he would tell Lord Gareth, if anything at all.

There was one thing that Lanton had come to believe in, and it wasn't Lord Gareth, although he carried out that charade quite well.

No, it wasn't Lord Gareth, at all. It was the visions that came to the seer that Lanton truly believed in, and he thought back to a night not too long ago.

His hostages were twins, he was sure of it. Both Light Skinned, tall, and blonde. The boy, he was reasonable, but the girl was a real spitfire. A warrior for sure.

He smiled for the first time in years. Even if he died, which he surely would, Lord Gareth's reign would soon be over. If the seer's vision was correct.

The only thing that bothered him was the mark on the girl's face. She definitely had a crescent shaped mark on her cheek.

Acknowledgements

A special thank you to Nathan for being a wonderful, gigantic, funny, easy going son and giving me the inspiration for Thann's character.

Of course, thank you to Natalie and Nicole for your advice and brutal honestly. Nicole, thank you for listening to my ramblings about characters, plot, etc. every weekend when you are home from college. And of course, thank you for your opinions. You are always spot on.

Thank you to the love of my life, Tony. My heart explodes with love for you. You never lose faith in me and are always by my side, even when you are far away.

A special thank you to Claudia of Phatpuppy Art for the fabulous cover. It was as if you knew Koree from the start. You are magic!

Thank you to Catriona from the Font Diva for your patience with me. I am learning!

A special thank you to Morgan and Landon. You keep me going with love. And Jessie, thank you for being such a wonderful mother to them. You are perfect!